Nefarious & Nightmarish 16 Tales of Terror

Meagan J. Meehan

Nefarious & Nightmarish

By Meagan J. Meehan

All rights reserved. No part of this book may be reproduced or transmitted in any form or by any means, electronic or mechanical, including photocopying or recording or by any information storage and retrieval systems, without expressed written consent of the author and/or artist.

Nefarious & Nightmarish is a work of fiction. Names, characters, places, and incidents are products of the author's imaginations. Any resemblance to actual events or persons, living or dead, is entirely coincidental.

Story copyrights owned by the author.

Cover art by Marissa Haynes

Cover design by Laura Givens

First Printing January 2024
Hiraeth Publishing
http://hiraethsffh.com/
@HiraethPublish1

Visit http://hiraethsffh.com/ for online science fiction, fantasy, horror, scifaiku, and more. Also visit the Hiraeth Publishing bookstore for paperbacks, magazines, anthologies, and chapbooks. Support the small, independent press...

~ACKNOWLEDGEMENTS~

This book is dedicated to my wonderful parents, Mary and Michael, and to everyone at Chilling Tales for Dark Nights, a company that shares my love of the horror genre and has steadily supported my creative writing for many years. I also dedicate this publication to musician James D. King; my fellow INFJ, horror-fan, inspiration, and creative collaborator whose friendship is the most profound that I have ever experienced. Thank you.

A special thanks goes out to Marissa Haynes who is a skilled writer and insanely talented author who did such an awe-inspiring job with the cover art for this book. Voice actor Otis Jiry and Jason Dube of Scattered Cat also deserve shout-outs for the remarkable support that they have given me over the years and everything that they do for the horror entertainment field in general.

~Author's Notes~

The ideas for these stories came from a spectacular array of places. They are listed in the order in which they were written. The first, "Reflections," was penned in 2011. The last, "Sire," was completed on January 26, 2020. Being a writer is my hobby and my passion. I am grateful to have had the opportunity to teach writing courses, the vast majority of which are conducted entirely online, and watch talented authors emerge via the talented participants. I have also been blessed to work with Craig Groshek and a range of talented writers, voice actors, and video creators associated with Chilling Entertainment, the company behind the immensely popular and entertaining YouTube channel *Chilling Tales for Dark Nights*. I am frequently asked where I get the ideas for my stories. Since this is my first anthology collection, I decided to include notes below on the inspiration behind each of the sixteen tales within this book.

- Reflections: A young boy is haunted by the ghost of his dead best friend. This story was written in 2011 and inspired by an array of excellent ghost-themed movies from Asia with both heart and tragedy at their center (*The Maid, The Eye, Dark Water*). The tale is meant to be set in the 1950s, something that was not initially clear but which I incorporated into this most updated edition of the story.

- Companions: A little girl summons more than she anticipated after the death of her mother. This was the first story I ever wrote for *Chilling Tales for Dark Nights* (CTFDN). It was inspired by a contest they ran which featured two creepy old photos: one of a teddy bear and one of a young girl in a white dress holding a mirror. I put the two images together and the result was this.

- Invitation: A lonely woman learns her place in society. This story was inspired by yet another

Chilling Tales contest based on photos of a creepy snowman, a set of keys, and a requirement to set that story in Nebraska. I also drew major inspiration from a classic painting titled *The Garden of Earthly Delights* by Hieronymus Bosch.

- Revelation: A paranoid truck driver fears aliens but learns that there are even worse things than being abducted. This tale was inspired by a CTFDN contest that offered two inspiring images: a noose and three faceless men in top-hats. I decided to make the main character a truck driver since I often watch trucks drive along the highway late at night from my apartment window. The alien theme came to me because I was just starting to work on my first Science Fiction novel when the call for this contest was announced so aliens were very much on my mind at the time.

- Jinnu: A wealthy bratty girl meets her match when she discovers a genie-like creature in a trunk. The 1st place winner of a CTFDN writing contest back in May of 2015, this story was inspired by a photo of an old trunk and an odd spider-like creature sitting in a large web woven between two trees. The mansion and garden themes were derived from my visits to lovely old Long Island manor houses, that are now state parks, such as Old Westbury Gardens, Coe Arboretum, and Sands Point.

- Collector: A boy is unnerved by the image of a skeleton in a vintage black-lit poster for good reason. This story was inspired by a January 2016 CTFDN prompt a la the image of a dinosaur and descending staircase. The grim reaper and neon-blacklight poster concepts were derived from the FAILE art show which was held at the Brooklyn Museum in the summer of 2015...a mere few months before this story was written. The excellent exhibit was a fun installation that allowed visitors to enter into a neon-wonderland. Many of the comic-book art style depicted grim reapers set against neon-hues so I knew I had to pay homage to FAILE via this story. I also wanted to include lava lamps because I think they're cool and have considered them aesthetically pleasing since I was a preteen.

- Oddity: A woman fears nothing more than being average and finds a way to ensure that her life will never be normal. Initially inspired by a CTFDN contest image featuring a girl staring into a pond only to see a reflection of twins staring back at her, I incorporated the history of side shows and the medical conditions of the "freaks" presented within them into this tale as well as "stage mother" lore such as that which followed Gypsy Rose Lee. Finally, the image of a *Face Off* makeup by Emily Serpico featuring a truly horrifying "rag doll" character immediately sprang to mind (the episode was titled *Deadly Dolls* and it was Season 8, Episode 12, for anyone who wishes to Google it). I envision the misshapen little doll in this story looking a lot like a tiny version of Emily's rag doll. The result of all these thought processes was this very dark, disturbing, and adult story which CTFDN would only air with a content warning and viewer age restriction.

- Summoner: A troubled child finds her place in the world. Inspired by a sketch of a demonic figure and a photo of a small green glass bottle, I modeled the dysfunctional family dynamic on a series of disturbing news reports. The story also pays homepage to "Pleasure Island" from Disney's *Pinocchio* which is as artistic as it is disturbing.

- Surrogate: A grizzled carnival worker finds an odd little creature that skyrockets him from carnie to showman. This story was specifically written for an incredibly talented filmmaker named Michael Davis who has been a longtime supporter and patron of CTFDN and who was the inspiration for one of the more fortunate characters presented in the tale. The inspiration for this custom-made story came as I walked through a county fairground, among the rides and games, and noticed that some of the plush toy carnival prizes looked very Halloweenish. That made me think of monsters and, somehow from there, this story emerged.

- Hexed: A beautiful young woman sets her sights on the wrong man and learns just how protective mothers can be. This story is based on the very strange and creepy true story of Rhoda Derry, a mentally ill woman who spent the majority of her life (1834-1906) locked in a wooden box in an insane asylum. The cause of Rhoda's insanity was her belief that she had been hexed by a witch. While this story is purely fiction, the true tale is much scarier, more intriguing, and incredibly sad. It's a classic example of truth being stranger than fiction.

- Decoy: Two hunters become the prey. Inspired by a camp-themed call for submissions, this is another tale created for CTFDN via the image of an abandoned campsite and grammatically problematic signage declaring "Welkome to Kamp." An ardent animal lover, I am not fond of hunters so this story was easy to write. To include an extra fun fact, the hilarious parody song *Goodbye Squirrel* by Cledus T. Judd was a major source of inspiration during my writing process.

- Ensorcell: A young woman and her pageant mother meet a beautician who can work magic. This story was penned upon request by CTFDN who put together a trilogy of anthologies to pay homage to the classic series *Scary Stories to Tell in the Dark*.

The story is intentionally written in a semi-detached, after-the-fact, third-person voice to mirror the tone found in the stories from the original series. The theme was inspired by the subculture of child beauty pageants which have long been the center of controversy. Originally titled *Beauty*, the piece was renamed to suit a research project for my doctoral studies concerning using stories to introduce readers to sophisticated and little-known words (a precursor to my dissertation on the same subject).

- Beastie: A disturbed and sadistic teen learns he isn't the only monster in his community. This story was born from a ridiculously entertaining headline from the now-defunct *Weekly World News* in which a man claimed to be kidnapped by Bigfoot for the purposes of sex slavery. I wondered what would happen if a predatory human were to meet a monster with similar appetites and this tale was subsequently crafted.

- Reaper: A security guard has been pursued by the grim reaper since babyhood yet, when it finally catches up to her, she is surprised by its ultimate intentions. Created to blend horror with comedic undertones, this story was written due to a CTFDN call for "school lockdown themed" stories.

- Tracker: An Irish doctor gets more than he bargained for during a humanitarian mission to Nigeria where fears of witchcraft have overtaken the population. This story was inspired by two things. Firstly, the news reports circa 2009 regarding accused "witch children" being abused, cast out of their homes, or killed—sometimes by their own parents. A documentary about the horrifying phenomenon was created to outline the causes, but the reality of the existence of such a situation, which is apparently ongoing, disturbs me deeply.

Secondly, this story is based on true events that occurred in Ireland in the early 2000s where a doctor suffered similar events to the man in the story. Until this day, I cannot recall his case without shuddering.

- Sire: A farm boy in Civil War-era America discovers that he has very unique neighbors. This was written for CTFDN as part of a "camping" collection.

I hope this background helps you enjoy the stories even more. If they unsettle you, linger in your mind, or give you nightmares then I have obviously done something right.

Sincerely,
Meagan J. Meehan
August 2023

Contents

13	Reflections
25	Companions
28	Invitation
42	Revelation
51	Jinnu
66	Collector
84	Oddity
101	Summoner
108	Surrogate
132	Hexed
140	Decoy
153	Ensorcell
163	Beastie
169	Reaper
176	Tracker
201	Sire
212	About the Author

Reflections

Peter first saw the girl three days after she died. She was clearly reflected in the bathroom mirror, staring at him scornfully while he brushed his unruly black hair. Peter screamed and spun around—but she was already gone.

Then his Mother was there; holding him, soothing him and reassuring him that it was all over now and that everything would be okay. Peter didn't believe a word of it.

Abby had drowned right in front of his eyes. They had been playing down by the creek, which was actually more akin to a deep lake. Although they were not supposed to go near the area, Peter and Abby spent nearly every hot summer day there. The lake, which he and Abby referred to as "the watering hole," was the best place to spend an afternoon pretending and dreaming and fending off the oppressive mid-summer swelter.

Few people actually knew about the backwoods location and even fewer would fight through the wood's thick foliage to get there. Thus, it was his and Abby's domain. Their parents repeatedly warned them that the watering hole was dangerous and instructed them to steer clear of it but they didn't listen. They both could swim, the lake was calm, and it wasn't as if any alligators were lurking. Nothing, they assumed, could possibly go wrong. Then one day Abby slipped and sank down into the murky waters of the black lake. Panic had overcome her and she lost her ability to think rationally or, apparently, to swim.

Peter had been right there with her but he couldn't remember anything that had happened. One minute she was there and the next moment she was suddenly gone. He must have tried to help her but he couldn't remember. It was as if he hadn't been there at all.

The doctors said he was in shock. Forgetting was one way that the mind defended itself from severe trauma, especially a young twelve-year-old mind like his. The explanation was one way to solve the mystery of how, ten minutes after Abby went under, Peter had shown up at his front door, soaking wet and slack faced. He was unable to explain to his Mother what had happened but she suspected trouble as soon as she saw his soaked swim trunks. It was Peter's mother who had found Abby's body floating face-down in the center of the lake.

Abby's remains went to the morgue and Peter went to the hospital. Although he remembered nothing of the event itself, or his mother's panicked phone call to 911, he remembered the hospital visit perfectly. By then he had come out of his shock enough to talk, and cry, and finally express dismay over what had transpired. He remembered the doctor's questions and he had answered them numbly; mostly just repeating himself over and over. He insisted that he didn't know what had happened or why it had happened. He couldn't believe Abby was gone. They had been swimming, splashing, laughing and then she had just...what? Sank? Had a heart attack? He didn't know.

The death was quickly ruled as accidental and Peter was allowed to go home that night. His Father drove along stony-faced as his Mother wept in the passenger seat and Peter stared out of the back window, dazed. The mild bruises on his body throbbed; from the examination the doctor declared that he had probably received them trying to help Abby. That served as some comfort; he had not simply allowed his best friend to die without even trying to save her.

Peter insisted on sleeping in his own room that night. He wanted to be alone despite his Mother's pleas that he allowed either her or his father, or both of them, to stay with him. Peter thought he would be all right—until he had a terrible nightmare.

In his dream, Abby was still floating alone in the lake in the dark of night. Slowly, her body—stiff and jerky, not lean and limber as she had been in life—started moving to the edge of the lake, crawling out of the water and sliding onto land. Every detail was impeccably vivid. Her wet hair dripped tiny streams along the dirt, her pale bloodless skin shone morbidly in the moonlight; her blackened rotting finger-nails gripped the earth. The Thing-That-Had-Been-Abby slithered into the woods, along the path, toward his house. She (It) was looking for him; searching, *hunting*.

Peter awoke screaming and crying hysterically. Within seconds his parents were there comforting him and, as they held him and rocked him, his tears of fear turned to ones of sorrow. He already missed Abby's smile and her companionship. She was a girl, but she didn't mind getting dirty or playing rough or reading comics. She befriended him when no one else had and now she was gone forever. His failure to rescue her brought on overwhelming grief which he knew was his to bear forevermore.

Peter's nightmares were relentless. Every time he fell asleep there was a continuation of the same dream. Abby's corpse crawled closer and closer to his house. In his last dream she reached the house and tapped on his window with flaxen fingers. He awoke with a start, covered in sweat, but there was nothing outside but the night. Now that The-Bad-Dream-Abby had reached the house he hoped the nightmare would cease. Then he took a shower to relax and—boom—as soon as he emerged from the water and looked in the mirror, he saw her behind him, following him in consciousness for the first time.

It terrified him beyond description to see her when he was awake and even as he screamed and stammered and told his parents insistently about what happened they simply reassured him that it was just a waking dream. Peter wished he could believe them but, deep down, he knew it wasn't true. Abby had reached him in his dreams and now she was reaching for him in his waking hours.

Peter briefly attended Abby's wake, but not her funeral. As soon as he looked down and saw her lying lifelessly in her stiff rectangular coffin he choked up and had to be removed. The room had grown cold and stuffy and he was both grateful and relieved when his parents took him home. Subsequently, they steered clear of the funeral, proclaiming that it was too traumatic to put their 12-year-old son through. As far as they were concerned, Abby was gone and they had to try and move forward.

What Peter's parents didn't know was that Abby was everywhere; Peter never got a moment's peace from her presence. He saw her behind corners, reflected in window panes and puddles; she even stared at him from the bottom of drinking glasses. At first, he only *saw* her but within a week she started speaking to him—calling his name and begging him to come back to her. It sounded like Abby's voice but there was anger and menace to it, nothing like the sweet nonthreatening girl he had known. In church he was told that people went to Heaven after they died...unless they were bad. Maybe Abby had been bad and God sent her to Hell. Death had made her insane and now she blamed him. One thing was of no doubt: her ghost was after him.

It was obvious to Peter that Abby was as lonely in death as she had been in life before she met him. Now she wanted him to join her wherever she was and keep her company once again. In his mind's eye he understood her plan perfectly; she would lure him to her and then drag him down so they could be dead together.

She was getting increasingly aggressive. He had seen her in his closet hiding and whispering to him from behind racks of clothes. One night as he lay in his bed, he felt her moving under the mattress, searching for him. Although he saw her constantly, she only came after him when he was alone. Thus, he made it his mission to remain by his parents' sides at all times. He insisted on sleeping on the floor of their bedroom. When they left a room, he followed. If he had to go to the bathroom or take a shower one of them had to stay with him. Even with his parents watching over him, Peter absolutely refused to take a bath. Whenever he was submerged in the water, he felt Abby's fingertips probing up from the drain, brushing against his ankles.

His parents—particularly his Father—were worried about his constant need for company. They took him to psychologists who badgered him with questions about his thoughts and feelings. Peter didn't mind. He was safe. He still saw Abby—she often glared at him from the ornamental mirror behind the doctor's chair—but he dared not tell the professionals that. Sometimes people who said such things got locked up in insane asylums. If he got locked up in the nut hatch, he might get lobotomized. That would be bad. What would be worse was getting thrown in a padded cell. If he got locked up in a padded cell, he would be alone...and totally at The-Thing-That-Used-To-Be-Abby's mercy.

Peter was an only child and he enjoyed a close relationship with his parents. They were his constant companions, allies, and protectors. He never imaged Abby —or her spirit—could extend to them. But Peter was only a boy and there were a great many things he did not know.

At first it was small incidents. His Mother lost her balance and nearly hit her head on the pavement while walking back to the car after leaving the grocery store. Then, his Father's hand slipped while he was using an electric knife to carve up dinner and he needed to get stitches. Although these things happened in close proximity to each other, Peter didn't connect them to Abby until the car accident.

January came in full force and it brought snow in massive quantities. It stacked up four-feet high and kept coming, turning the world into a landscape of ice. Peter's parents owned a brand-new Plymouth Belvedere—his father's pride and joy—and the car handled well in snow so the weather didn't prevent them from going into town to do their errands. One day, as they were standing in line at the supermarket, the snow started coming down in heavy drifts. By the time Peter and his parents piled into their vehicle and headed home the streets were nearly invisible. Peter's Mother sat rigidly in the front seat, anxiously watching the road, as his Father cautiously navigated through the near-white-out. Peter was the most relaxed one of the three as he sat in the backseat and nibbled on a candy bar. He was with his family, he was fine, he—

Abby appeared out of nowhere. She stood in the middle of the road still wearing the bathing suit she had worn on the day she died. Despite the freezing temperature she was dripping wet.

Peter's parents didn't see her. Before Peter could scream, Abby held her arms out and touched the hood of the slow-moving Plymouth. The car instantly spun out of control. Peter's Father turned the wheel fanatically as the vehicle careened off the pavement and landed in a snow bank. No damage was done and no one was hurt but Peter saw Abby smiling menacingly at him through the rearview mirror as his Father reversed the vehicle and continued the journey home. It was then that Peter realized that he needed to face her, for his parent's sake if not his own.

That night, for the first time in months, he told his parents that he wanted to sleep in his own room. His Father was supportive but his Mother was suspicious of her son's new-found bravery, especially after the frightening incident merely hours before.

"Are you *positive*?" she questioned.

Peter assured her that he was.

That night, as the snow fell heavily outside, Peter confirmed that his parents were asleep and safe. Then he went back to his room and faced the window. Abby was outside, as usual, tapping on the glass with her finger. She was so close to him that he could see the irises of her eyes. Once they had been a beautiful bright blue, now they were black and emotionless. Peter trembled with fear as he put on his warm coat and boots. He fully believed that he was about to die at The-Thing-That-Used-To-Be-Abby's hands but, strangely, the idea of freezing still bothered him. Once bundled, he took a deep breath and opened the window.

He expected her to attack him right away—perhaps rip his neck out with her long fingernails and then drink up his blood—but no such thing happened. Instead she simply stood still and watched him climb out of the house. Then she turned and walked into the woods with that stiff and jerky gait of hers. Peter followed.

She led him to the lake. It was now completely frozen over but the sight of it sent a wave of terror through him. He had not been there since Abby's accident. The-Thing-That-Once-Was-Abby walked out to the lake's center which was right around the very spot where she had drowned. Then she turned and beckoned to Peter who stood shivering on the embankment.

Tentatively he stepped onto the ice and met with his departed companion. As soon as he was next to her, she spoke. He was relieved to hear Abby's voice, not ranting or raving, but curious—maybe a bit sad—and undeniably *his* Abby.

"I miss you," she declared, loneliness lacing her words.

"I miss you, too!" Peter gushed emotionally. "You were my best friend, Abby! I'm really lonely without you. I miss you every single day. I'd give anything to have you back!"

"Why did you do it?"

"Do what? I can't remember any of it! Honestly, I can't! I wish I could but I can't! I don't understand how you could've drowned! You were a better swimmer than me! I'm stronger than you were so I should have been able to save you! I could've gotten you to the shore! I—"

He couldn't finish his sentence. He was tongue-tied and his gut wrenched; his words were choked and blocked by deep and seemingly ceaseless sobs.

Then Abby turned her face directly to his and Peter immediately noticed that her eyes were her own pretty light blue, not the startling black holes he had seen in the reflections. Aside from the bluish tint to her once-tanned skin, she looked and acted exactly like the Abby he had known; not vindictive or emotionless or soulless but sweet and loyal and good. Tears streamed openly down his face. Abby took pity on him as soon as she saw the extent of his genuine torment.

"I'll help you," she crooned.

Gently, she slid her arms around him. She was surprisingly warm—actually everything was warm...hot... scorching. Peter suddenly realized that it was July again; the lake sparkled blue and his and Abby's laughter filled the air.

They had delighted in sneaking off to the forbidden lake since it made them feel like rebels. Peter would bring his transistor radio and the songs of Elvis Presley, Sam Cooke, Jimmie Rodgers and all the other musicians that made adults mad would fill the air. Typically, they would assume the roles of the characters from their favorite horror films--*Voodoo Island*, *The Curse of Franksenstein*, and--Abby's personal favorite--*Daughter of Dr. Jekyll*. Sometimes they even pretended to be Bonnie and Clyde.

That's what they had been doing on that fateful Monday. Abby had been playing the part of Bonnie, prancing around the muddy marsh and showing off her long legs, pretending to distract bank clerks so Peter—Clyde—could take off with all the loot in the vaults. Then she had given the game up and gone for a dip.

"It's too hot for this," she declared while submerging herself in the cooling water. "Besides, Bonnie and Clyde happened like 200 years ago. We should think of something else."

"Bonnie and Clyde wasn't 200 years ago, it was twenty at most!" Peter retorted as he followed Abby into the waist-deep water. "My Dad was a teenager when it was all over the papers and he's not old."

He put his arms around her. To his surprise, she quickly shoved him off. He fell backwards, parting the water like Moses.

"What are you doing?!" She sounded as outraged as a nun in a brothel.

"I wanna kiss you again."

"Don't."

"Why not? We did it last week! Remember Friday?"

Truthfully, Friday had been an accidental incident which actually started on Tuesday. On Tuesday they had been playing Bonnie and Clyde and after a successful robbery Peter had leaned over and kissed Abby lightly on the lips. It was a purely spur-of-the-moment action which had surprised them both, but nothing more. Quickly, they had gone back to playing as if nothing had happened. Yet, on Wednesday, they started talking about Abby's older sister, Helen, who was an understudy for the part of Juliet in the local theater's presentation of Shakespeare's famous play.

"If the lead actress gets sick Helen will have to play the role and at the end, she'll have to *kiss a boy!*" Abby reported this information as if it was the most scandalous thing that she had ever heard. "I'd be too scared, especially on a stage in front of a *whole audience!*"

Then the discussion had turned to wondering if kissing—real kissing—was hard to do. Somehow, by the end of the day, they had tried it. It seemed that both of them liked it because on Thursday they practiced again. On Friday they repeated the process...this time lying down on the sandy, marshy embankment. Weekends were reserved for family, at least in Peter's household, so they didn't see each other on Saturday or Sunday. Peter had eagerly awaited Monday so that he could touch Abby again.

Previously, Peter had regarded Abby as a tomboy from a rough family. She climbed trees, spit, and knew how to defend herself from anyone who riled her. Yet she was also thoughtful and funny. She was an outcast because she was poor and he was an outcast because he was short and skinny. They both came up against snickers and jeers and constant exclusion from practically everything. In each other they found solace. Even though their friendship was prime ammunition for bullies, they were able to withstand anything as long as they had each other to talk to. Their vivid imaginations connected and combined in the ultimate sharing of minds. They allowed each other to escape and for years that had been their only desire.

Recently, however, Peter had started to notice how pretty Abby was—her wide eyes, her dark hair, even her nice long legs. Normally her body was well hidden in the baggy hand-me-down clothes that she was given by her sisters who were all older and at least three sizes bigger than she was. Yet, in the summer, Peter had instantly seen how nice her legs were as she paraded around in shorts and swimwear. And so, that Monday, he had yearned to feel her lips on his once again.

"Come on, we can pretend to be Popeye and Olive Oyl, or Lucy and Ricky! They kiss, right?"

Abby shifted uncomfortably under the weight of his gaze. "We shouldn't have done that. I think lying down while kissing can be dangerous. Mommy's always screaming about staying away from boys or we'll end up like Susie. She has no idea how much time even I spend with you."

Susie, he should have known! Abby was the youngest child in a family of seven girls. Susie, the second oldest, got pregnant when she was fifteen and now lived with her drunk husband and bratty son in a shack on the bad side of town.

"I don't think it's the same thing," he protested. He was, in fact, pretty *sure* it wasn't the same thing but there was an underlying connection, somehow.

Abby shrugged. "Either way, it's better not to, just in case."

She turned and headed toward the lake's deeper depths and something inside of Peter snapped. He was good to Abby. He bought her movie tickets, candy, cheeseburgers and milkshakes that she never would have been able to afford otherwise. He let her watch *I Love Lucy*, *Leave It to Beaver* and *The Honeymooners* on his television set since her family didn't even have one. Last Christmas, his mother had even knitted her a poodle skirt because her own couldn't be bothered. Hell, he was even considering getting her a pair of blue suede shoes for her birthday--if they even made them for girls--since she admired his so much. That was more than anyone else ever did for her and now she was denying him a mere kiss. It wasn't fair. It wasn't right. It wasn't acceptable. Peter seized her by the arm and pulled her to him, roughly running his hands through her hair.

"Come on, one kiss!"

"No! Let go of me, Peter, you're hurting me!"

"Just one! We're too young for you to be like Susie!"

"We're too young, period! Stop it!"

She kicked at him and her feet connected painfully with his shins. Peter released his grip, yelping in agony as Abby ran deeper into the water. Cradling his injured leg, anger boiled up inside of him. Ignoring the throes and throbs and hurt, he swam after her. He was bigger and stronger than she was and he caught up with her quickly. They were now swimming in the middle of the lake where the water was too deep to feel the muddy bottom.

"Come on Abby," he pleaded. "Don't be a bitch!"

"Don't call me that!"

"Bitch, bitch, bitch!"

Rage consumed them both at once. She took a swing at him. He retaliated by grabbing her. They struggled against each other, splashing and kicking and shouting in a violent embrace that was not at all like the pleasant cuddle he had been hoping for. They tussled for several minutes before Abby got still. Peter assumed she had given up and was playing possum. Then he realized that she was under the water. She stared blankly up at him with the same empty gaze he saw in the eyes of dead fish at the market.

He spent several minutes trying to wake her up to no avail. He had been screaming shrilly but then he seemed to tune everything out. Stony-faced, he emerged from the water and started walking down the woodsy path towards his house, leaving Abby's corpse floating listlessly in the center of the water.

The doctors had been right; he panicked and set off a defense mechanism in his brain. He had blocked everything out and was unaware of what he had done. No wonder she wanted to reach him—he had taken her life himself! He had murdered Abby!

"ABBY!" Peter wailed aloud; the awful realization felt as if it was ripping his insides to shreds and he wished that he too was dead. "OH GOD, ABBY, I REMEMBER! I'm sorry, Abby, I didn't mean to! I'm so sorry! ABBY!"

It was cold; the warmth of the world was suddenly replaced by a biting chill. The air was no longer still and muggy but gusty and freezing; its inconsolable wails mixed with his own. Peter fell to his knees and thought that he heard his Mother's voice as a sharp cracking sound filled his ears. Suddenly he was falling, descending down into the cold and the wet and the darkness.

* * *

Doctor Auburn stared down at the unconscious boy who was lying stock-still in the hospital bed. It had been unpredictable for a while—hypothermia had set in and they nearly lost him a few times—but now he was in stable condition. The medical staff had been monitoring him carefully for hours and his vital signs indicated that he would make a full recovery.

The boy was lucky. His mother had woken up and realized that he was out of the house. Instinctually, she had known where he had gone and had been level-headed enough to sense that something was very wrong. She had called the operator and requested help even before she ventured down the woodsy path and found her son standing on the frozen lake. The emergency personnel arrived seconds after he had fallen through the broken ice. In the ambulance he had come to enough to repeatedly declare: "*I did it!*"

The boy's worried parents huddled together next to the bed. Doctor Auburn knew that his patient was Peter, the same boy who had lost his best friend six months earlier. The poor girl had drowned in the same spot where the ice broke. Undoubtedly, the boy was traumatized from witnessing such a thing. Obviously, he had made his way out to the lake in what was seemingly a suicide attempt; a result of misplaced guilt. The poor kid probably really believed that he had killed the girl who had been his one and only friend.

The strain of the initial accident's aftermath had affected his parents as well. Upon being brought to the hospital, his Mother insisted that Abby's voice had woken her and told her that Peter was in trouble. Abby—the dead girl—allegedly told her to go to the lake and call for help immediately. When Peter's Mother checked his room and found his bed empty, she listened to the voice.

The doctor was sympathetic. He gave her a Valium to calm her nerves and re-checked the boy's chart. Finding nothing amiss, he gave the parents a wan smile, reassuring them that their son would live. On the way out of the room he reflected on the irony of fatal accidents. Death was often quick for victims; it was the survivor's psychological agony that lingered.

Companions

Although she was only seventeen, Rose knew more about Emma's odd behavior than anyone else in the village since she was dating Emma's older brother, Edward. Her parents weren't pleased about the relationship because they believed that mental abnormalities ran in families. Yet Rose refused to stop seeing Edward. She felt sorry for him and his Father since Emma's condition was a hardship and hearing everyone snicker behind their backs only made the situation worse. Of course, sometimes it was hard NOT to laugh at Emma's strange antics.

Emma spoke to mirrors, chatting to her own reflection as if it was another person. She even had a name for her imagery companion: Hazel. Moreover, sixteen-year-old Emma still carried a teddy bear everywhere. No one knew exactly what was wrong with Emma. Rumors circulated that she went crazy when she was six after her Mother succumbed to tuberculosis.

"It worsened when she was eight and found an old book about séances in the attic," Edward told Rose. "Granny believed in that nonsense and Emma thought she had found a way to contact Mom. After that she started playing in the woods all day, just her and Teddy."

The mention of the woods sent a chill down Rose's spine. The woods were creepy. Witches had been hanged there a long time ago and Rose was sure that their evil spirits still walked between the trees.

Emma went steadily downhill.

"At first she tried to hide her behavior," Edward confided, "but now she's lost even that sensibility. You've seen how she walks around chattering to that mirror; she takes the damn thing everywhere!"

Rose had indeed witnessed Emma wandering around talking to herself with Teddy in one hand and a portable silver mirror in the other. As funny as these scenes looked, Rose never laughed.

At first Emma's behavior was weird, yet harmless. Then she became violent. She shouted at the postman.

She threatened the paperboy with an axe. Whenever Emma screamed at someone, or spat at someone, or threw a tantrum she claimed that it was at the whim of Hazel, her companion. When Emma killed her neighbor's incessantly barking dog her Father finally had her committed to the psychiatric hospital. She had fought furiously; it took several orderlies to carry her away. After Emma's committal Edward gave the mirror and Teddy to Rose.

Initially, Rose was delighted by the gifts, especially Teddy who was made of soft brown wool and had big button eyes. But soon she sensed that something was amiss; sometimes Teddy's wool felt coarse and his eyes looked vindictive. Most unnervingly, Teddy seemed capable of moving by his own volition and had a strange affinity to mirrors. On numerous occasions Rose had left Teddy on her bed only to later discover him sitting beside her dresser mirror, staring fixedly into it as if searching for something.

Each night, Rose was plagued by terrible nightmares. Teddy whispered awful things in her ears as *something* watched from the dresser mirror. Rose would sit bolt upright in her bed, panting with panic, only to find nothing wrong.

Then Emma died.

She had taken ill at the asylum. An autopsy confirmed that heart failure was the cause of death. Rose attended the funeral but she dared not go near the coffin.

She's mad at me for taking her things, Rose thought as she stood among the mourners.

* * *

That night, Rose was awakened by the sound of scratching noises outside her bedroom door. Whispers echoed throughout the room. Rose's heartbeat quickened and fear welled up inside of her. She gripped Teddy tightly, seeking comfort. Suddenly the bear recoiled from her grasp, turned towards her, and hissed venomously!

Rose didn't have time to scream before the door burst open and Emma—or what was left of Emma—staggered into the room. The long white gown that she had been buried in dragged listlessly behind her. When the corpse reached for her, Rose clearly saw autopsy stitches embedded in its flesh. Emma's nails were caked with dirt. She had dug herself out of her grave to reclaim her beloved bear.

Rose attempted to run but what she saw next made her stop cold. There was a witch—*Hazel*—crackling from inside the dresser mirror. Her ancient face was filled with malice. She called to Emma's body—controlling her in death just as she had in life—but the voice didn't come from the mirror, it came from Teddy.

"Pick me up!"

Emma's remains snatched Teddy from Rose's quivering hands. Instantly there was a flash of light. Then the witch vanished from the mirror.

* * *

Hazel gazed into the mirror, studying her new body. It felt wonderful to be back in human form again! Rose's figure was a divine vessel; much better than being trapped in a teddy bear or wandering as a formless spirit!

Hazel glanced down at Emma's corpse which lay beside Rose's bed. Situating herself beside Emma's rotting ear, Hazel whispered:

"Your body shall serve me well, Rosie."

With one final wretched cackle, the witch that possessed Rose's body climbed out of the window and descended into the woods.

* * *

Rose helplessly watched everything from the floor, her soul entombed in Emma's remains. She watched the sun rise. She watched her mother scream and faint. She watched the police come. She listened as Edward organized a search party. Yet she could not move or give a single sign of life.

She couldn't even scream as she was placed back into Emma's coffin and reburied in Emma's defiled grave. Emma, the grieving little girl who had once tried to summon her Mother's spirit and instead called forth a witch's ghost.

Then there was only darkness and Teddy, Rose's final companion.

Invitation

The sun was setting. Jane watched the glorious colors splay across the sky from where she stood in her antique shop, staring out the dusty window at the world beyond. The sunsets in Brereton, North Dakota, truly were magnificent; certainly, more beautiful than anything else in the sleepy and dilapidated town.

As she basked in the glow of the sunset, Jane caressed the mysterious key in her hand. Where had it come from? More importantly, where did it lead to? Jane would give anything to find out the answers to those questions.

Beginning after the first snowfall in early November, the residents of Brereton had begun finding grotesque-looking snowmen in their yards and small silver keys inside their mailboxes, carefully placed in sealed, unmarked envelopes. No one knew exactly who had made the snowmen or left the keys but nearly everyone blamed local teenagers. With merely 800 residents Brereton was an especially small town and young people often found the oddest ways to amuse themselves, even if it was at the expense of others...

When 87-year-old Tyler Perrison spotted one of the figures on his lawn he had been so surprised that his heart started to race—subsequently resulting in his hospitalization. Amy Harrison had screamed herself hoarse at the sight of hers. Even Rodney Rickson, the most dedicated hunter in town, had been so alarmed that he shot his snow figure with a bow and arrow, convinced that some sort of mutant had crawled onto his property. When he realized that it was just a mound of sculptured snow, he humorously put red dye all around the spot where the arrow struck and posted the photo on the Internet.

Although the majority of Brereton residents were horrified and angered by the sight of the monstrous snowmen, Jane found the situation rather amusing... perhaps even somewhat thrilling. It had obviously taken a great deal of time and effort to construct the snow demons and whoever had done so possessed incredible artistic skill—they really were gruesome. Jane knew that better than anyone since she had taken a brisk walk all around town just to see every single one.

Jane had also discovered a dreadful snow figure on her property but she hadn't screamed or shot at it. Truth be told, she had rather admired it. It was a noticeably larger figure than the others with several arms, numerous eyes, and rows of sharp and pointed teeth. She was planning to keep it for as long as possible and she was extremely annoyed when Officer Henley and Officer Palmer arrived unannounced on her property and promptly kicked the snow figure until it disintegrated into a formless pile. As Jane watched the snow creature—which oddly appeared to be hollow on the inside—disintegrate she had a sudden urge to kick the officers until they were nothing but bits of blood and bone. She *always* suppressed violent impulses, of course, yet she did wish that she had taken photos of every ferocious figure.

The presence of the police led Jane to consider the possibility that there could be a lunatic loose in town. It would certainly be exciting if there was because nothing interesting ever happened in Brereton. An active sugar mill provided the majority of the town's employment but, to Jane, it was little more than a decaying ruin. In the summer there were two tepid town fairs, "Riverfest" in July and the "Modern Corn and Apple Festival" in August, but Jane rarely lingered long at either. The villagers were quite tiresome with their petty gossip and that was precisely why she also never joined any bingo nights or "Bone Builders" group exercise classes.

By far the most enjoyable occasions were the rummage sales where Jane both sold and bought things. She was always hopeful that at least one item would turn out to be possessed by some dark force but, thus far, all objects appeared to be quite normal. The only other occasions that the town residents seemed to get excited about were related to baseball and football and such things did not appeal to Jane. She hated sports.

Secretly, Jane was addicted to watching "True Crime" programs on television and so she knew all about homicidal maniacs. She thought the topic was quite interesting, although she kept her obsession to herself since she knew many of the townspeople might think it was morbid or strange and such perceptions would not fare well for her antique business. Undoubtedly the church women would think her media preferences were downright scandalous—just like the church folk had thought her teenage preoccupation with heavy metal music was reprehensible.

Jane had always hated attending church services and she often dreamed about burning the church to the ground. When she was younger her fantasies had been so intense that she could practically smell the smoke and feel the heat of the flames. But it was all in her mind, of course, she would never actually *do* such a thing. Truthfully, she had never actually done much of anything. She had never journeyed out of state or had neither a nemesis nor a kiss. When she was a girl, she had escaped into fairy tales and films like "Labyrinth," hoping that one day something special would happen to her.

Yet nothing exciting ever did happen—until those snow figures appeared. They were, by far, her highlight of the year, maybe even the decade, and that was why they intrigued her. It was also why she had lied to Officer Palmer about the key. Like everyone else she had received one in her mailbox but she swore to the police that she hadn't. They were collecting them to test on every lock in town and, although Jane was desperately curious about their purpose, she didn't want to surrender hers. It was so shiny and small and *captivating*. Jane never tired of gazing at it.

Officer Palmer had given her a funny look when she denied having a key and Jane knew that he had pegged her for a lair. Perhaps she was now a suspect, maybe they thought she had been behind the whole affair! Jane didn't mind, there was no evidence against her and, at 46, she was an unlikely candidate to go around building hundreds of frightening snow creatures in the dead of night. Officer Henley was more accepting of her claim. Jane's house was on the edge of town, perhaps it was the last one that the perpetrators had gotten to and they had either run out of keys or simply forgotten to leave one.

In the days that followed, Jane wondered if the police would come back and arrest her. She hadn't done anything to warrant such an event, of course, but she anticipated the *possibility*. Getting arrested would certainly be a new experience and one that would undoubtedly prove to be quite memorable. Yet Jane did not get arrested and now, nearly two weeks since the snow figures appeared, the authorities still had no leads on who had left the keys or what they unlocked. Jane was bitterly disappointed and she seriously considered starting her own investigation—it would certainly help her pass the time as the winter approached. Brereton had particularly long and bitterly cold winters and Jane spent most of the months of December thru March home alone.

As she stared down at the small silver key, Jane smiled. It was a present from some unknown giver yet it might just grant her the gift of adventure, something she had never known.

* * *

That night Jane locked up her shop and drove home as usual. She kept the radio tuned to her local country music station. That was a perfectly acceptable choice of audio in Brereton. Yet as soon as she got outside of the town limits, she slid an old Black Sabbath CD into her aging car's player and bobbed her head to the sound of *Lady Evil*. Over the past ten days Jane had started listening to the beloved music of her long-lost youth once again. It both revived and soothed her. Mostly, it helped her block out the voices.

Normally, Jane only heard the voices in her dreams. Ever since early childhood she had recurring visions of dancing with monsters. Upon the arrival of the snow figures those dreams had come back in full force except, this time, she was dancing with demons made of snow. Although most people would categorize such dreams as nightmares, Jane adored them. The macabre land of her dreams was so enticing—so *enthralling*—compared to the bleak world she awoke to daily.

Jane smirked as she glanced into the rear-view mirror. Saint Edward's Church was disappearing into the background. She remembered how the churchgoers had reacted to her "wild stories" and "fantasies" when she had been young and foolish enough to confess them. But Jane really did hear things. Sometimes the whispering voices told her to play with knives and turn on the stove's gas. At first, she had obeyed them and carried out whatever whims they instructed but she had quickly learned that listening to those nighttime whispers in daytime hours was a bad idea—specifically when you were being raised by people like Elmira and Andy Weston.

Jane didn't know who her real parents were since she had been left on the steps of the church, bundled up in a blanket. Preacher Warren had found her and intended to take her to the orphanage until Elmira had begged him to let her and Andy adopt the abandoned child. The Weston's were religious, churchgoing, childless folks and Preacher Warren readily surrendered Jane to them and thereby sealed her fate.

Elmira and Andy never let Jane forget her mysterious roots.

We saved you from a life of destitution, they said.

You owe us, they accused.

You best remember where you come from, they scolded.

Elmira and Andy always had a lot to say to Jane—mostly unflattering speculation about her parentage. Eventually they decided that her mother was probably a teenaged prostitute and her father a criminal who had escaped from prison. They forever watched over Jane and scolded her whenever they even imagined that she might be considering taking something that didn't belong to her or wearing her skirt even slightly above the knee. The Weston's had always been very firm about one thing: Jane's bad genes would not be justification for poor behavior.

Jane had no idea if her mother really was a woman of easy virtue and her father a brute but as she got older, she grew increasingly tempted to do naughty things, *wicked* things. She tried to be good but sometimes her urges pushed her to behave most incorrigibly.

At church she gazed at the beautiful stained-glass windows and wondered what they would sound like shattering. At age 11 she had used a payphone in the center of town to call 911, and then remained silent on the line, just to see if ambulances would arrive. Much to her delight, they did with the lights flashing and sirens blaring. Another time she had faked being sick until the EMS came and took her to the hospital. It had been a marvelous experience for Jane who had soaked up all the attention of the doctors and nurses, but Elmira and Andy were so angry about the steep bill that she never dared to feign illness again.

Andy had been a mechanic who restored and sold old cars and tractors and Elmira had quit her job in the post office mailroom to become a stay-at-home mom. Their limited finances were often attributed to Jane, their "extra mouth to feed." For over a decade Jane toyed with the idea of setting fire to one of Andy's beloved restored cars but she never got the nerve. Alas, that was usually the case with Jane—she often had wonderful ideas for making mischief but she simply lacked the will to carry out acts of mayhem.

As a child she had written letters to fairies and trolls and placed them in the letterbox, hoping someone *(something)* would find her and take her away. Every time she saw a freight train, she fantasized about hopping on and heading to a big adventure. As a teenager she had seriously considered jumping off the bridge and plummeting into the icy water below where her body would mingle with all the fish that Andy frequently hunted. Her suicidal inclinations had been so strong that she had actually stood up on the bridge once and very nearly jumped but balked when she considered the physics of the matter. The bridge was low and if she had jumped, she would probably have just ended up cold and wet, not dead. Besides, such an endeavor could certainly have landed her in a psychiatric hospital and that was an experience that seemed too unpleasant to risk, even for someone as bored as she was.

Jane's eerily quiet nature had made her especially solitary yet she never felt lonely. Truthfully, she didn't think that she was capable of feeling most of the emotions that other people did. She didn't want to go to school dances, or flirt with boys, or giggle at sleepovers. She was much more inclined to take long walks alone through Skjeberg Cemetery. The name Skjeberg enthralled her; it sounded so exotic…so *otherworldly*. She had spent hours there fantasizing about being the Empress of the Dead. Jane had always possessed a vivid imagination.

Sometimes she wished that the long-distance truckers passing through town would make eyes at her like they did to the local waitresses. There were occasions when she had intentionally loitered around the highway rest stops, hoping to attract some rough shaven character, but her mousy appearance left her perpetually unnoticed. From time to time she even walked past the Elm Crest Motel, looking for some new and interesting faces, but no one outstanding ever seemed to materialize. Monotony was the calling card of her existence.

For a while Jane had gotten away with her peculiarities but, in 1983, everything changed after Andy barged into Jane's blandly decorated bedroom and discovered her dancing to Black Sabbath's *Lady Evil*. The Weston's were a God-fearing couple and they were not at all pleased about the "ward" in their care listening to the devil's music. And so, 15-year-old Jane had been forced into one Bible study group after the other—all of them led by Preacher Warren.

In the years since he had found her abandoned on the church steps Preacher Warren had aged prematurely. As the lines on his face deepened and his hair thinned, his temper got shorter. Most of his Bible study groups included fevered screaming about damnation and eternal suffering. Yet Jane never complained about attending his sessions, she enjoyed it, especially all the fire and brimstone stuff. Preacher Warren's rants were extremely entertaining and it was thanks to him that she had discovered the artwork of Hieronymus Bosch.

Preacher Warren firmly believed in the power of fear and he obsessively searched for unique ways to terrorize his congregation—especially the poor souls who attended his Bible studies. One day, Preacher Warren had passed around postcards portraying an oil painting titled *The Garden of Earthly Delights* by an artist named Hieronymus Bosch. The painting was filled with depictions of deprivation—most of it sexual in nature—and many demonic figures of assorted shapes and sizes. Most of the unfortunate churchgoers were horrified by the artistic hellscape but Jane was nothing short of enraptured.

Brereton was not a town that placed much emphasis on art. Had it not been for the furor of Preacher Warren, Jane most likely never would have found out about the 16th-century Dutch painter who had so aptly illustrated the creatures in her dreams. As soon as she saw his work Jane immediately understood that Hieronymus Bosch had obviously seen the same beings that she did. Some of the depictions had been so exact that they had taken her breath away! Although Preacher Warren had been trying to scare her, he had actually provoked her curiosity in all-things-demonic and turned her into a life-long admirer of Bosch. Years later, when she acquired the Internet, she spent hours observing each and every one of his demon-laced pieces.

As Jane pulled into her modest home's driveway and switched off her car's engine she smiled, just thinking about the mesmerizing painting delighted her. The postcard was now sitting atop her mantle, claiming the honorable position that it deserved. Jane always took time to admire it as soon as she got home. She hoped it would manifest her dream of dancing with the demons every night which was usually the highlight of her otherwise loathsome days.

* * *

That night Jane awoke with a start to the sound of the wailing wind. She clutched instinctively at the silver key which she kept hidden in the pocket of her pajama top —no one was going to take her treasure! When she glanced out the bedroom window, she saw a distant light in the woods. Jane still lived in the house that she had grown up in. She had inherited it from Elmira and Andy when they passed on. Andy first from a sudden heart attack at age 68, Elmira seven years later after a long bout with emphysema. Jane didn't miss them nor had she felt much pain or grief at their departure. She had been rather relieved, in fact. Life was less troublesome without them. But in all the years spent in the house Jane had never known anyone to light a fire in the woods especially on cold, windy, snowy nights. This was something very unusual—something that warranted immediate investigation.

Jane hopped out of bed and quickly dressed in her warmest parka. Donning gloves, she bounded out into the snow holding nothing but a flashlight. In the back of her mind she knew that she ought to be afraid but, on some deeper level, she knew that she was going to be okay. That light was intended for her. It was calling to her. It was *inviting* her.

Jane trudged through the snow for what seemed like an eternity but she barely felt the air's bitter chill. She heard movement all around her and, from the corner of her eyes, thought she saw misshapen snow figures scurrying between the tree trunks, snickering. Jane giggled too—this was quite an adventure!

As she fought her way through the ever-climbing snowbanks, Jane spied a small ramshackle cabin that the light was emanating from. She thought that she had explored every inch of the woods but clearly, she was mistaken because she had never seen the old cabin before. It looked quite ancient. As she got closer to it Jane could smell a fireplace mixed with something else—something that smelled absolutely exquisite, like roasting meat.

The door was made of wood that looked as old as time. Jane gripped the iron door handle and pulled only to discover that it was locked. At first a crushing sense of disappointment rained down upon her but then she remembered the key! As her fingers shook with anticipation, she slid the key into the lock and turned. With a "click" the door creaked open. She had solved the riddle of its purpose.

Jane stepped into the cabin with excitement pulsing through her veins. To her surprise, the cabin was empty except for a small lit fireplace embedded in the right wall and a spiraling staircase that led downward. This was something entirely unexpected since Jane could have sworn that cabins rarely had basements. From the bowels below came the sounds of music and laughter mingled with bright lights and good smells. Jane immediately started her descent.

The steep and seemingly endless staircase twisted and turned like a conch shell. Carved between walls of pure red rock, the steps glowed gold. When Jane eventually got to the bottom she gasped in disbelief at the scene before her: she was standing in a landscape that looked very similar to the "Garden of Earthly Delights" from Bosch's painting. There were dark caverns but there were also patches of oasis filled with beautiful clear water and lush green vegetation. The creatures from her dreams abounded in the abstract scenery. Most of them were naked, dancing and singing, or drinking and eating.

As soon as she stepped off the staircase, they all turned to face her.

"JANE!" they serenaded and bowed down to her.

Before Jane could react, booming footsteps shook the cavern and the sea of demons parted to make way for a huge creature with blue skin and several arms, numerous eyes, and many rows of sharp teeth. The creature wore a silky black cape and a thorny crown. Jane instantly recognized its shape as being the same as the snow figure that had graced her lawn. The creature approached her and extended one of its hands. Jane noticed that its fingers were adorned with dozens of sparkling rings.

"I am Zaakdor, King of the Underlands," he declared. "You have seen me in your dreams, yes?"

Jane nodded ecstatically.

"Did you make all of the figures in the snow and leave the keys?" she questioned.

Zaakdor nodded.

"In Brereton?" Jane stammered. "There must be better places than this!"

Zaakdor shrugged. "There's sugar here. We like sugar. Some might even say that we are addicted to it."

Jane observed that most of the demons were covered in sugar; many were greedily licking it from their hands and garments. They reminded her of kids in a candy store.

"I do hope that you liked our snow sculptures," Zaakdor continued. "Each one was the exact likeliness of my most devoted followers. They were sent as an invitation to you."

"But *everyone* in town had a figure on their lawn and a key in the mailbox," Jane protested.

Zaakdor waved his arms dismissively. "It was just a bit of fun," he answered. "Scaring mortals is amazingly amusing. Besides, I knew that you would be the only one clever enough to catch on...the only one *special* enough. After all, I am searching for a queen."

"But surely there are female demons!" Jane exclaimed, awestruck. "Wouldn't they be better matches for you than I, a mere mortal? Why would you bestow such an honor on me?"

"Haven't you always heard our whispers and visited our world in your dreams?" Zaakdor replied. "You *are* one of us, Jane, and you've known it all your life."

Jane felt herself blush and hoped that her crimson complexion would be unnoticeable in the hot landscape. It was Hell but it was beautiful and alluring. Jane already knew that she never wanted to leave.

"Imagine a world without boredom or routine or monotony," Zaakdor commanded. "Every moment of every day here is a festival! Come, my prize, let me show you!"

Jane allowed the demon to take her in his arms. They spent what seemed like an eternity dancing to heavy metal tunes, frolicking amid the forbidden fruits of the twisted trees, and drinking from the plentiful fountains. Then they dined on the most exquisite and exotic meat that Jane had ever tasted. It was pure bliss.

After the meal was finished, Zaakdor handed Jane a crumpled piece of paper with dried blood on it. Jane squinted as she strained to read the strange language printed on the paper.

"Drevozpracujici druzstvo is a company that produces wood lumber and board materials in the Czech

Republic," Zaakdor explained. "One of my Lordesses got her human mate from there. He's here with us now."

A chill crept up Jane's spine. Vaguely she remembered watching a news report about a Czech lumber worker who went crazy and murdered a number of other loggers before killing himself.

Most of the bodies had been dismembered, some were never found. Jane was fairly certain that the company the man worked for had been the same as the one printed on the bloodied piece of paper.

"I can give you everything you want," Zaakdor declared. "Riches, power, everlasting excitement.... even youth."

As he spoke, a smaller demon with a stick-like body, six eyes, and a birdlike beak held a mirror in front of Jane. To her amazement she looked thirty years younger, sixteen at most! She squealed with glee as Zaakdor continued his speech:

"This can be your home too," he proclaimed. "Would you like that?"

"Yes!" Jane exclaimed.

"Provided that you agree to my terms I think we can reach an agreement," the demon king replied.

"ANYTHING!" Jane wailed.

Zaakdor chuckled.

"Eagerness, I like that in a lady. What I most desire are people, preferably pure and innocent ones. The sinless tend to provide the best souls and most delicious meat... as you now know."

Jane recoiled. She had not considered that the meat she had dined upon was human. Then again, what did it matter? A meal that delicious was nothing to scorn no matter where it came from!

"Some generations are tastier than others," Zaakdor said conversationally. "We had grand feasts in 1930 and 1990. Now I think it's high time for another."

Jane remembered looking up Brereton's population record and seeing severe dips in the populace in both 1930 and 1990. She had always assumed that it was due to people leaving town during the depression and recession yet now it was obvious that some unfortunates had also been devoured by demons.

"How about children?" Jane suggested. "Would they be tasty enough for you, my love?"

Zaakdor licked his lips, clearly pleased. Apparently, children were an especially desirable flavor.

Jane knew what needed to be done.

* * *

Reluctantly she ascended the staircase, knowing that the quicker she finished her earthly duties the faster she could return to the euphoria of the demon's realm. It was already dawn when she ran through the snowy forest, unmindful of the cold and ice, determined only to reach the wood shed and fetch her axe. She had already sharpened the blade. It was ready for action.

After years of fixatedly watching media associated with murderers Jane finally understood their motives. The Czech man hadn't been crazy—he'd been *enlightened*, just like she was now. Nothing ever happened in Brereton but now SHE was going to MAKE some *things* happen!

There was carnage in the hours that ensued.

She went to Gullander's Hardware Store first. The grizzled owner barely had time to register her presence before she sank the axe into his chest. Relieved that there was no one else present to massacre, Jane rummaged through the aisles collecting plastic bags and the ropes that she would need to restrain the children who she intended to bring back to the Underlands alive. The demons would decide whether to keep them as slaves or eat them. Jane had no preference one way or the other.

Next, she went to Lefty's Liquors. She couldn't imagine returning to the Underlands without booze since the demons would surely savor alcohol. Lefty's Liquors was busier than the hardware store. Several lapsed A.A veterans—not that there was anything actually *anonymous* about who were alcoholics in a town as small as Brereton—always seemed to be stumbling around nearby regardless of the weather conditions nor the time of day. Jane dispatched two drunks and Lefty himself easily. Then she scooped up dozens of bottles of vodka and whiskey and gin.

Before exiting Lefty's, Jane butchered the corpses of the slaughtered winos and collected their meatiest parts in a large plastic bag. Although such characters could hardly be called sinless, their constant intake of liquor might have marinated their flesh to tender perfection. Jane assumed that the demons would know how to make a lovely potluck out of such human remains.

Trudging through the snow in her blood-soaked boots, Jane ventured into Drayton Drug. The shop was already decked out in Christmas décor and the festive atmosphere irked her. She had never cared for Christmas. Santa had never come to her because, as her adoptive parents said, she was evil.

"Lady Evil," Jane whispered and crackled as she hatched a blue-haired elderly shopper and split the young pharmacist in half.

She proceeded to raid the prescription medication counter. She strongly assumed that the demons would be delighted by the pills.

Lastly, she headed towards the school, her final earthly destination. Jane's joy was indescribable. Once these deeds were done, she would be gone from Brereton forever, having acquired her ticket back to Hell—her wicked little slice of heaven.

* * *

The following day the news relayed the story to the shocked public. Jane Weston, 46, had gone on a murderous rampage in the tiny town of Brereton, North Dakota, leaving ten people dead and fourteen wounded. Before being fatally shot by the police, Jane had attempted to kidnap several small children from an elementary school. Local residents claimed that Jane had long battles with depression and mental instability and had spent her last hour alive ranting about demons...

She had accepted her invitation.

Revelation

The night was clear and cloudless enabling the moon to illuminate the winding country road that was otherwise devoid of light. Reece Hanlon had been driving for over nineteen hours, the past six of which had been spent navigating narrow backwoods roads. It was difficult to steer an eighteen-wheel truck along such narrow lanes and by the time Reece emerged onto a mainline highway he was undeniably exhausted. He easily could have pulled over and checked into one of the many cheap motels that were situated right off the highway but Reece didn't believe in staying in hotels. He didn't like the idea of checking into anyplace since that would make it so much easier for *them* to find him.

Reece knew all about *them*—the invaders, the aliens, the *extraterrestrials*—and that was precisely why they were out to get him. At first the signs had been subtle, almost unnoticeable. He repeatedly caught every red light on the roads. He got pulled over for speeding twice. He found it increasingly difficult to drive at night because lights seemed brighter and blurrier than they ever had before. At first these things all seemed like coincidences. It wasn't until he started hearing the buzzing in his ears that he realized every little misfortune was connected. The invaders were on to him; they were after him.

Reece had first started to seriously suspect the invasion when he was in his mid-teens. He would stand out in the woods behind his childhood home and stare up at the planes going by...well, what everyone *assumed* were planes. Reece's father had always suspected something more sinister and soon Reece began to see his point of view. After all, many of those planes did have odd shapes...*otherworldly* shapes.

Reece's father didn't trust the United States government. In fact, he didn't trust governments anywhere. Governments were full of power-hungry men who were the precise kinds of people that highly advanced aliens could easily manipulate. Politicians were corruptible and undependable. The police were the same way as were judges and military personnel. Any and all authority figures were individuals to be scrutinized. After all, they had even gone so far as to cover up the events that defined Area 51.

Mitch, Reece's father, had spent his final years living in constant fear of abduction. He knew all the stories about the unfortunate souls who had been beamed up into space never to be seen or heard from again and he was determined to avoid such a fate. Mitch barricaded himself into his ramshackle house and packed a pistol whenever he dared to venture outside. Mostly, he sat in his favorite ragged armchair and drank whiskey morning, noon, and night. He had finally succumbed to liver failure, at the age of 44, when Reece was 19.

No one had been surprised by Reece's father's death. Mitch had been drinking himself silly for years, getting really bad after his wife left him for a used car salesman when Reece was only three. Most people took his warnings about aliens to be the ravings of a lunatic and, at first, Reece had felt the same. As a preteen he had been resentful of, and embarrassed by, his father's behavior but now, as he approached 40, he understood his father more and more since he had slowly but surely started to see the same patterns of insidious invasion that the old man had.

Reece yawned and surveyed the roadside. He was thick in the woods of West Virginia now, surrounded by the mountains and hills that encompassed coal miner territory. It was a world in which Reece was familiar. He had been born in Appalachian country and his father and uncles had all been coal miners as were many of his cousins. Reece had been the one male member of his family to escape such a fate. He liked trucking for a number of reasons, but most of all since it was a profession that didn't require men to burrow down into the bowels of the earth until their lungs were blackened and rotted.

The road he was on had a scenic layby. Reece pulled over and parked the truck. It was already after midnight and, even though most truckers drove straight through the wee hours, he was too sleepy to go any further. He gazed up at the sky suspiciously. He knew that the UFOs were flying around above, lurking. He had disabled his GPS system and his phone to stop the invaders from constantly monitoring him but they always seemed to follow him regardless. They were bound to have access to advanced space age technology, after all, and he supposed that they had already put a tracking device somewhere on his truck. They were determined to destroy him and yet he didn't have a clue how to protect himself. Heck, he couldn't even decipher which planet they were from, although he strongly assumed that they were visitors from a different galaxy altogether.

Reece climbed into the back of the truck's spacious cab and lay down, attempting to sleep. He tried to ignore the ever-present buzzing in his head and remained acutely alert for any sounds that might indicate spying aliens. He was keenly aware of the creaking of the surrounding trees and the low wail of the wind. He was also reminded of the many mines that most of his kin had spent their lives toiling in, especially, and most notoriously, Uncle Harlan.

Reece supposed that his Uncle Harlan had a lot to do with why he had aimed to do something different with his life. Reece's daddy had been a drunk but Uncle Harlan, his daddy's half-brother, was outright crazy. Most folks assumed it was on account of all the dust and gas that he had inhaled while digging deep into the earth—or maybe there were just faulty genes in the bloodline—but Harlan had well and truly snapped before he reached the age of 30.

Harlan's downfall had begun when he had gotten trapped under the earth after a mine collapsed. For two and a half days he had endured the damp and dark, although he was the lucky one; the sole survivor. In fact, most of the bodies of his fellow miners had never even been found. From the time that he was rescued, Harlan hadn't been right in the head. He constantly ranted and raved about monsters under the earth. He called them "mole people" and swore that they had been the reason behind the cave in. He also claimed that they had attacked and eaten several of the other miners. Harlan insisted that he had been the sole survivor simply because he had remained motionless, playing dead while buried under a pile of rock and mud.

"*Them things had sharp claws and teeth,*" he had stated repeatedly. "*I could hear them moving all around me, scratching at the walls and making high pitched whining sounds and low growling noises. And the screams! I could hear the screams of the other men as those things tore into their flesh.*"

About a week after the cave-in, inspectors had descended into the mine and searched for evidence of carnage in all of the accessible passageways. Truthfully, the inspectors had been nervous; if there was evidence of gore then it was likely that Harlan had suffered a psychotic break and had murdered his fellow miners. Sometimes the harsh working conditions and the earth's gases damaged men's minds. Back in 1923 a man had slaughtered eight of his fellow miners; just enough body parts had been found to have him hanged for murder. That miner had blamed monsters—just as Harlan did—all the way to the gallows.

When the inspectors found no trace of flesh or blood, Harlan had been declared insane and spent the rest of his life in the state psychiatric center, mercifully doped up on medication that helped him forget whatever he thought he had seen. Reece hadn't visited his uncle or known much about him but he got quite a kick out of the stories concerning Harlan's delusions... "mole people," could anything be more laughable?

When he had first heard the term, he had been seven years old and immediately envisioned people with gross skin conditions, not horrifying monsters. When he was a teenager he had stumbled across a tacky B-list movie from 1956 titled "The Mole People" and he had laughed all the way through it, wondering what crazy old Uncle Harlan would have made of its scenes of men in mole masks digging themselves up and out of the ground. Of course, there were real "mole people." Reece knew that term was sometimes used to describe the homeless in New York City who took shelter in defunct subway tunnels, but West Virginia was a long way from New York and the creatures that Harlan thought he had seen were definitely not human.

The hoot of an owl made Reece jump; he was always extra sensitive to noise when he was about to go to sleep. He could never be too careful. Ground-dwelling monsters were a ludicrous fantasy but extraterrestrials... now they were a force to be reckoned with. He held his breath and listened carefully for sounds of ray guns or strange languages transmitting over the radio but there was nothing but the hoot of the owl and the trees swaying in the breeze. Normal sounds, *earthly* sounds. Reassured, Reece exhaled and fell into a turbulent slumber.

He rarely slept well. Every night he was plagued by nightmares of space crafts and probing devices, unknown planets and little green men. However, this night was particularly bad. First, he dreamed of a group of four abducted people floating in midair. When they turned towards him and tried to scream in agony their heads started shaking so violently that their features became indistinguishable until each individual face disappeared; morphing into twisted and tormented blurs. Obviously, these unlucky victims were having a superbly negative reaction to whatever weird chemicals the aliens had pumped into them during their ungodly experiments.

Suddenly, the dream switched tracks and Reece found himself standing in a dilapidated auditorium with peeling paint on the walls and one single dull lightbulb illuminating the bleak room. Before him stood an aged wooden stage with blackened and tattered drapes pulled askew to the right side. A faceless man in a dark suit and bowler hat stood on the stage beside a noose which hung from the ceiling and served as the stage's single macabre prop. Three figures—which could have been men, monsters, or aliens—stood facing the stage, their backs turned to Reece. These three ominous figures also wore dark suits and bowler hats and Reece suddenly got the feeling that they were the judge, the mayor, and the sheriff —the mining town's three most powerful residents back in 1923 when the homicidal miner had been hanged. Suddenly, the executioner standing on the stage looked up —although his face was nothing but a blank oval—and beckoned to Reece, summoning him toward the noose. Then high-pitched nonsensical chatter, mingled with snarls and growls, filled the air and the three men (monsters) started to turn around—

Reece jolted awake, sweating profusely. He checked his watch; it was 3:21am, well before sunrise. There was a familiar and foul coppery taste in his mouth; it was a despicable flavor that he had grown accustomed to after waking from nightmares so frequently. Reece strongly suspected that his chronic night terrors were beamed into his brain courtesy of the invaders. Hence, the bad dreams indicated that the aliens knew where he was and it was time to get moving.

Reece crawled into the front of his cab and looked up at the sky. All he saw were stars and the moon...but there were also strange noises outside, whistles and clicks that sounded a bit like chattering. Although everything looked fine, the sounds could be an alien dialect; invaders communicating with one another via invisible airways. It was better to be safe than sorry so Reece started up the truck. He intended to drive through the night and make it to his destination in Wisconsin by noon. Despite his lingering tiredness, he resolved to meet his schedule and deliver his cargo of canned-food early; then no one could say that he didn't do his job.

Reece had a growing suspicion that the aliens had gotten to his boss, his whole company, in fact. He had heard whispers in the loading docks between fellow truckers; murmurings that were about him even if not directed towards him; just fragmented bits of words and phrases that alerted Reece to the fact that most of his coworkers were not on his side.

"*Losing his mind...*"
"*Going crazy...*"
"*Something's not right...*"
"*Seriously wrong with him...*"
"*Strange character...*"
"*Odd duck...*"
"*Creepy...*"

On and on such denunciations went.

Unsurprisingly, his boss appeared to be the ringleader. Reece was getting increasingly nervous about the very real possibility of losing his job—his only source of income—since his boss, a robust and balding middle-aged man named Frank Finkle, was constantly interrogating him. Frank asked Reece more questions than a game show host. He was particularly interested in knowing if he was feeling all right or if he had been sleeping well. And then there were the comments, the *accusations*. Frank told Reece that he didn't look too good; he hadn't shaved and had taken on a scruffy appearance; his eyes were red-rimmed; he was jittery and nervous. The worst part of it all was that Frank seemed to enjoy these spiteful conversations, these *belittlements*. He smirked—not smiled or grinned but outright mean-spiritedly *smirked*—whenever he interacted with Reece.

The cause of Frank's endless debriefings had quickly dawned on Reece. There really was only one suitable explanation: the aliens were mind controlling poor balding Frank Finkle. They were planting ideas in his head and making him think about firing one of his most efficient long-distance truckers. After all, if Reece was fired, he would soon end up homeless and be even more vulnerable. Reece knew that it was all part of their conspiracy to persecute, and ultimately abduct, him. Yet despite the aliens' persistent intentions they would not take his job, his livelihood, from him. Reece vowed to continue doing his job, and doing it well, until they finally succeeded in either killing him or beaming him up into space.

Determined to foil the aliens' wicked scheme, Reece steadily accelerated down the backwoods highway. He longed for a little company and switched on the radio for the comforting sound of human voices. "A Country Boy Can Survive" was playing on the country station and both the words and rich voice of Hank William Jr. encouraged Reece—a red-blooded country boy himself—to keep going, keep driving, keep fighting.

Reece was getting into the music and starting to relax, even enjoy himself a little. Then, suddenly, he hit something. The impact was exceptionally forceful. Reece felt and heard the crush of the truck's metal front grill and the shattering of the headlights. He was thrown forward violently and his body slammed painfully against the steering wheel; if he hadn't been wearing his seatbelt his head probably would have gone straight through the windshield.

A deer! He thought instantly, *I hit a goddamn deer!*

Or maybe it had been a bear, or even a moose. The front end of the truck was engulfed in smoke; whatever he hit must have been bigger than a deer to have done such extensive damage.

Trembling, Reece exited the cab to survey the destruction. Chills shot up his spine as soon as his feet hit the tarmac. There was no one around for miles but the woods seemed to be alive with sounds. Guttural wails and clicks and sputters seemed to come from every direction, as if seeping out of the very tree trunks. A terrible thought suddenly struck Reece: perhaps this was all a ploy—*a trap*—set by the aliens. With fear welling up inside of him, Reece backed up. But then, out of the corner of his eye, he spotted a lump of brown fur lying still and lifeless in front of his truck. Whatever he had hit was some kind of animal, it definitely wasn't a menacing little green man or an invincible robotic soldier. Relief washed over Reece. Whatever he had hit was a creature of earth and that alone was enough to quell his tortured nerves.

Damn critter, Reece thought as he stared at the dead beast. He couldn't help but feel a pang of pity for it even though he was also indescribably annoyed. Frank would undoubtedly blame this latest mishap on Reece's supposedly questionable sanity...it was possible that this would be the incident that finally cost him his job. Maybe the aliens were behind this misfortune after all; perhaps they had intentionally spooked this poor beast, provoking it to run out into the road and right into the grill of Reece's truck.

I best see what it was, Reece thought. *If it's gonna cost me my job I should at least know what the damned thing is.*

Reece walked over to the creature. If it turned out to be a buck, he intended to keep its antlers. He had always admired taxidermy. Yet the creature was no buck. Its fur was brown and caked with both mud and blood. It didn't look like any animal he had ever seen before. It looked almost like an ape, maybe a Sasquatch, but it had a tail that seemed far too long for a primate. When he turned the corpse over, Reece recoiled in horror.

He had struck some kind of monster. Its dead eyes were still open, colored an unnatural shade of red. Its nose was elongated and it had rows and rows of yellowed razor-sharp teeth. It didn't have hands; instead it had extended claws with five long and extremely sharp talons. Even though it was as big as a man, the creature looked just like a mole...the precise kind of monster that both Uncle Harlan and the long-dead condemned miner had described.

Panic consumed Reece. His stomach felt like it was full of lead and it was difficult to get air into his lungs. He started to move back toward the safety of the cab inside his ruined truck but his legs were shaky and unreliable causing him to stumble. Suddenly the wails and grumbles and growls got louder and louder. Branches snapped and leaves rustled from every direction as dozens of figures scurried out of the woods and descended upon Reece. Apparently, the creatures traveled in packs.

The grisly beings were covered in thick and matted brown fur that was laced with mud. Their eyes glowed red. Their pointed teeth gleamed in the moonlight, illuminated by the salvia flowing from their open and snarling jaws. Claws dug into Reece's skin as the creatures took hold of him and hauled him—screaming and shrieking—into the woods towards the long-abandoned mines...their precious caves.

As Reece was dragged first through the forest and then down the muddy tunnels by the vicious monstrosities, he had a revelation: mole people, not aliens, were the true threat after all.

Jinnu

The estate was opulent, a palace among mere mansions. Yet to Chelsea Blackbourne it was a miserable prison of boredom and routine; grand yet familiar...and familiarity bred contempt.

The manor was evidence of the great wealth and privilege that had once belonged to the Blackbourne family; a lifestyle Chelsea had never known. It had been nearly a century since the clan had been truly prominent; even Chelsea's father had not experienced the majestic heyday of the family legacy. Unlike their ancestors, they had never been invited to balls or galas. They existed in the shadow of excess, devoid of the pleasures of extravagance that the house portrayed.

It had high ceilings and winding staircases, thick stone walls and grand fireplaces, dozens of rooms and quarters for servants—spaces that were now empty. The manor's décor was aging yet lavish which enabled the house to maintain its dignity despite its present owner's problematic financial circumstances.

Chelsea roamed halls covered by lush Persian carpets and lit by glass chandeliers that glowed golden. There were dozens of oil paintings, mostly portraits of well-dressed and long-dead relatives, and intricately carved wooden furniture that would last for centuries. Once, there had been considerable quantities of jewelry, silverware, and porcelain but the majority had been sold over the past 50 years. Now all the remaining treasures were in the attic—a place Chelsea was barred from but infiltrated whenever she could.

Chelsea's father, Henry, inherited the mansion and the acres of land it stood upon from his Uncle George, an eccentric bachelor who had lived his life in the lap of luxury and spent his fortune traveling to far-off locations like Asia, Africa, and the Middle East, where he amassed various artifacts. Uncle George, a private person, built a huge stone wall around the grounds and ensured that there was only one entrance onto the premises, which was guarded by a wrought-iron gate painted the darkest shade of black. Throughout his life he embarked on his own adventures and shirked all traditional roles.

Chelsea had never met her Great Uncle George, he died before her parents married, but she assumed that he had been completely bonkers. To his credit, he hadn't been responsible for any of the terrible investments that had ultimately bankrupted the Blackburne's. In fact, Uncle George had been quite the businessman. He created a business out of his "assorted oddities" collection by opening and operating an antiques shop in the city's downtown. Of course, most downtown dwellers couldn't afford to buy anything so George changed tactics; he turned the shop into a curiosities museum and charged the public admission to enter. When George passed away, he had left all his worldly goods to his favorite nephew, Henry.

Henry had been cared for by George since the age of sixteen after his father committed suicide and his mother had a nervous breakdown. Insanity, Chelsea noted, plagued all the Blackbourne women. Even her mother, Agatha—who had married into the family —hadn't been quite right. Apparently, mental instability attracted Blackbourne men.

Motherhood hadn't suited Agatha. The scarce memories Chelsea had of her were not fond ones. When Chelsea was three, Agatha had fallen off the roof to her death...at least that was what Henry said. Now older and wiser at age eleven, Chelsea strongly suspected that her mother had purposely thrown herself down, wishing to die. Agatha's death had turned Henry cold and standoffish. Chelsea, meanwhile, hadn't been dismayed; they hadn't liked each other and so she had no reason to mourn her mother's passing.

Since then, Chelsea spent her days confined to the house or languishing in its sizable gardens as her father locked himself in the study. Her only company was her tutor, Miss Iverson, and Sara, the wretched maid. Chelsea utterly disliked dowdy old Miss Iverson, who constantly pestered her to polish her pianist skills, but she outright hated beautiful perfect Sara.

While Miss Iverson was only the latest in a string of tutors—few lasted long with Chelsea—Sara had been a near-constant presence, and enemy, for over four years. Sara worked at the estate three days a week and as much as Chelsea tried to ignore her there was something about the servant that captivated—and enraged—her.

Sara was nineteen and much prettier than Chelsea which seemed woefully unjust considering that Sara was also much poorer than Chelsea. In spite of how far the Blackburne's had fallen in high society circles, they were still undeniably privileged—utterly unlike Sara who toiled away as a maid for three different households six days a week. Once, Chelsea asked her where she lived and the maid confessed to calling a small row house, cramped with several younger siblings and a sickly mother, home. Sara was a pitiful creature burdened with a difficult life; the sole advantage she held over Chelsea were her looks. Sara was undeniably beautiful and Chelsea was indescribably jealous.

Chelsea had first noticed her unfortunate features at age ten. Prior to that she hadn't thought much about her pudgy belly, frizzy hair, and bucked teeth. She barely registered her broad nose, too-far-apart eyes, and dull brown hair until one day she looked in the mirror and realized that she didn't look anything like the fairies illustrated in her storybooks. Fairies were dainty and delicate; stubby Chelsea resembled the depictions of witches. Sara, however, was tall and slim with long blonde hair and bright blue eyes; the incarnation of loveliness.

One day Chelsea had been in town with her father on a rare outing to the curiosity shop and heard a group of young men whistling and shouting. Several stable boys were desperately vying for the attention of Sara as she hurried down the street, wicker basket in hand, obviously on an errand. The sight had filled Chelsea with envy. She knew she was too young to be courted but one day she would be expected to marry...and how was she to marry when she didn't look like Sara? Moreover, why should common Sara be graced with good looks when she—a Blackbourne! —was not? It was simply unacceptable! Sara hadn't as much as glanced in the boys' direction, clearly such attention was too common an occurrence to warrant a reaction.

Chelsea had never been fond of Sara but her indifference turned to loathing after witnessing that scene. She vowed to punish Sara for her blessed features and tormented her every chance she got. She switched the labels on the salt and pepper shakers. She threw mud on newly washed sheets as they dried on the line. She hid the broom and misplaced the kettle and, when questioned, denied everything. Sara started avoiding Chelsea, a fact that elated the younger girl and filled her with an intoxicating sense of power.

Chelsea felt a similar sense of accomplishment every time she frightened off a tutor. Chelsea disliked learning and she threw wild tantrums whenever anyone tried to make her sit for a lesson. Her father did nothing to quell her and the tutors dared not strike her—she was still a Blackbourne, after all—so they simply left to find greener pastures...or at least more agreeable students. The same thing happened with the nannies. From age three to seven Chelsea had been burdened with several minders whom she successfully sparred with until her father finally stopped hiring them.

Miss Iverson was the sole teacher she hadn't managed to banish. An elderly spinster, Miss Iverson always looked after Chelsea whenever her father had an appointment. Henry rarely took Chelsea along with him since she acted up relentlessly and had a tendency to make a spectacle of herself at formal events. Chelsea didn't mind staying in Miss Iverson's care since she had diligently studied plants and herbs and she knew precisely how to spike the old woman's tea and make her fall into a long, deep, slumber.

Whenever Miss Iverson drifted off to sleep Chelsea seized the opportunity to ascend into the attic; she had even taught herself how to pick locks solely for the purpose of exploring it. Chelsea was inexplicably enticed by the attic—it was as if something inside of it called out to her incessantly. She liked its dim light and its musty smell. She liked sight of cobwebs and dust. Mostly, she was fascinated by the masses of objects stacked on top of each other; all things from Uncle George's collection that had not been selected for display at the curiosity shop. Chelsea thought deeply about the treasures; who were the original owners? How had Uncle George come to possess them? Unanswerable questions but divine food for thought.

The attic was a portal into a world of wonder and mystery and it was also the beginning of the end of Chelsea Blackbourne's life.

* * *

Time drifted idyll as she wandered aimlessly among ancient armor and dulled swords, fierce looking carved masks and odd fleshy objects in jars filled with yellowed liquids. Chelsea was especially fond of the jars which contained half formed pigs and eels and cows; one jar even looked as if it held a human baby...although she couldn't imagine how a baby could have possibly ended up in a bottle.

She had been rummaging through the attic looking for more jars—or, better yet, papers confirming what they were and where they came from—when she stumbled across the trunk. It was medium sized, upholstered with aging brown leather, and fastened with brass buckle-like locks. It was an unremarkable thing that Chelsea would normally cast aside without a second glance...but something about the trunk pulled her toward it magnetically. She crept closer, unable to take her eyes off of it. On a whim she reached out and touched the lid. As soon as her palm connected with its surface an odd dizzying feeling came over her, as if she was being lifted out of her body while another presence entered her head.

Out...out...out!

Chelsea was aware that the voice was in her mind but, somehow, it also seemed to be emanating from inside the trunk. Her sudden intense urge to carry the trunk down three flights of stairs and into the garden seemed ludicrous considering that it was nearly as big as she was. Yet, apparently, the chest was lightweight because the next thing Chelsea knew she was sitting on the garden's lush overgrown grass, under her beloved hemlock trees, fiddling with the trunk's locks. Strangely, she had no memory of actually carrying it downstairs or of leaving the attic.

The final lock came undone with a SNAP and Chelsea eagerly lifted the lid. She was instantly overcome by a thick grayish white cloud—at first, she thought it was dust or smoke, but it had a strangely intoxicating aroma that was both timeless and exotic, it was like no other scent she had ever known.

Then, with a sound somewhere between a gasp and a yawn, a lithe creature rose from the confines of the trunk. Its body was white yet vapid, like a ghost, although it was more akin to insect than human. It had long spindly limbs—arms, legs, fingers—and large black eyes. Its nose was nonexistent, its mouth merely a small straight line near the bottom of its oval head. It had no hair or clothes. Its gender was indeterminable.

Chelsea tumbled backwards but excitement quickly overcame her initial fear. She had read books about these creatures before and, although they traditionally emerged from sealed fancy bottles, it could only be a genie!

"You've got to grant me three wishes!" Chelsea shouted at the creature. "I'm entitled to three wishes!"

The creature cocked its head to the side, examining her.

"I said—" Chelsea continued but then the being spoke.

"I heard you, small one, but I do not understand why you want only three wishes. You could have so much more."

Chelsea's brow furrowed. "What do you mean?" she demanded.

The creature stretched. "You freed me; I've been in there for ages. I must show my gratitude."

"Good! I want a new music box; a gold one inlayed with diamonds and pearls!"

"But that's not what you *truly* desire, now is it?" the creature challenged.

"Of course, it is!" Chelsea spat. "I wouldn't have asked for it otherwise."

"Material things may be pretty but getting your way is so much more satisfying, don't you think?" crooned the creature. "I specialize in fate. If you want something to happen, I can assist you."

Chelsea stared at the creature wordlessly, intrigued.

"If you let me live in your lush garden, I can help you with all your problems," the creature explained. "My advice is golden and my magic is potent. I can help you with all that ails you but my presence must be our secret. You wouldn't want to share my attentions, now would you?"

Chelsea vigorously shook her head.

"The only other task I ask is that you bring me food, preferably meat. I don't eat much but when I'm hungry I'm *ravenous*."

Chelsea skeptically considered the offer.

"Tell me this," she tested, "how do I rid myself of my tutor? I'm tired of her and I want my father to fire her at once."

The creature's mouth twisted upwards in a sinister grin.

"That's easy," it replied. "Spread rumors about her, tarnish her supposedly pristine reputation. Tell your father that she's aging and she is starting to disclose scandalous little secrets. Perhaps she had an affair—or two—with men, or boys, or maybe even *other ladies*. That wouldn't be proper at all, now would it?"

Chelsea had never thought about spreading nasty untruths regarding Miss Iverson but it could certainly work; she was aging and did mumble on and on from time to time. Who's to say that she couldn't have confessed some dark secrets?

"And what about our horrid maid?" Chelsea hissed. "She's even worse! Scurrying around, flaunting her beauty, mocking me with her existence; she must be stopped!"

"If you really want to punish her take away her beauty," the creature replied. "Scarring her face will be a fate worse than death. After all, if you make her lose one of her pretty eyes she'll have to suffer as an invalid for years...decades...*forevermore*."

"How do I do it?" Chelsea pleaded, trembling with glee and amused by the creature's cunning ways. She already felt a stronger kinship with it than with any human she had ever known.

"I'll guide you," the creature promised. "I aid those who are loyal to me. Have we a pact?"

Chelsea did not hesitate to accept the creature's terms.

* * *

The next thing Chelsea knew she was back in the attic, sitting on the floor with the trunk in its original position. She didn't remember bringing it upstairs or pushing it back into place; it was as if she had done so in a trance. A sudden wave of sorrow washed over her.

It was all nothing more than a daydream!

Yet, when Chelsea glanced out the attic window, she was elated to see the oddly elegant creature coiling itself around the branches of the hemlock trees.

A dream it was not.

Within a week Miss Iverson was fired. Henry had been horrified by his daughter's accusations of the tutor's unladylike behavior—especially when Chelsea told him about how Miss Iverson had caressed her. Needless to say, the old woman was not provided with a reference.

Yet the ultimate glory came three days later when the hated Sara was finally permanently marred. Following the creature's advice, Chelsea tightened all the piano strings and partially cut several with a kitchen knife. Then she ordered the maid to dust inside the piano. As soon as Sara opened the cover, the steel strings popped off and slashed her face. Her screams were music to Chelsea's ears.

There had been a lot of blood. Sara's right eye was completely ruined and the skin across most of her face was covered with deep gashes that would definitely leave lifelong scars. Sara had spent weeks in the hospital, stitched up like a rag doll, and never returned to work. Several months after the maiming, Chelsea had spotted Sara in town walking with a black veil over her face to conceal her disfigurement. Young men stood on the corner yet not one whistled, clapped, or called. Chelsea was pleased.

* * *

Over time, Chelsea learned the creature's name, Jinnu, and accommodated its feeding requirements. During dinners of chicken or steak—prepared by the new housekeeper, a quiet woman who was neither beautiful nor bothersome—Chelsea saved some morsels and sneaked them out to Jinnu. Neither her father nor the new maid ever complained...which was good since anyone who annoyed Chelsea was guaranteed to meet with misfortune.

Jinnu's presence ensured that Chelsea always got whatever she wanted. After feigning trauma from the alleged assault by Miss Iverson, Chelsea convinced her father that she was educated enough for a girl of her status. Without any scheduled activities, Chelsea spent her days learning how to mix potions to rid of her pimples and to straighten her frizzy hair.

Jinnu was quite satisfied in the garden. It nested in the darkest portion of shrubbery, hidden away among the hemlock trees and poison ivy and built an elaborate nest by weaving silky white tendrils together, creating a web just as spiders did. It was also eating more; when the leftover scraps were no longer enough Chelsea started capturing birds, squirrels, rabbits and the occasional stray cat for the creature to dine upon.

The massive grounds of the Blackbourne estate were unkempt since the family no longer had the means to afford the gardeners that the property required. Due to the wild and undisturbed conditions of the land, Chelsea was utterly shocked when her father managed to catch a glimpse of Jinnu one day...several years after its arrival.

Henry had been pacing around the grounds, worried about the cost of the curiosity shops' rent. He got too near to the hemlock trees and spotted Jinnu slithering around the upper branches. Henry Blackbourne screamed and ran into the house, hysterically ranting about snakes. Chelsea found him in the living room, searching for his old Crimean War sword, fully intending to slay the creature in the trees. She calmed him and accompanied him back to the garden and eventually convinced him that there was nothing there.

Yet Henry remained suspicious and continued searching around the garden, so Chelsea decided that he had to go. Chelsea fixed him tea laced with cyanide and told the doctors that he had died in his sleep. They had no reason to be suspicious; Henry was aging and financial stresses often weakened older men's hearts. Chelsea, being of legal age, inherited the entire estate. She felt no qualms about what she had done since she had done it on behalf of Jinnu. After all, the creature doted on her far more than her father ever had.

Once named the proprietor of the estate, Chelsea promptly sold the curiosity shop and its remaining items. She fired the housekeeper and lived like a hermit off her dwindling inheritance. She took up gardening zealously, planting additional hemlock and spindly trees along with deadly flowers such as foxglove, ragwort, oleander, and yellow jessamine. She even started a makeshift greenhouse in an upstairs bedroom, cultivating Venus fly traps and other assorted poisonous vegetation until the house was surrounded by a prism of colors. Sometimes it seemed like the garden was enchanted, alive; trees whispered, petals snapped, vines coiled and roots twisted and pulled.

In her spare time Chelsea explored Uncle George's library. He had collected books about uncommon yet fascinating, subjects: histories of wars and dead languages, medieval medical practices, instructions on potions and spells...One book regarding human escapades with supposedly mythical beings included an illustration that depicted a Middle Eastern knight slaying evil jinns— dark forms of genies somewhat akin to Jinnu. Below the artwork read the caption: *Imam Ali Conquers Jinn, unknown artist, 1568.* Chelsea paid it no mind.

Time ticked by; its rules non-applicable on the Blackbourne property. Chelsea never seemed to age a day over 30 but Jinnu grew bigger and hungrier and, unable to hunt effectively on its own, depended on Chelsea.

She started traveling to the poor side of town at night, frequenting the dingiest pubs and the shabbiest inns to prey on the rabble of society. Initially she pretended to be a charity worker and tricked working girls, destitute widows, and hapless orphans into following her home where Jinnu feasted upon them. Authorities never came to the estate asking questions; the poor were seldom missed.

During the course of her rare interactions with other people, Chelsea came to the realization that she was no longer the plain, borderline ugly, child she had once been. She subsequently learned how to use her beauty to woo men back to the estate. At first, such seductions had been risky as only the true dregs of society—like men newly released from prison—would accept such an improper offer. However, with each additional trip into town, such propositions were met with increasing ease. Apparently, the decency of the commoners was being eroded at an astounding pace.

Chelsea wasn't sure exactly how many times a year Jinnu had to eat; the creature simply got hungry when it got hungry. Gradually Chelsea learned that its meals were extremely infrequent, occurring every few years—perhaps every few decades. She supposed it was possible that a human body could fill Jinnu up for thousands of days, just as a large rat could fill a snake for months. All the clocks on the estate had long since stopped working and time was a riddle, but indications of change abounded whenever Chelsea ventured into the village. On one trip she would spy a newly constructed building and, on the next, the same building would be decrepit with age—if it was still there at all!

The fashions changed even more dramatically. Topcoats and corsets turned into casual suits and sequined dresses, then blue jeans and poodle skirts, followed by bright obnoxious colors that Chelsea heard referred to as "tie dye." That changed to pastels and black leather jackets worn by men and women with enormous hairstyles. Next, men paraded around in baggy pants and women stuffed themselves into impossibly tight jeans. Chelsea was not a fan of any of these styles but she made sure to occasionally entice a female victim back to Jinnu's lair merely to acquire clothing in which to blend into the crowds. Yet, no matter what she wore, her outfits always seemed to be slightly dated each time she exited her estate.

Another telling sign of the passage of time was the gadgets that the villagers used. The days of horses and carriages had morphed into a world full of cars, radios, and loud blaring boxes called televisions. Most recently, people walked around staring at small rectangles of light that they held in their hands, sometimes they even spoke into them. Chelsea hadn't the slightest idea what these devices actually did, but they were called "phones" and most people seemed quite reliant on them.

Although Chelsea shunned most technological advances, on one fairly-recent trip she acquired a brand-new Bakelite radio and she took great pleasure in dancing to the music known as "jazz." Of course, every time she switched the radio on the stations were different, as if the programming changed overnight. What was the value of one night in the mansion to the outside world? A year? A decade? A century? Chelsea couldn't say.

She lived to amuse the creature. She sang and danced for it and, in return, it kept her young and vital. After years of listening to Jinnu speak of the sumptuousness of human flesh, Chelsea decided to sample it and quickly named it her favorite meat. She took to joining Jinnu in its meals; devouring everything but the bones which she used to decorate the manor's interior; she was especially fond of human skulls.

Eventually, Chelsea was forced to alter her hunting methods. The new world was full of security cameras and it was no longer easy to quietly obtain victims. Jinnu knew exactly how to change tactics. The creature convinced Chelsea to start rumors around town about the Blackbourne estate being haunted by the spirits of mentally ill persons. It was a silly, juvenile story but it was also the stuff of urban legends. Chelsea assumed the fictitious tale would catch on like wildfire...and she was right.

Approximately two weeks after Chelsea's latest visit to town—which could have been as much as two decades in the outside world—four teenagers scaled the fence and stormed the garden like Vikings set on pillaging a village. It was a dark moonless night and the uninvited guests blindly stumbled through the tall untamed grass, shouting and giggling and reeking of alcohol. They were all holding their phones but technology was useless on the Blackbourne estate so the entire group was swearing at their blank unresponsive screens.

None of them saw Chelsea coming until it was too late. She swept down upon them like a storm, expertly dispatching all bodies in seconds before they could as much as scream. Jinnu and Chelsea both ate well that evening. Chelsea supposed that she would have to purchase a freezer to store excess meat since she assumed their meals would be coming to them quite regularly in the future.

She assumed wrong.

**

Chelsea was entirely unaware of the emergence of social media and this ignorance proved to be her downfall. Four teenagers vanishing at the same time raised alarms throughout the village. When the police checked the missing youths' webpages, they discovered that the group had been planning a trip to the long-abandoned Blackbourne estate.

Approximately twelve hours after the teens' disappearance, a police search party descended upon the mansion. Chelsea had been asleep in her bed, belly full and satisfied, when she was jolted awake by the sound of the intruders cutting through the locked wrought-iron gate. She glanced out her window, saw the flashing lights, and heard several voices speaking in tense tones. Extreme fear immediately seized her; the plebeians were breaking in—perhaps intending to riot or loot!

Maybe the world is at war again, Chelsea thought as she ran to the garden. Her panic was palpable as she imaged the villagers' discovery of the array of bones placed throughout her home.

Jinnu was resting (hibernating) in its shroud-like cocoon which glistened silver against the dark green branches of hemlock. In desperation, Chelsea violently shook the web. Jinnu awoke, hissing furiously.

"Commoners are storming the grounds!" Chelsea wailed, "Too many for me to slay! Protect me!"

For several moments Jinnu remained still and stared at Chelsea, studying her. Finally, it beckoned to her with its long limber fingers.

Chelsea had never entered the creature's nest before but she eagerly crawled in, surprised to discover that the dwelling was warm and cozy—more like a tent than a web. Chelsea was starting to relax when Jinnu turned to face her. Its eyes were black and cold and utterly merciless.

"Our pact is resolved," it hissed and promptly attached its gaping mouth to Chelsea's pale neck.

* * *

Jinnu knew its survival depended on disguising itself amid the treetops and waiting for the chaos to subside. It summoned all of its energy and moved away from its silky nest; knowing full well that it would be difficult to find such cushy accommodations ever again.

All of its human keepers—*slaves*—eventually faltered and had to be destroyed but Chelsea had been the cleverest and longest lasting of all its caretakers; ironic considering that Jinnu had initially been disappointed by how young and small she was. It had greatly underestimated the girl who had *rottenness* in her deep core; a trait that was fairly rare in humans but indescribably useful to beings of Jinnu's ilk. The creature knew it would be fortunate to ever master another such host...but it also knew that it needed to start looking. As soon as the humans saw the conditions inside the manor, they were likely to have the building condemned. Remaining in the garden was simply not an option.

Jinnu crept along the tree branches, staying close to the estate walls. It slithered toward the back of the garden where the overgrown shrubbery was thickest knowing that it could probably climb over that section of the wall, undetected, if need be.

Suddenly, Jinnu heard voices.

"I can't imagine what they've found," a male declared.

"That place is an enigma," a female replied.

"I'd love to see its garden though," the man admitted. "It's probably the only private property in the county with more plants than mine."

This statement piqued Jinnu's interest. It originally came from a land of sand and heat; an abhorrent environment which it had no fond memories of...it much preferred greenery and gardens.

Jinnu peered over the wall and saw a man and a woman. Both were holding cameras and standing beside cars. The trunk of the man's car was ajar. As soon as they looked away from the wall, Jinnu snatched the opportunity. It hurried over the stone barrier and slunk into the invitingly dark trunk.

A few minutes later, the man bid the woman goodbye, placed his camera in the trunk, and shut the lid. He was completely unaware of the presence of Jinnu, lurking in the back corner. This pleased the creature. It would wait for the man to pop open the trunk. Then they would make a deal...

Collector

Before the poster entered his life, Ethan didn't believe in monsters or ghosts or anything supernatural. Even at the tender age of eleven his mind was deeply rooted in the real world. Science was his passion and he dreamed becoming a paleontologist. The very thought of uncovering dinosaur bones filled him with glee.

Science class was the highlight of his life. For starters, there was a replica of a dinosaur skeleton that took up residence on Miss Ashby's desk. Ethan was so enthralled by it that he sometimes dreamt about it. And then there was Miss Ashby herself; she was young and nice but, moreover, she *liked* Ethan. She didn't just accept or tolerate him, she genuinely *liked* him. She also encouraged him to pursue his dreams. Miss Ashby made Ethan *want* to succeed. He was good at drawing, which was important because paleontologists sketched a lot, and he was good at remembering information which was imperative for any class--especially science.

Some people considered dinosaurs to be monsters-- and that was fitting since some dinosaurs were predatory carnivores. Ethan supposed that was why they so fascinated him; dinosaurs were monstrous but they were *monsters that had actually existed*...unlike the stupid zombies that staggered around in the crappy horror movies which James was so addicted to.

James was both Ethan's cousin and the bane of his life. Ten years older than Ethan, James was a perpetual slacker who continuously found himself out of work and out of luck. James had never been what one would have called a "straight shooter." At age five, his claim to fame was his penchant for sticking crayons up his nose--but anyone who spoke to his mother would think that James was destined to become the next Einstein. Both Aunt Samantha and Uncle Hector doted on their only son and either chose to ignore his many flaws or were truly blind to them. Ethan found the latter hard to believe.

For his part, James blamed Ethan for everything that went wrong not only in his life, but in the world at large. As far as James was concerned, his life had been permanently marred when he was sixteen and Ethan--then six--had come to live with the family.

Ethan wasn't a bad kid but he came from bad circumstances. Ethan's mother, Susan--Aunt Samantha's little sister--had gotten pregnant by the town drunk, a man aptly named Joe Barr. Joe repeatedly found himself in and out of prison--or "the crowbar motel", as Uncle Hector called it--throughout his and Susan's tumultuous two-year marriage. When Ethan was three, his father took a bottle of whiskey on a hike in the woods and proceeded to fall into the river and drown. By that time, the Barr family was living in a run-down shack and his mother resorted to government assistance to get by.

Ethan often wondered why Aunt Samantha and Uncle Hector--who had a nice split-level home and two cars--never tried to help more. He had occasionally seen Aunt Samantha and Uncle Hector on Christmas Eve or Easter Friday when they dropped off some gifts and warm meals but James never accompanied them on these trips and they never appeared on the actual holidays. Ethan later learned that Aunt Samantha thought her sister's house had bugs and mold and she didn't want such a place to contaminate her precious son. The first time Ethan met James was when he moved in with him after his mother dropped dead of a heart attack whilst shopping for groceries. Ethan had been in school at the time, but he heard that she'd been dead before she hit the tiled floor of the chilly dairy aisle.

Ethan admitted that Aunt Samantha had been right about the bugs. His old house had been so completely infested with spiders and ants and roaches that he had actually come to consider them pets. But she was totally wrong about her "precious son" since there was nothing particularly precious--or even likable--about James Paul Sinclair.

James had a mile-wide mean-streak laced with sneakiness. Deep down, James was jealous of his baby cousin--his *invader* baby cousin. Uncle Hector had long since ceased complaining about the perpetual guest and simply accepted the situation--something James apparently found impossible to do. He missed his life as an only child; a peaceful existence that Ethan had stolen from him and, subconsciously or otherwise, James determined to make the little brat pay.

Ethan didn't believe that his aunt and uncle outright hated him, but he was not equal to their precious son and he was reminded of that fact all too frequently. Once, two weeks after moving in, Ethan got up to get a glass of water in the middle of the night and caught James trying to sneak out. Ethan threatened to tell on him which proved to be a colossal mistake. James had grabbed him by the collar and yelled for his parents, claiming that he had caught *him* trying to sneak away. Even though Ethan was in pajamas and James was fully clothed at 3am, neither adult ever questioned their son's version of events. That was simply standard practice in the house of Sinclair.

Of course, everyone had their limits--even Aunt Samantha. James instinctively knew that if she saw him openly harassing his much younger cousin, she would pitch a fit. Hence, James minded his manners in front of his parents. Everything he did to the younger boy he did on the sly and disguised it so well that any suspicions on Ethan's part would seem baseless at best and paranoid-delusional at worst.

Already an adored only child, James kept in his parents' good books by doing errands--he would mow the lawn and "accidentally" plow over any figurines Ethan had left in the front yard. He would start the dishwasher and "accidentally" melt Ethan's favorite plastic crazy straws. He would help with yard sales and "accidentally" sell Ethan's favorite puzzles and earth science books. Oh yes, James was a master of seemingly innocent "accidents." It had gone on for so many years that Ethan had slowly but surely adapted--making sure to hide his most cherished items and keep as much distance from his older cousin as possible.

Material grievances aside, James was just pure annoying. When Ethan was in fourth grade, he had learned the definition of the word "intolerable" and it described James perfectly. His mean smirk and slit eyes, his too big clothes and too small brain, the way he ate, the way he talked--*intolerable*, all of it. James liked weird music and bad movies; what Uncle Hector called "B listers" but Ethan thought they seemed more like Z listers...and even that was being generous. James had a habit of sitting up late, hogging the TV with his weird gory movies that had scared Ethan to death when he was little. As he got older his interest in science assured him that monsters didn't exist--although idiots did, idiots like James.

 As the years wore on, James stopped wrecking Ethan's toys and instead settled for minor physical aggressions like closing doors in his face, tripping him when he walked by or occasionally slapping him when nobody else was looking. Ethan upped his avoidance techniques and often evaded assault for weeks at a time. Forgoing college, James started working a series of odd jobs and--although he didn't actually move out--he spent more time away from home. Sometimes Ethan did too, he'd managed to make some friends at school and attempted to have sleepovers whenever he could...always at someone else's house, of course. He couldn't imagine subjecting one of his few friends to James' endless passive-aggressive wrath.

 It was after he arrived home from an awesome sleepover at his friend Michael's house that Ethan first saw the poster. It caught his eye as he was walking down the hall towards his room since its colors blared obnoxiously from James' slightly ajar door. It was one of those cheesy black-lit pieces consisting of neon hues on black velvet. James' room was a shrine to such materials; his walls were lined with similar posters, most of which showcased skeletons in some form: playing guitars, riding motorcycles, sitting atop horses...the new addition was in the same aesthetic vein but it was somehow *different*, there was something dark about it--something *bad*.

 The new poster depicted a skeleton in a grim reaper robe. The Grim Skull was holding a fierce looking spiked staff and had a pile of skulls lying at his feet. This was standard horror-movie-illustration-faire except there was something deeper to it, something *darker*. Perhaps it was the Grim Skull's malicious smirk, or maybe it was the purple robe that looked as if there were faces trapped within its fabric, writhing in never-ending agony. The sight of it made Ethan shudder, a reaction that James instantly seized upon.

"What's the matter, squirt, don't you like it?"

Ethan hated being called 'squirt' but complaining would only egg James on.

"It's not my style," he replied simply, never taking his eyes off it.

"Not enough rainbows, eh pansy?" James sneered.

Ethan wasn't exactly sure why James sometimes called him 'pansy' but he sensed it was an insult and refused to take the bait.

Ethan made a point not to show fear or weakness in front of James again but the poster disturbed him on a number of levels. For one thing, he couldn't stop looking at it. Every time he walked down the hall passed James' room, he stole a peek--and every time it seemed as if the Grim Skull was situated differently and the faces in the robe sometimes looked as if they were *squirming*. Ethan knew this was just a trick on the eyes, what Miss Ashby called an "optical illusion," but it sent chills through him nonetheless.

Then there was the matter of why he could even see it in the first place. For years James had consistently kept his door tightly shut but since he got the poster, he kept it cracked open just enough for Ethan to get a glimpse of the Grim Skull several times a day. This, he assumed, was done purposefully. James knew he didn't like the poster and therefore made it his mission to expose him to it as much as possible. The whole thing was silly, ridiculous even. He had never been afraid of skeletons before!

You want to study them for god's sake! Ethan told himself whenever he felt as if the Grim Skull's bony fingers were tracing his spine.

As the days wore on, Ethan became increasingly convinced that something was basically wrong with the poster. It didn't only move--it *beckoned*. And it was hypnotic. At night he dreamt about the Grim Skull standing over him, probing his sleeping brain for stray thoughts. On the fifth day of its presence in the house, it enticed Ethan to do something he never thought he would: he entered James' room.

From the start of his residence in the house, one thing had been made very clear--James' room was off limits. Once when he was seven, he had made the terrible mistake of walking in to investigate, spellbound by the lava lamps that James kept on a shelf above his bed. No sooner had he stepped two feet into the room than James ran in, grabbed him by his shirt and screamed: *"Get out of my room, you fucking halfwit!"* Ethan, surprised, had started to cry which only made James shake him harder and yell louder. Then Aunt Samantha had run in. She'd gotten James to let go of his little cousin but she had also sided with her precious son.

This is James' room, she'd scolded Ethan. *We set up a nice room for you! You should be grateful and respect your cousin enough to leave his things alone!*

But I didn't touch anything! Ethan had protested.

It's a personal space issue you dimwit, James had sneered, smugly satisfied in the knowledge that the adults had his back and he would always have the upper hand. Since that fateful day four years earlier, Ethan had lost any desire to venture into James' room...until the poster came.

It was a sunny afternoon and James was out with friends. Ethan hadn't known he was planning to enter the room until he found himself opening the door. It was messier than he remembered; the carpet hadn't been vacuumed in a while and there were old clothes and dirty dishes everywhere--apparently Aunt Samantha hadn't been in to do her daily cleaning yet. Even at the age of twenty-one, precious James was not expected to pick up after himself.

If I left my room like this, they'd drop me off at the orphanage, Ethan thought and the idea unsettled him because he knew that it was true. Despite the overall disarray of the room, the lava lamps and the posters remained. Actually, there were many more posters than Ethan remembered--they were taped up so close together that it was impossible to see the wall behind them.

The Grim Skull poster was the only one separated from the gathered mass on the wall. It hung from James' closet door, presiding over the room like a gatekeeper, grinning malevolently.

It's cursed, Ethan thought and then quickly chastised himself. *Don't be stupid, it's just an ugly piece of art some hippie did when he was jacked up on LSD! It's just a picture painted with neons. There's nothing special about it!*

He glared at it, searching its surface for any sign of movement. It didn't budge.

It's just a drawing. Touch it and you'll see that it's just fabric and paint, nothing more and nothing less.

He inched closer. The poster didn't move.

Closer...no change.

Closer... it didn't stir.

"It's not real," he whispered aloud as he got within an inch of it. Then, as if in response, the Grim Skull winked at him!

Ethan jumped back and uttered a scream of surprise. He closed and reopened his eyes; the Grim Skull stared back, unflinching.

It was just your imagination! You're freaking yourself out! James is right, you are a pansy!

Suddenly anger and self-disgust surged inside of Ethan--he was supposed to be a scientist in training! He was supposed to be rational--and yet here he was nearly having a panic attack over a piece of artwork!

"I'm not afraid of you," he growled as he touched the center of the poster.

The pain was sudden and intense, causing him to yelp and jump backwards so quickly that he lost his balance and fell to the floor with a resounding BANG! Heart pounding, he stared down at his tingling hand.

It shocked me! It gave me some kind of electrical jolt--but it didn't feel like a shock, it felt like a bite! He glanced up at the poster and the Grim Skull--which was undeniably smiling wider--stuck its blue snake-like tongue out and wiggled it at him. Ethan screamed.

Aunt Samantha burst into the room within three seconds, her face a mask of rage, and literally dragged

Ethan out. Yet his angry aunt was the least of his concerns--the poster WAS alive...or at least it contained something that was alive and menacing and very much supernatural. The idea that the seemingly logical scientific world could evaporate so fast made Ethan's mind feel like it was tearing at the seams. For the first time in his life, he questioned everything.

The situation worsened that night when the Grim Skull escaped from the poster. Ethan awoke in an uneasy sweat at 1:36am to the sound of rustling. He turned towards his door--sure that James would be standing there, perhaps holding a plastic bag and poised to smother him in a fit of rage. When he glanced across the hall into James' room, his stomach dropped a mile--the Grim Skull was gone. The poster was there, as was the heap of skulls, but the Grim Skull itself was missing...and something was moving around the house.

It's a burglar, Ethan thought. *You've got to get up and call the police!*

Except it wasn't a burglar and Ethan knew it. Uncle Hector had the house alarmed better than Fort Knox--whatever was wandering around hadn't broken in...at least not through a window or a door.

It's just James or Uncle Hector or Aunt Samantha getting a midnight snack.

Before he was aware of his intentions, Ethan got out of bed. The carpet felt like ice--the whole house felt colder than a freezer and, if not for the moonlight, there would be no light at all. Tentatively, he crept out of his room and stole a look at James who was sprawled on his bed snoring loudly. Ethan continued his journey down the hall towards his Aunt and Uncle's room.

He saw it happen. Too afraid to move or scream, he bore witness in a state of near paralysis. The Grim Skull was leaning over Aunt Samantha, as if whispering in her ear, and making odd smacking noises, like it was absorbing the air around her. The sound terrified Ethan because it reminded him of a noise that he often thought he heard in his dreams...and the position of the Grim Skull reminded him too much of all the nights when he had come half-awake believing it was hovering above him.

Now he questioned if those occasions had been dreams at all.

Suddenly, the faces stitched into the Grim Skull's robe noticed Ethan. They locked eyes on him and turned their tormented faces towards his. Then, in unison, they started wailing--warning their master that he was being observed. Ethan retreated down the hall as quickly as possible, feeling a shroud of cold creeping up behind him. The Grim Skull's guttural laughter filled his ears.

It knew I was there and it didn't care! For some reason it didn't mind me seeing it!

That theory made no sense, but neither did anything about the situation. Once Ethan reached his room, he slammed the door and slid his heavy dresser draw in front of it, bolting himself in.

This won't work, he thought franticly, *but I'll at least get an A for Effort!*

'An A for Effort,' was one of Miss Ashby's favorite expressions.

I wonder what Miss Ashby would say if she saw me now, Ethan thought and then, for no apparent reason, he broke into a frenzy of hysterical laughter. Unable to gain control of himself, he lay on the floor and howled until he cried.

This is what it feels like to lose your mind, he realized.

Insanity was certainly the basis behind all of this, perhaps it was contagious. James never actually told him where he had gotten the poster but Ethan knew that he and his loser friends snuck out at night and broke into abandoned buildings to drink and smoke and fool around with girls or whatever else lost causes in their 20s did. Perhaps they'd collected it on one of their illegal excursions into the recently closed Peyton Psychiatric Hospital...or maybe they'd found it in the dump where they sometimes went to shoot at rats with BB guns. Its origins were not traceable but whoever had previously owned it had certainly had their share of problems. In his gut, Ethan knew the poster was not store bought and whoever had once owned it was dead. He also knew that his days of pursing science were over. There was no point in devoting himself to logical endeavors when he now had proof that horror movies were much closer to reality than anyone wanted to believe.

Ethan laughed himself to sleep. The next day he awoke in his sunny room to the sound of Aunt Samantha furiously banging on the door. Ethan tried to tell her about his nightmare but she wouldn't listen. He had missed the bus and he was late for school and she was angry.

You're too old to be acting like this, she hissed as she marched him off, sans breakfast.

Ethan couldn't concentrate on anything that day. Thoughts of the poster clouded his mind even in Miss Ashby's class. His friends noticed something was wrong but Ethan declined to tell them about the poster. He didn't want them thinking he was crazy, especially Michael whose Dad was a shrink. By recess he made up his mind-- he couldn't live like this anymore. He decided to confront the Grim Skull.

That night, he waited until everyone was asleep. James didn't drunkenly stagger in until after 2am and it was 2:43am by the time Ethan felt comfortable enough to tiptoeing into James' room.

What if it's gone creeping around the house again?

But he knew it wouldn't be--it was waiting for him. And tonight, its eyes were glowing red.

Ethan had already prepared himself to die. It knew that he had seen it and he understood that his estimated chances of survival were little to none. What he didn't understand was how any of this was possible in the first place. Before all of this happened, he had wanted to be a scientist--to explore and discover and indulge his natural curiosity. If he was condemned to die, he might as well spend his last doomed moments investigating.

Faintly aware of James' snoring, Ethan locked eyes with the Grim Skull as he reached out and touched the poster. He fully expected to get sucked into it but, to his surprise, all he felt was cloth and paint, just like a normal poster. Yet there was nothing normal about the Grim Skull's bony hand that reached out of the frame and snaked down to the closet's door handle. It gripped the knob and turned until the door clicked open. Then the Grim Skull drew its hand back into the poster, looked down at Ethan, and grinned.

James' closet was no longer James' closet. Instead of a small space containing jackets and hockey sticks, the closet now opened up into a strange world of trees and paths, valleys and mountains; rivers of neon yellow, overgrown mushrooms and tiny suns. Everything in the surreal landscape had an unnatural neon glow but there was no sky--just blackness.

Perhaps this is where all the boogeymen live, Ethan thought. *It's the realm of monsters.*

Or the realm of the poster, to be precise; as he stepped into the domain and heard the closet door slam shut behind him, Ethan felt his sanity waver. There was no way to logically or scientifically explain this; therefore, he *must have* gone crazy. It should have been a frightening thought but instead it was comforting, freeing.

Dead men tell no tales but crazy ones have a ton of them, he thought and brayed laughter.

He walked through the fluorescent maze like a tourist exploring a new city. Everything seemed pretty in a psychedelic way but there were threats and menaces everywhere; sharp toothed jesters beamed at him from behind purple tree trunks, floating blue eyes watched his every move and unknown things crept in the pink and orange bushes. The world was filled with odd noises; choruses of calls and growls and clicks and the unmistakable sound of a guitar riff somewhere far, far away. As he descended deeper into the dreamscape, he noticed neon versions of Aunt Samantha's favorite flowers and the car models that Uncle Hector most admired; he even saw a few of James' beloved cigarettes dancing the jig under a towering crystal ball.

This is what it took from their dreams, Ethan realized. *The Grim Skull creates the stuff in here from what he steals from people's imaginations.*

As if to verify this hypothesis, Ethan turned a corner and was met by the dinosaur skeleton from Miss Ashby's class...except this one wasn't a replica, it was vibrant neon green and very much alive. It turned and stared at him briefly before wandering off towards a field of flowers that looked suspiciously like giant Venus fly traps. As the dinosaur bones shifted themselves away from him, Ethan realized that they had been blocking the entrance to a deep cave; its darkness akin to a black hole amid a palette of color.

Ethan entered the cave and quickly felt himself falling--descending like Alice down the rabbit hole. He landed with surprising grace in a foggy gray landscape that was utterly unlike the manically colored world above. The ground was damp and muddy; it pulled on Ethan's shoes like quicksand, threatening to wrench him down into its murky depths. There were a few puny trees protruding from the land, their deformed branches twisted in misshapen poses. The area looked like a desolate wasteland in the aftermath of a nuclear bomb. It reminded Ethan of photos from World War II.

"*Boy....*"

In the distance, the Grim Skull beckoned. Situated amid the dreary landscape, its cloak looked black instead of purple; a proper Grim Reaper.

As Ethan approached, the groans from the faces in the cloak wailed sounding like the wind on a winter night. Ethan assumed he would be one of them soon but he was too numb to care. He just wanted this to be over. He wanted peace and death would provide the ultimate rest.

Up close, the Grim Skull was tall and terrible. It was gaunt and haggard as if it had dug itself out of a thousand graves. Yet its cloak was brilliant as were its red eyes.... eyes that showed an undeniable intelligence and cunning.

"Do you like my lair, boy?" the Grim Skull questioned. Its voice was like sandpaper, as if it hadn't spoken aloud in eons. "I suppose this is a surprise for you, O one of science, but there is much to the world that you don't know. Both in your realm and others...Oh yes, boy, there are *many* other dimensions."

Ethan felt his mind wince again in the final throes of complete and utter breakdown.

"You and I are alike," the Grim Skull explained as it circled Ethan. "You are an artist and so am I. Everything that you saw I created from the dreams of humans. Your species is my muse."

Ethan remained perfectly still as the Grim Skull leaned into him and whispered into his ear: "In fact, *I used to be one of you.*"

The revelation horrified Ethan. He glanced up at the creature in shock and couldn't ignore the thin mask of flesh that still clung to its bones. Indeed, at some point, this thing had been a man.

"I've waited *ages* to find someone with your skills," the Grim Skull crooned.

"Wha-what do you mean?" Ethan mumbled in a meek, trembling voice.

"You will take my place," the Grim Skull declared.

Ethan recoiled. "No!"

The Grim Skull slid its scaly tongue over its prominent teeth. "This fate has its merits. There are much worse things that can occur in the course of a life."

"Name one," Ethan challenged.

"Well, something *unfortunate* could happen to dear Aunt Samantha and Uncle Hector. Then it would just be you and James."

The Grim Skull's words struck a deep dread into Ethan's very core. The idea of being left at the mercy of James was his worst nightmare.

"You can't leave me with him," Ethan pleaded. "He would kill me."

"Indeed, he would," the Grim Skull echoed. "That's why it would be so much better for you--not to mention your aunt and uncle--if you would simply accept your fate."

Ethan looked into the Grim Skull's red eyes and, for the first time, noticed that they were bloodshot. The creature that had once been human looked tired, weary, exhausted. It needed him to take its place.

It wants to die, Ethan realized and, despite the revolting circumstances, he felt a pang of pity for it.

"I'm only eleven," Ethan whimpered. "Won't I be more useful to you when I'm older?"

The Grim Skull thought for a moment and nodded.

"True, a man is stronger than a boy but a boy needs time to become a man and time is something I am in short supply of."

"Is there anything I can do?" Ethan begged.

After what seemed like an eternity the Grim Skull replied.

"Fuel," it said.

"What?"

"FUEL! I need fuel! If I'm to maintain my post until you have morphed from boy to man then I need fuel so I can keep the higher realm looking as it does. That is my duty."

"What kind of fuel?"

"Take a guess," the Grim Skull hissed.

Ethan stared at it, terrified of saying the wrong thing.

"Energy! I need energy and humans are the best source of it. They are the perfect mix of meat and, shall we say, *mental* stimulus."

"You want me to bring you a *person*?" Ethan exclaimed in dismay, unable to comprehend doing such a thing.

The Grim Skull chuckled. "I think you'll find it to be a much easier task than you imagined. Leave now, you are missed in your dimension."

"What do you mea--"

Before Ethan could finish the question, the Grim Skull raised its hand and a giant gray stairwell suddenly appeared behind Ethan.

"Go," commanded the Grim Skull and Ethan found himself bounding up the stairs towards a door, fully aware that he was not entirely in control of his body. Weakening or not, the Grim Skull still had a great many powers of persuasion.

A strong gust of wind pushed Ethan through the door at the top of the stairs. He tripped over his own feet and landed with a THUD on the floor of James' room. As he came back into familiar surroundings--*the human realm*--he felt his mind recoil, still unable to fully accept the new reality that it had been exposed to. Then rough hands grabbed him and painfully yanked him up by the hair.

"What the fuck are you doing in my room you little bastard?"

James was awake. Judging by the smell of booze on his breath and his unsteady gait, Ethan surmised that he was still considerably intoxicated.

"I-I--"

There was no possible way to explain.

"You were in my closet!" James roared. "What were you doing in there? Blowing one of your little boyfriends?"

James threw Ethan to the floor; he landed hard and whimpered. Unsurprisingly, neither his deep-sleeping aunt nor uncle stirred.

"You're such a little pussy ass baby, you know that?" James sneered. "We all would've been so much better off if you died with your drunk ass parents. Now, *what were you doing* in there? Stealing my stash of booze?"

James stumbled towards the closet as Ethan glanced up at the poster and noted that the Grim Skull was still missing. That was when the idea came to him.

"You're gonna be just like your dead mom," James continued, "If something's wrong with the bitch then something's wrong with the pup. Those are just the facts, squirt."

James swung open the closet door and was greeted by the sight of the gray staircase.

"What the hel--"

Before James could even finish his sentence, Ethan leapt up and shoved his cousin as hard as he possibly could. James propelled forward and plummeted down the stairs. As he descended into the foggy realm below, Ethan bellowed:

"Fuel coming through!"

Then he shut the door and hurried back to his room. Somewhere in the distance he thought he heard James screaming and the Grim Skull laughing. He jumped into bed and entwined himself in the sheets, trembling furiously. Eventually, he slept.

Ethan awoke to the sound of Aunt Samantha frantically screaming James' name. She couldn't find him so she woke Ethan up and--of course--he couldn't find him either. Then Uncle Hector came home and looked. He found James' collection of liquor in his otherwise very unremarkable closet, but his son was nowhere to be seen. The police were called and the story made its rounds via local news media but James Paul Sinclair was never seen again. Ethan had never been suspected and the police listed James as a runaway.

Life after James was much easier for Ethan, serene even. No one bothered him or bullied him and Aunt Samantha and Uncle Hector were so grief-stricken that they barely paid their nephew any attention at all. It gave him incredible freedom to perfect his newfound passion in life--art. After James vanished Ethan lost all interest in science and instead dove head-first into art. His grades plummeted in all classes but drawing and, by age sixteen, he had dropped out of school to focus on his artwork. His specialty--his obsession--was black-lit posters.

Ethan grew from a boy into a man and every day he expected the Grim Skull to come for him but it never did. He continued to live with his aunt and uncle until they both died prematurely in their mid-60s. The coroner said a stroke had taken Samantha and a heart attack had felled Hector but Ethan knew the truth--they had both died of grief. They had both been as good as buried since the night that James disappeared more than 17 years prior.

Ethan lived off their inheritance for several years but after more than a decade he could no longer afford to keep up payments on the house. Unable to work on anything but his drawings and paintings, he had applied for welfare and public assistance but ended up in a state-run psychiatric facility--not that he was complaining. He liked the center. It was clean, his bed was soft, and he was allowed to sit quietly and draw all day. Of course, sometimes he had outbursts. Luckily, the nurses had medication that calmed him. Without the medication to sooth him, Ethan would have killed himself long ago.

The outbursts often came when he thought about James, whose life had been ruined by his little cousin's mere existence. Ethan saw James every day; not in the ward or in the cafeteria, but in his paintings. James' image emerged from the trunks of trees and on the tops of mushrooms--sometimes he even showed up on the petals of flowers. But his face was always contorted and tormented; a mask of misery.

James appeared most frequently with the other faces in the Grim Skull's cloak of victims since that was the subject that Ethan focused on the most. Ethan liked to decorate his room with his posters even though they frightened some of the nurses. Sometimes he joked with the young women and assured them that the paintings didn't bite--because even though he knew that they *could and did*, he also knew that they *wouldn't* because they didn't need to. The Grim Skull had him so it didn't need anyone else to do its bidding.

The years crept by. Ethan's brown hair grayed, his smooth checks wrinkled and his steady hands started to shake. Still, he drew, he painted, he *created*. When he was in his forties the stomach pains started--and persisted. The hospital doctor eventually ran some tests and told him that he had stomach cancer. Ethan wasn't surprised. Frankly, he was amazed that he had lived as long as he had.

It showed mercy to me, he thought. *It let me live longer than I needed to as some kind of thanks for agreeing to carry its burden.*

On the night after he received his diagnosis, Ethan taped the old Grim Skull poster up on the door of his room. Then he lay down to sleep. Within an hour he heard the Grim Skull calling his name. Ethan was ready. He rose from his bed, opened the door, and descended down the stairs--out of his world and into the other dimension to take his place as the wearer of the cloak and the collector of souls within the neon realm.

* * *

Ethan's disappearance was a source of both mystery and shame to the mental facility where he had resided. No one understood how he had simply gotten up and walked away. He wasn't violent and so the ward wasn't high security, but there were still safety protocols and how no alarms went off was more than perplexing, it was downright unnerving.

Orderly Georgia Harrison was particularly upset by Ethan's disappearance. She had liked him, heck, she had even liked his creepy artwork. The black-lit stuff might have gone out of style before she was old enough to tie her own shoes, but it still looked cool. Two months after Ethan's disappearance the investigations started to wane and rumors started to circulate that Ethan had simply traveled elsewhere. Most of the staff believed that he would eventually turn up in some homeless shelter, cold and hungry and broke and sick; begging to come back. Georgia wasn't so sure. She had a weird sense of conviction that Ethan was gone for good.

Eventually, they started cleaning out his room. Georgia couldn't bear the idea of his detailed artwork lying in a trash heap so she gathered it up and brought it all home. One piece in particular got her attention. It had been taped to the back of Ethan's door and depicted a grinning skeleton draped in a robe with skulls at its feet. It looked like a grim reaper except its robe was purple and there was something very familiar about the shape of its head. It was scary looking--heck, there even seemed to be screaming faces embedded in the robe--but her son would love it.

After all, Randy was into horror movies and he was quite the budding artist.

Oddity

There was nothing strange about Amber. She wasn't too tall or too short. She was of average height and weight. She wasn't ugly but she wasn't pretty either and her grades, although passing, were never top marks. She lived in an average house, with an average family, in an average town. Her father worked an average job in insurance and her mother sold Avon to other average housewives. They drove an average Toyota and listened to average music. Everything about her childhood had been bland, stable and entirely *average*.

That was why Amber strove so hard to be different.

When she was three, she pitched dramatic tantrums in stores to get attention. When she was five, she delighted in wandering away from her parents so she could hide and watch them panic. She discovered heavy metal at six, black nail polish at eight, and the occult at ten. She first dyed her mouse brown hair jet black at the tender age of eleven. By thirteen she had gotten several ear piercings and by fourteen she also had a nose, tongue and bellybutton ring. By use of a fake ID, she got her first tattoo--a skull reclining on a red rose--when she was fifteen. Morbidity fascinated her. She ritualistically wore black clothes and black makeup--with the exception of her penchant for dark red lipstick--and stared down anyone who dared to shoot her a dirty look.

Amber's strait-laced parents were mortified by her appearance as were most of their very-clean-cut neighbors, yet they were even more horrified by her attitude and behavior. They could not understand why she was so interested in misfortune and they urged her to be thankful for her good health and stable life.

Such suggestions enraged her.

Throughout her teens she drank, she smoked, she skipped school and she stayed out late; sometimes she even ran away. On three separate occasions the local police had brought her home after finding her passed out on a park bench or fighting at the mall or hanging out with the other cut-ups. Worst of all, she liked the wrong kind of boys.

Amber was no Miss America but she knew how to flirt and she had no trouble attracting men who liked her particular brand of sexy. Specifically, Amber was into musicians. Any guy who had cool hair, a loud band and a bad attitude was just her kind of man. In her mid-teens she had switched boyfriends frequently; quickly tiring of each one, bored by their inability to provide the kind of exceptional and exciting lifestyle that she so craved.

Then, when she was nineteen, she met Jaxson.

Jaxson was three years older than her and ten times poorer. Yet she envied him because, despite growing up with next to nothing, he had what she always wanted--an abnormal childhood. Jaxson had been raised on the carnival circuit and had traveled from place to place with no formal schooling and little respect for authority. She had met him at a rock concert when his fledging band--known as "Bloody Scum" --was opening for an equally eloquently named group, "Spit Spewers." Whilst standing at the edge of a mosh-pit, she had admired his drumming skills. Yet she only decided to cozy up to him after she watched the group's grand finale which involved Jaxson repeatedly slamming his head down on the cymbals. Any guy who did that was hardcore, and Amber liked hardcore guys.

Jaxson rode a motorcycle, drank like a fish, cursed like a sailor and disregarded every rule known to man. He had even been arrested for disorderly conduct a few times; bailing him out gave Amber the hots. He was wild--nearly feral--but he was also considerably less intelligent than she was, thereby making him much easier to manipulate--another trait that Amber liked in her men.

Jaxson was a certified redneck and he could be as mean as poison when he drank, but Amber gave as good as she got. They fought constantly but after they smacked each other up good and plenty the quality of the make-up sex was worth every punch, every kick, every bite. For nearly three years things were good--or what qualified as good in their very un-traditional (totally *non-average*) relationship--until Jaxson discovered OxyContin.

By then his band had broken up and he had gone back to his family on the Floridian carnival circuit, taking Amber with him. By that point she had graduated from groupie to girlfriend and she was downright ecstatic to join the carnival--feeling right at home amid the tattooed carnies and pink-haired ticket takers. The show even had some genuine freaks--fat ladies, bearded ladies, and contortionists amongst them. Jaxson even admitted that his late Great Uncle had been part of the sideshow courtesy of having been born with a parasitic twin growing out of his back. This tidbit of family history was what *really* made Jaxson sexy in Amber's eyes. For a girl who desired difference, a guy with freaky genes was the crème de le crème.

Although Jaxson's family was less than impressed by Amber, they begrudgingly came to accept her--in part because she could curse better any of them which was a highly esteemed skill in their circle. She was also pretty good at reading palms, tarot cards and tealeaves. She had yearned polish her skills, but the ancient fortune teller was a shriveled old hag who delighted in being a complete bitch to everyone. Had that attitude not extended to include her, Amber might have admired it. Despite such early tensions, Amber was starting to settle in--really get with the groove of the nomadic lifestyle--when Jaxson had started popping pills.

It began insidiously. He was depressed by the failure of his band and, on the road, the cure for depression was often found at the bottom of a bottle--a pill bottle, in Jaxson's case. He went through periods of agitation followed by days when he was completely lethargic. Their fights increased, his family blamed her, and after the police were called in to break up one particularly bad row, Amber packed up her things and moved back up north.

By then, she was twenty-two and hadn't spoken to her parents in over four years. Instead, she crashed in a small apartment with her friend Lara and didn't even bother to tell her family that she was living less than an hour away from them. Her stomach was already wrenched enough due to stress and tension.

That was when things got weird.

* * *

"I wanna see if they have any more rodent skulls."

That sentence instigated the trip to Vera's Vintage. Amber had been playing roommate to Lara for barely a week and she was already in the mood to redecorate. Lara's apartment was small and cramped but it didn't need to be anywhere near as *bare* as it was. Lara worked nights' stripping under the moniker "Lithium" and she slept in everyday--leaving her with little desire to make an effort to search for home goods. Amber, unemployed and insanely bored, was desperate to add some flare to her surroundings and Vera's Vintage was the ideal location since it carried some seriously strange--even sinister--items.

"Go yourself, you weirdo bitch," Lara half whined, half yawned, making no gesture to rise from her nest of bedsheets.

"Look who's talking, trashy ho," Amber retorted and leaned down to flick Lara's nose.

Abusive bantering was part of their bond--it seemed strange, but both women *liked* strange things.

"Seriously, it's almost 4pm. It's open until 5pm. If you get your ass up now, we can make it and maybe I won't go insane and slaughter us both."

Lara buried her face deeper into the pillows but she was noticeably more awake than she had been a minute earlier. "I've been working all night."

Amber had briefly considered joining Lara as a stripper using the moniker Morphine but she was too flat chested for it and deathly scared of medical procedures, doctors, and anything even remotely related to hospitals, so plastic surgery was out of the question.

"Please?"

"Maybe, I'll think about it...Just get out of my room if you want me to get dressed."

"Oh, like I haven't seen tits and ass before."

"Lesbian."

"Prude."

They both started giggling and that sealed the deal, they were going to go to the store. It was pretty remarkable that they got along so well, especially since Amber liked so few people. She had been called cold and callous; attention-seeking and argumentative--a user. Jaxson's aunt had even suggested that she was a sociopath which Amber regarded as a compliment even though she was fairly certain that it had been meant as an insult.

Part of the reason that Amber and Lara got along so well was that they were practically duplicates--two Goth chicks in their early 20s who hated normalcy, loved rough boys and horror movies and were fascinated by all things dark and weird. They had met when they were eighteen and working at an alternative bookstore. They bonded over volumes on the occult and freak-show history. Truthfully, they also bonded whilst parading around town together looking like two witches heading to a conference on black magic. Plus, Lara had a car and, as old and decrepit as it was, it got them from Point A to Point B. Amber appreciated that bonus, she wouldn't be caught dead taking the bus. Public transportation was just so *common*.

Once in the car, they blasted their self-proclaimed anthem, "Black No. 1" by Type O Negative, all the way through town, giggling at the looks of suspicion and scorn that they garnered from every granny and soccer mom that they passed, and subsequently decided to play Nine Inch Nails "Closer" on the way home.

Vera's Vintage was a dumpy little corner shop that's basement expanded into a sprawling labyrinth of nicks and knacks. The owner--Vera--considered herself to be a psychic medium and she never looked twice at Amber's dark appearance; if anything, she seemed more startled by Lara who was a rare Goth blonde.

It had been over a year since Amber had steeped foot into the store and she was instantly elated by its musty aroma. Thrift shops were akin to comfort food for her, a treasure chest of nostalgia. As a kid she had messed with her parents by buying old weird antiques-- like taxidermy busts and books of potions--and decorated her room, sometimes the house, with them. She had learned that the best way to navigate a thrift shop was to search the top and bottom shelves since those nooks and crannies were where the coolest items were left to rot, overlooked.

Most of the things for sale were the standard junky fair--ancient trinkets that kinless spinsters had left behind. She had almost given up on finding anything worthwhile when a taxidermy owl caught her eye. When she reached up to grasp it, she accidently knocked over an unremarkable cardboard box beside it--which contained the most remarkable collection of items that Amber had ever seen.

Freaks. Deformities. Oddities. The box was filled with stuff from old-time side-shows, mostly photos. Four legged girls, men with tails, bearded ladies, pinheads, conjoined twins...some of them Amber recognized. She had been obsessed with freaks since grade school and she knew Pip and Flip, Myrtle Cobain and Stephan Bibrowski on sight. The Camel Girl, the Elephant Man, the Ape Woman--all had been popular attractions in their day. Yet the box contained other images that she hadn't seen before: a two-faced man, a boy with an eye embedded in his forehead, a woman with horns sprouting from her neck. Amber's hands shook with excitement as she rooted through the box. The photographs were obviously authentic and probably ranged from the 1860s to the 1940s--the golden age of freak shows.

That was when she found the doll.

It was an ugly old thing yet Amber's hands grasped it eagerly. It was made of a material as coarse as burlap and while it was probably originally white it was now frayed and dirty. Oddly, its stringy black hair was surprisingly smooth--probably horse, or maybe human. Tattered and featureless, the doll would have been completely unremarkable if not for the strange lump on its side. Unlike lumps caused by misshapen stuffing, this one was stitched onto the doll intentionally as if a tumor was growing from within it.

Someone did this on purpose, Amber thought. She immediately understood that she had to have it. She took the box to the front of the store, prepared to haggle for a good price.

I'll just get the doll if I don't have enough for everything, Amber thought...and she would slip the doll into her back pocket and walk away with it if need be. She had never wanted anything as badly as she wanted that weird, creepy, deformed doll.

Vera didn't haggle about price; in fact, she sold everything for five dollars, seemingly happy to be rid of it. Lara wasn't nearly as impressed.

"Why'd you want *that*?" She asked, wrinkling her nose in disgust at the sight of the doll.

"It's cool, check out these photos! I think some of them are from Coney Island back in its heyday."

"Seriously?"

"Yeah."

"We gotta take a road trip there sometime."

"Undisputed."

The history of Coney Island was something that Amber and Lara were fascinated by along with films like *Freaks* and the photography of Diana Arbus. Amber eagerly leafed through every image, hoping that one would be such a snapshot, but none of the photos looked like the work of Diane Arbus. They looked more like images that were intended to be used for postcards and newspapers, icons of the freaks that the non-deformed could ogle at long after they left the show. One particular photo commanded Amber's attention--it depicted a little girl of nine or so staring sadly into the camera. She was naked from the waist-up and had a huge lump on her side...a lump that had visible arms and legs--shriveled and half-formed but arms and legs none the less. Amber turned the coarse yellowed paper over; "Opal and Pearl" was scripted on the back in browning, aged, ink.

"They're parasitic twins!" Amber squealed gleefully. "Isn't that awesome?"

Lara glanced at the photo and squirmed. "Gross."

"Parasitic twins are my favorite kinds of freaks," Amber continued, ignoring Lara's reaction, "I bet this was their doll!"

"You think some store sold dolls like that?" Lara exclaimed, unable to veil her shock.

Amber rolled her eyes. "No, dummy, this is obviously homemade. Someone stitched this doll to make it look like that girl."

"Someone must've really loved her to do that," Lara replied, with an audible edge in her tone. Lara had a horrible relationship with her parents and she resented anyone who had been even remotely cared for as a child...including the deformed little freak in the photo who had undoubtedly died decades earlier.

When they got home, Amber leaned the doll against the lamp on her nightstand and reached for an aspirin. She was starting to feel queasy again.

I hope this isn't the flu, she thought. Without insurance, antibiotics would cost a fortune. Yet the queasiness passed and she and Lara spent a pleasant evening eating ramen noodles and watching "Paranormal Witness" reruns.

The weird shit started at 2:43.

She was vividly dreaming...*a tall man in a top hat and a fancy coat is standing at the foot of a grand stone staircase, beckoning to her. There is something unnerving about him--unnatural--but alluring. She steps closer and closer and when she gets near to him, she sees that his face is made of nothing but burlap. He reaches for her, urging her to ascend the stairs towards a regal looking brick building....*

Amber awoke with a start, keenly aware that shadowy figures were moving around her room; she could see them out of the corners of her eyes but no matter how swiftly she swiveled her head she couldn't focus on them. Uttering a little scream of surprise, she switched on her bedroom light. The rag doll stared back at her, neither accusing nor sympathetic.

"Fuck," Amber said aloud and immediately felt a deep aching sense of loss. She missed Jaxson, if he was lying next to her, she'd be able to cuddle up beside him and sleep. Junkie or not, he made her feel safe, secure and sexy. She missed being desired.

She switched off the light and burrowed back under the sheets, unwilling to let her imagination turn her into a hysteric. Her stomach lurched and she wondered if she had a tape worm, a big fat one like the kinds she sometimes saw in tequila bottles. It was a possibility. She was always hungry no matter how much she ate and yet her stomach still complained. She also felt bloated but had a weird craving for fried onions--which was beyond strange because she normally hated them, she even forbade Jaxson from eating them near her. He loved the damn things.

Maybe the worm is missing him too, she thought and felt another pang of loss.

The room suddenly seemed very warm. Amber kicked off the comforter but still felt like she was sweltering.

Roasting and queasy--an all new low, she thought as she begrudgingly rose from the bed and walked over to the window.

The evening was chilly; a cool breeze blew forth from the lake directly across from Lara's apartment complex.

I'll open the window wider and that'll get me cooled off enough to sle--

There was someone standing by the edge of the water. It was a little girl in a white dress, illuminated by the moonlight; her eyes were as black as her hair. Then Amber noticed something incredibly strange--impossible, even--although there was only one girl standing by the waterside, the reflection showed two; a duplicate so precise that it could only be an identical twin. The little girl on the water's edge beckoned to Amber and her twin water reflections mimicked the gesture; a triple threat.

Amber screamed.

Lara burst into the room within seconds. Amber pointed out the window and babbled about the figure but when Lara looked there was nothing to see but water and reeds and distant trees.

"You're crackers my dear bitch," Lara opined but she did agree to stay in the room that night so Amber was eventually able to descend into a deep--and thankfully dreamless--sleep.

* * *

Three days later, a pregnancy test came back positive. She had brought it on a whim after her bouts of morning sickness weren't responding to Tylenol. She hadn't believed it at first but when three others came back likewise, she begrudgingly accepted the situation--she was likely one month pregnant. The dates worked out; although she was surprised that Jaxson still had such virility given his newfound pill habit. Lara saw immediate opportunities given the circumstances.

"You can totally get him on child support," she said.

"Unless he ODs and dies first," Amber muttered, staring miserably down at the hateful blue line.

"So? Then his family will pay. Carnie freaks or not they make steady money running the circuit, right?"

"True," Amber agreed. "You know for someone who's never been knocked up, you've got this whole baby daddy thing well thought out."

Lara shrugged. "I know a lot of girls who make good money from having kids. You'll be able to get welfare way easier now and you can feel free to stay with me. That money will come in handy."

I can stay here, good.

That was comforting. The last thing Amber wanted to do was admit to her parents that they had a grandkid. They would almost certainly try to remove it from her care and that would be the end of any money to be had. It was a fucked-up situation but if she could make pay out from it, she wasn't one to complain. People like her took what they could get.

After a few moments of silence Lara asked, "Do you think it's a boy or a girl?"

Amber shrugged. "Doesn't matter."

"You should get a sonogram."

"No!" Amber practically shouted, glaring icily at her best friend. "No doctors. You know I can't stand hospitals; those places are just fancy slaughterhouses."

"All pregnant women see doctors; you can even get free care--"

"I don't need it. I'm not going to a hospital; if I can pop this kid out right here, I swear I will."

"No way," Lara replied, horrified. "Do you have any idea how disgusting that would be? Birth is akin to pure gore!"

"Anything's better than hospitals. Besides, women gave birth at home for centuries before there was medicine and the human race survived. Plus, the women in my family always have easy births and healthy kids. It'll be fine."

"And if it's not?"

"If I start bleeding to death during a breeched birth in the bathtub you have my permission to call 911."

"Thanks for that lovely image, *mommy*."

The weeks went on and, as Amber's stomach grew, the dreams intensified. In them, she was always in a crowded place--sometimes it was a big building and other items it was a tattered tent but there were always people catcalling and screaming. Some were well dressed and others looked like bums but they were from a long time ago--their clothes and hairstyles conveyed an era long past. The dreams came every night and showed Amber more and more. A tall man in a top hat and tails--*a caller*--always stood outside enticing people--*the rubes*--to come in, and those very crowds were always amused but also shocked, even horrified, as they pointed and stared at a stage. Amber always awoke before she could see what was on display, but--on more than one occasion--she opened her eyes to find the odd little doll resting on her tummy, as if embracing the life that was growing inside of it.

In the sixth month of her pregnancy, Amber's dream finally allowed her to see that a little girl was being exhibited on the stage...a little girl who had a much tinier half formed body--two arms, a torso and two legs--hanging from her side, her clothes had even been tailor-made to fit her odd anatomy. Amber instantly recognized her as the little girl from the photo in the thrift store box--the doll's original owner. As soon as Amber looked upon her, the girl stared back--her gaze was fiery and unforgiving. Seemingly oblivious to the rest of the crowd, she pointed at Amber's belly with all four of her arms and sang the word "*Mommy*."

Amber woke sweating profusely; pain seared her belly and she rolled onto her side. As she did, she uttered a scream of surprise--the little ragdoll was twirling around on the bedroom floor, dancing as if in a ballet. Amber blinked hard and then saw that the doll was simply lying on the floor, somehow staring at her in spite of its lack of eyes.

Despite the unsettling dreams and odd waking moments, Amber continued onwards with her regular routine. She continued to crave fried onions and jam out to bands like Kittie, Rob Zombie and Soil. She also continued to smoke and drink, figuring a kid with fetal alcohol syndrome could get her disability benefits.

"You better be careful," Lara warned. "If you keep smoking and drinking after junior's born those bastards from social services will pay you a visit."

Amber sneered. "And do what? Take the little brat? Come on, foster care kids cost the state money and in lieu of the Great Recession the government likes to save money. They cut corners wherever possible--letting some white trash rug-rat fall under the radar is the norm.

Besides, I could always say I'm a Christian Scientist or something and can't do all that medical shit. At least I'll be a cool mom which is more than I can say for my folks."

"When are you gonna tell Jaxson?"

"Soon."

Truthfully, she had decided to tell Jaxson about the baby after it was born...provided that Jaxson was still in the land of the living.

The dreams kept on, frequently following her into her waking moments. Sometimes she'd open her eyes to see the doll coming towards her, life-sized as if in the form of a grown woman, reaching towards her, groping at her. Other times it was the girl with the misshapen body who she awoke to, standing at the foot of the bed--sometimes weeping, sometimes glaring. It was unnerving but the apparitions always vanished within a few seconds. Amber supposed that she might be losing her mind...but being crazy was better than being boring so she tolerated her circumstances.

One day when Amber was eight months pregnant, she awoke to the sound Lara screaming. Amber willed her cumbersome body up and lumbered into the living room to find Lara shaking badly and pointing at the change dish.

"Why did you put that out here?" she shrieked.

The little doll was sitting in the dish with coins stacked up all around it. Amber hadn't put it out there nor had she any idea how it had gotten there. She suspected that the doll had a mind of its own.

Possession--either demonic or ghostly--was the ultimate in interesting and thereby peaked Amber's curiosity.

She decided to uncover the origins of the doll; beginning with the history of Opal, the deformed child who she believed it had initially belonged to. Opal's life did not have abundant records like those of many other freaks, but diligent googling eventually revealed the whole strange, sad, story.

* * *

Opal Pearson was born on February 9, 1908 in Pennsylvania to impoverished farmers Gemma and Tobias Pearson. Gemma was widely regarded as being an oddball around her village so no one was overly surprised when Opal emerged from her womb entwined with a malformed twin, Pearl. Some people believed that Gemma--who was rumored to have dabbled in witchcraft--had cast a spell over her womb, willing her child to be born malformed. Certainly, Gemma instantly saw a means of making money out of her baby's physical misfortune and quickly started exhibiting her deformed child--*children*--off to her neighbors for a penny a peak--or food, or fabric...whatever they had to give. Tobias was horrified by his wife's behavior but was seemingly powerless to stop it. He fell into a deep depression and died nine months after the birth of his first born--*borns*--although rumors were whispered that he had been poisoned. Gemma reportedly kept great quantities of arsenic around their shabby home, allegedly to deal with an ongoing rat problem.

After Tobias' death, Gemma started showing her odd little child--*children*--off to circuses and even museums, Amber recognized the large stone building from her dreams as the Smithsonian. Throughout the duration of her childhood Opal and Pearl were touted around the county being mocked by crowds or laughed at or feared. Gemma, raking in the cash, didn't seem moved by her daughter's unhappiness. Aside from tailor-making the misshapen little doll for her, Gemma showed little love for the being which she had birthed.

When Opal was fifteen, she was touring around with Sigfried's Circus; a second-rate sideshow that just so happened to be the home of Merv Gilman--more commonly known as "Rat Man". Merv was famous for having a tail and, although he was twenty-three years older than Opal, Gemma immediately seized upon the ultimate publicity stunt--she arranged to have Opal marry Merv in a grand hoopla ceremony that was open to the public for a fee. In fact, over the course of a year, Opal and Merv got "married" in several different states with new guests at every show. Opal and Merv were wed only fourteen months before her death. According to the records, her demise was the result of accidental drowning.

After Opal's untimely departure, Merv continued touring with the troupe but Gemma was quickly cut out of the show-business lifestyle. She lived another fifteen years, desperately trying to hang onto the carnie way of life, even by performing meager duties such as selling tickets and making popcorn before succumbing to alcoholism. She died whilst living in a flop house, destitute--likely with nothing but the doll and some pictures left to hold onto.

Knowing Opal's history made Amber feel closer to her memory--and also envious. She had lived a life of exception; a life devoid of normalcy and filled with excitement...just the kind of life Amber had always wanted.

The final dream was the most vivid. Amber had gone to bed tired, sore and swollen. She was, by her own reckoning, approximately three days past her due date. She had lain down, sure that sleep would be fleeting, but instead fell into a remarkably deep slumber.

* * *

The dream started like all the others. It was the 1920s and she was at the freak show--except this time she was on stage. People were pointing at her, staring at her; screaming and laughing and *ogling*. She was the freak, *this* is what it felt like and, surprisingly, it didn't feel good.

Suddenly the scene jumped to a tiny bedroom. Amber--or Opal, as she seemed to be--was sitting on a bed. A tall raven-haired woman--Gemma--handed her a glass.

Drink this, it'll help you relax.

The dream skipped again and suddenly she was lying flat, naked and unable to budge, as an older man--Merv--moved atop her; sweating and panting and thrusting, raping her. Opal tried to scream, to beg him to stop. Their marriage was a sham, she was too young, and the pain--the searing unbearable pain! Yet she couldn't move. Her mother had drugged her, seemingly the driving force behind this consent-less consummation of the marriage of the freaks.

The dream skipped again. Now Opal was standing on the ledge of a tall stone bridge. It was nightfall and she could both hear the water below and see it reflected in the moonlight. She had snuck out of her sleeping quarters and was dressed in her fine white nightgown, the one she had gotten in New York. Her hands caressed her belly which was hard and firm, swelling in a rounded way that could only indicate the early stages of pregnancy. Her mother was pleased about the child; it was her will for Opal (and Pearl) and Merv to welcome a baby into the world.

It'll be a real stunner; Gemma had crooned to her sobbing daughter on the day that the doctor had confirmed her condition. *Surely, it'll be an instant crowd pleaser; perhaps it'll have both a twin and a tail! Your freakish brood will make us a fortune!*

Then she had laughed in her hard, cawing, witch-like way. But Opal hadn't laughed since she saw no humor in the circumstances. She hated her life--she detested her mother and her husband and the whole sideshow business. She couldn't imagine subjecting an innocent life to it...Death was the most merciful option.

And so, Opal jumped off the bridge and hurdled downwards; taking her parasitic sister, unborn child, and mother's ambitions with her.

Amber awoke right before she--Opal--hit the water. She was shaking and had a coopery taste in her mouth.

That was no dream, they were her memories! It was some kind of a flas--

There was a woman hovering over her bed. She was shriveled and sharp-featured with dark hair and tattered clothes--undoubtedly the spirt of Gemma. A clear vision suddenly formed in Amber's mind--Gemma right before she died, poor and mostly insane, pulling her hair out and using it to fill in the ragdoll's thinning lochs...Gemma who had practiced witchcraft and surely knew exactly how to attach herself to such an object--therefore living on in spirit long after her body died.

Before Amber could move or utter a sound, the spirit reached down and rubbed her exposed belly as if it was a crystal ball.

"You're going to get what you always wanted," she crackled.

With that said, the labor pains started. They were stronger than Amber had expected and far more painful; although she had fully intended to give birth in the house, her wails of agony quickly frightened Lara into calling an ambulance. Amber was rushed to the hospital where she gave birth slightly over eight hours later.

* * *

The condition was rare in modern times, at least in first world countries. The doctors said that Amber's daughter (*daughters*) was the first parasitic twin they had ever seen outside of a medical book. Although one twin was little more than a spine, an arm and two limp legs, Amber decided to name it. And so, she became the mother of Crystal and Jade. The doctors said it didn't have to be this way, they said they could surgically remove Jade and let Crystal lead a normal life but Amber would have none of it; normalcy was a far worse fate. Oh no, this baby would bring flavor to the world...*difference.*

Lara was mortified. "I told you to get a sonogram," she babbled. "You could have seen it! You could have done something--"

But Amber wasn't nearly as concerned. She assumed that Jaxson's family would be amused, maybe even downright pleased. After all, such occurrences were in *his* genes.

"You're not serious about the freak show, right?" Lara asked a few weeks later as Amber packed up to visit Jaxson. "I mean, you're not really gonna show the kid off for cash...are you?"

"Try me," Amber replied as she placed the old ragdoll in the car seat where it lay against the soft skin of her sleeping offspring. She had long since surmised that the spirits in the doll had sensed the difference in her baby (*babies*) and had purposefully found her in the thrift shop during the first days of her gestation. She had also surmised that she and the late Gemma Pearson had much in common.

And so, Amber packed her child (*children*) into the car and headed back towards the carnival circuit. As she drove along, singing aloud to Hole's *Asking For It*, she stole a peek at the rearview mirror. Gemma's spirit was hovering over the tiny freak, smiling wickedly and making the old ragdoll dance in midair. The baby (*babies*) laughed and Amber smiled. Her life would never be normal again.

Summoner

Sadie had first summoned the Sandman when she was eight years old. She had done it by accident whilst dancing around her sparsely decorated bedroom, chanting nonsense words at midnight, pretending to be a witch, willing herself to learn the ability to curse Tom and Lila. Somehow, she had managed to utter a certain sequence of sounds exactly right--or wrong, depending on one's perspective--and brought him forth. He had come through the mirror and danced with her. Despite his inhumane face and scary-looking hoofed feet and big horns, she hadn't screamed because he danced so beautifully. Besides, he was gentle in comparison to Lila who was entirely human but far fiercer.

Looking back, she understood that he wasn't the actual Sandman but she had called him that because he had helped her sleep. When she knew he was there she felt safe and slept easily; a relief for a child who regarded slumber as a fickle tease, an enemy to be reckoned with.

Sadie was what psychiatric professionals referred to as "a problem child" who frequently threw tantrums and rarely complied with even reasonable requests. She threw her dinner across the room if the carrots so much as touched the potatoes. She kicked and screamed in shops if she wasn't allowed to buy candy and if anyone denied her a trip to the playground they would be met with her glass-shattering shrieks. Sadie's behavior would be difficult for any parents to deal with but she was a foster child, which severely complicated matters. Her real parents were unfit but no one would tell Sadie precisely why. She didn't remember her father at all and her only memories of her mother were fleeting--she'd been very fond of screaming and Sadie clearly recalled her punching the mailman once, a scene she'd found hilarious.

Eventually, Sadie's mother had gotten so angry that she had hurt someone and lost custody of her daughter. With no other family to take her, Sadie had been passed through several temporary homes, growing angrier and angrier. She hated rules. She hated boundaries and, most of all, she hated people--especially adults.

Adults made up all sorts of weird rules, the kinds of rules Sadie didn't abide by. She had been moved from school to school after fighting with her teachers--and the occasional pesky peer--and she had similarly been moved from one foster family to another. Sadie had what her social worker called "a bad reputation." She had gotten into so many fights with other foster children that her file declared her to be best suited with a childless couple. Of course, she fought with them too. Her last foster family consisted of a preacher and his wife and she had misbehaved so fiercely that they suggested she undergo an exorcism. The foster program responded by removing her from their care.

And that was how she came to live with Tom and Lila Wilkerson who were, by far, the toughest nuts to crack. The Wilkerson's were a strange pair. Tom was portly and near-sighted, balding and mostly silent. Lila was slender and blonde and quite attractive despite being deep within the throes of middle age. She was also much bossier and vocal than her husband, something that irked Sadie to no end.

The Wilkerson's were not religious enough to go to church--nor had Sadie noticed as much as a crucifix in their home--but they used more religious phrases and threats than the mellow preacher and his meek little wife ever had. They did not scare easily and her tantrums seemed to have little effect on them. Lila even seemed to take Sadie's misbehavior as a challenge and refused to let the child win.

"Bad kids get taken away," Lila hissed at her after a particularly brilliant outburst at the supermarket. "You better start acting right or you'll get locked up!"

At first Sadie had scoffed, sure that she could break them...but as time went on, she grew less and less sure. They were *difficult* people.

She couldn't scream or kick or punch them into submission. They refused to surrender her back to the state even when she smashed mirrors and shouted at strangers. As a last resort, she had etched the image of two voodoo dolls into her desk and repeatedly stabbed them with pencils and pens, since she had no access to more effective items like scissors or knives. Both Lila and Tom had seen the voodoo doll renderings but seemed to be totally unfazed by them--something that would have sent the preacher's wife screaming from the room.

"You'll be damned for life if you keep this up," was all Lila had said. Sadie reckoned she was already damned whilst under their lock and key.

She felt incredible dismay at the couple's apparently unbreakable nerves and so finding the Sandman in the mirror was something truly uplifting--exciting even. He was big and he was scary looking so Sadie asked him if he would like to eat the Wilkerson's but he shook his great horned head, preferring that she was the only one to see him. Yet even though Sadie couldn't *show* the Wilkerson's her friend didn't mean that she couldn't *tell* them about him...which she did, gleefully.

She hoped that they would think she was crazy and have her locked up in the mental hospital. She would stay there for a while, playing on the nurses' sympathy and getting them to do whatever she bid, and then she would get checked out and sent to another couple; hopefully ones who were lenient with rules, liberal with money and easily manipulated. Yet neither Tom nor Lila seemed remotely interested in her stories, let alone disturbed by them.

"Liars lose their soul with every untruth they tell," was Lila's sole response. As usual, Tom merely scowled and said nothing to the odd little child that he had agreed to foster.

When her descriptions of the Sandman failed to produce the desired outrage, Sadie started sketching images of him everywhere--she even etched his likeness into the side door of the couple's mini-van--and always illustrated him to look as menacing as possible. Alas, such displays of extreme misbehavior were still not enough to scare off the Wilkerson's.

Sadie's days were miserable but her nights were enjoyable since the Sandman came to see her; he smelled like a fireplace--all ashes and soot--which Sadie thought was a divine aroma. Although he never spoke to her, she told him about her burning hatred for the Wilkerson's and her unwavering desire to escape from them. The Sandman offered no assistance but he did listen, Sadie supposed that made him her first and only true friend.

Several months after the coming of the Sandman, Sadie had secretly listened in on Lila and her equally dreadful sister having a conversation. They thought she was lying in bed sick with the flu but Sadie had faked the illness just to see if Lila would buy it. Surprisingly, she had; it was Sadie's sole victory against her. As expected, Lila and her sister were discussing "bad kids" aka all-things-Sadie related.

"I warned you not to take in a foster," Lillian snipped. She was several years older than Lila and had a skin condition that made her hands and cheeks crack and peel; a real-life boogeyman--or *boogey woman.*

"We need the money," Lila replied. "Tom's hours at the garage got cut and the state is paying us extra for this one."

"I told you not to marry him," Lillian retorted. "You didn't listen to me that time either. And now look where it's gotten you. That little brat upstairs could kill you. Have you even considered that?"

Lila waved her hand dismissively. "I can handle her."

"Can you? Can you *really?*" Lillian persisted. "You have no idea what that kid saw or experienced before you got her. Think about what happened to that poor woman who spent all that money adopting a little boy from Russia. She returned him a few months later because he was planning to kill her! He was hiding knives under his bed and even tried to burn the house down. He was only six years old! God forbid that could be your fate."

"It's not that serious, she's just bitchy," Lila replied.

From her perch at the top of the stairs, Sadie's heart raced. Murder! Of course! Why hadn't she thought of it before? Right there and then she decided she would have to kill them, or at least really make them think that she was trying to kill them. Yet this was easier said than done since the Wilkerson's owned no guns and forbade her from going near sharp things. Hence, she would have to be creative.

Over the course of the following week Sadie tried to arrange a series of little "accidents" for Tom and Lila. She left rubber balls around the kitchen floor, hoping that Lila would trip and fall and crack her skull open on the tiled floor. She attempted to trip Tom down the porch steps but he was surprisingly agile and grabbed ahold of the railing, therefore securing his safety. She got a hold of some aspirin in the school nurses office, ground the tablets up, and sprinkled them into Tom and Lila's teapot. She'd hoped they would overdose and die but--maddeningly--the pills seemingly had no ill effects at all. The Wilkerson's were indestructible.

"It's not fair!" she wailed to the Sandman one night as they twirled around her room to music that only they could hear. "I'd do anything to get rid of them!"

The Sandman had looked at her inquisitively and Sadie hoped he would offer her guidance but instead he simply nodded, sympathetic to her plight but unable or unwilling to assist her. Perhaps it was a language barrier; Sadie didn't even know if the Sandman *could* speak.

The night started out as usual, he went back to his mirrored realm--refusing to let her follow even when she begged and cried and pleaded--and she went to bed and fell asleep as soon as her head hit the pillow.

But then something odd happened...she woke up.

It was the first time since the coming of the Sandman that she failed to sleep a full night. The clock on her bedside table said it was 2:46am. Her stomach knotted, afraid that the insomnia was returning, but then she smelled soot and ash--the scent of the Sandman! She turned towards the mirror, fully expecting to see his great horned figure, but instead two items sat in front of the glass; a box and a bottle had been left there like offerings...or presents.

Sadie scrambled to the mirror and eagerly grasped the items. The box contained a standard pack of matches but the bottle was green and fancy...it looked quite ancient. She uncapped it and inhaled an unmistakable scent--gasoline. The bottle smelled exactly like a gas station. Gasoline and matches...a recipe for fire. Sadie immediately understood what the presents meant and the realization filled her with glee--the Sandman had listened and he was going to help her after all! The presents were more than mere gifts; they were tools--keys to her freedom!

Sadie knew exactly what needed to be done. She uncapped the bottle and carried it and the matches towards the Wilkerson's bedroom. It occurred to her that she might be dreaming--the Sandman was the master of slumber, after all--but it didn't feel like a dream as she opened the door and watched the Wilkerson's sleep and listened to their snores. It didn't feel like a dream when she doused the gasoline all over their bed and witnessed them squirm, startled awake by the liquid. And it *certainly* didn't feel like a dream when she saw the fear in their eyes as she lit the match.

"You'll go straight to Hell for this," Lila said right before Sadie threw the match upon the bed, instantly setting both Lila and her spouse ablaze.

The intensity of the flames was what really and truly convinced Sadie that she was not sleeping and this was no dream. The fire roared to life; the heat soared as the smoke suffocated the air making it impossible to breathe. Still clutching the bottle and matches, Sadie ran back to her room and saw the Sandman standing in the mirror--just as she knew he would be. He was grinning and beckoning, finally inviting her into the realm of the mirror.

Sadie blissfully glided towards him. She fully expected to be gently twirled into the next dimension but instead the Sandman reached out and grabbed her roughly.

He callously pulled her downwards into a hole of jagged rocks, caverns and fire. When they reached the bottom of the deep pit the Sandman--or what Sadie now realized was a demon--threw her into a blackened cage and locked the door, laughing as she withered.

Lila was right; Sadie had condemned herself to Hell.

And so, Sadie remained in the cage and--over time--her nails grew long and curled, her tongue forked and her skin hardened. Her ears elongated, her hair fell out in clumps and--slowly but surely--she sprouted tiny horns. Her teeth sharpened and her ability to speak diminished until all she could vocalize was a series of howls and growls; grunts and snorts.

Yet Sadie was not alone. There were other cages containing other children in varied stages of metamorphosis. For the creature that she had called the Sandman was really a demon--a summoner of naughty children. After all, if devils were fallen angels then it made sense that demons were damned children. Sadie assumed that one day she would look just like a breasted version of the demon and perhaps she would start her own collection of lost souls...

Eventually, when her human features were all but gone, Sadie was allowed out of the cage; free to run amuck--and fly amuck, courtesy of her newfound wings--and exist in a world devoid of rules. An ideal dwelling, really...essentially her dream come true.

So, perhaps Lila hadn't been entirely right after all. Sadie was in Hell but she surely wasn't burning or particularly unhappy. She belonged. She was home to where she had been summoned.

Surrogate

Sometimes he dreamed. Not regularly, not often, but sometimes. The content was usually mundane or silly, like arriving at the carnival wearing nothing but swim trunks or wandering through abandoned towns looking for open bars, but sometimes the dreams were scary instead of silly ...especially since, occasionally, they had deeper-rooted meanings and, deep down, Hank Bott knew it.

Sometimes he dreamt of Holli--spelled with an "i" as she always made sure to point out--who was perpetually young and always nine months pregnant. In those dreams, his foster-turned-runaway old flame was homeless and dirty and staring at him hatefully amid a makeshift home of cardboard boxes, pointing an accusatory finger in his direction. Those dreams always ended in gore when her swollen belly popped and projected all its bloody glory onto him, the cause of all her troubles.

Of course, Hank had no idea if he had actually impregnated her all those years ago. She *said* he was the father but that had been back in the 1970s before DNA testing so there had been no way to prove it. Hell, for all he knew she hadn't actually been pregnant at all and had just made the whole thing up for attention; there had certainly been a lot of drama queen in Holli. Either way, he had hightailed it out of town less than a week after she told him--months before she would've started to show--so he had no idea what had become of her or her (*his, their*) alleged child. He didn't think about it much, except when he dreamt. Hank wasn't the fatherly type.

He'd had the dream tonight and jolted awake; squinting in the harsh sunlight and wincing from the sharp pains in his back as his muscles and discs complained about spending the night on the floor. Hank supposed he probably should have made more of an effort to get to the bed, but he'd been too lit last night to give a flying rat's ass. Truthfully, he was somewhat surprised that he had managed to make it back to the motel at all; many nights he hadn't been so fortunate and had spent the evening on park benches, in doorways, in abandoned buildings or--worst of all--homeless shelters. Once in a blue moon he had even wound up in the county jail drunk tank.

He glanced toward the clock; it was 1:23pm. He'd overslept, badly, and the boss would be pissed. The carnival opened at noon and he was, technically, supposed to be there at opening. It got busier at night though and they needed all the hands they could get. Hank forced himself to get up. If he came in two hours late it was better than not going in at all and, slave wages or not, he needed some money if he wanted his nightly whiskey. Hank Bott was never one to turn down whiskey.

* * *

The carnival was loud and riotous and an assault to his senses, especially so since he was hungover--although being hungover had become habitual for him and he supposed, to some extent, his body had adjusted to the perpetual toxicity.

Morton carried on as if he was pissed off but Hank knew he was happy to see him. Carnies often skipped town and bosses like Morton were happy to get whatever help they could. Hank had been working the carnival circuit for years and he knew how to handle most of the duties, but he wasn't exactly thrilled when Morton threw a bag of sawdust at him.
"Some kid puked a few feet off the tilt-a-whirl," he growled. "Go clean it up! The barf's right outside Mike's tent."

Mike, great.

Mystic Mike was one of the star attractions of the carnival who made his money by telling old ladies whatever they wanted to hear about long-dead husbands, and promising starry-eyed teenage girls that they would meet Prince Charming one day. It was all hogwash, of course, but well-done hogwash.

Deep down, Hank admired Mike. He was a conman, but a damn good one. He was a smooth talker, skilled at his craft, and a surprisingly sharp dresser to boot. Whereas most fortune tellers paraded around in bandanas and golden earrings, Mike rarely deviated from tailored suits and shiny black dress shoes with matching socks. His strength was in his ability to observe people's clothing, mannerisms, speech, and give cold-readings on the spot that were usually just accurate enough to awe the rubes to their core.

Mystic Mike was the personification of everything Hank wasn't. Even standing next to the star-covered tent made Hank feel inferior and cleaning up some brat's spilled cookies outside of it did nothing to improve his standing.

Mike's tent was crowded, as usual. A line had formed outside of it and was growing rapidly. Several patrons had sidestepped the puke in disgust and were clearly relieved to see Hank trudging towards it with the sawdust.

"Look, mommy, a pirate!" a little boy shouted from somewhere in the crowd and pointed his grubby little finger at Hank, eliciting a chorus of snickers. It wasn't the first time that Hank had been mistaken for a pirate although he wasn't sure why. He didn't have an eye patch or a peg leg and he despised parrots, but he did have an uneven gait and shaved rarely. Perhaps that was the problem.

Hank cleaned the mess and then slandered off towards the tilt-a-whirl. Blake, it's operator, was an asshole but he sometimes let Hank help out...and subsequently sneak peeks up girls' skirts. Hank didn't have too many joys left in life and so his perversions provided fleeting entertainment.

Unfortunately, Blake didn't need any help. He was even more hungover than Hank was and in a meaner mood than usual. With no rides to set up or take down, Hank wandered through the carnival, hoping to get through the day with as little hassle--and as much pay--as possible. He had wanted to be trained as a ride operator so he could keep busy--and earn additional bucks--while on duty, but Morton was sluggish in taking him on. Hank supposed he had smelled booze on his breath once too often.

Guys like Hank were at the bottom of the food chain on the carnival circuit, not to mention society at large. Wandering aimlessly around the carnival made

Hank acutely aware of his own misfortunes and shortcomings; the way his life had unfairly played out to plot against him. Sometimes Hank daydreamed too, mostly about what it would be like to have talent and prestige and poise; a way to become one of the acts rather than a background groupie.

The day turned out to be more of a disaster than usual. There was a grand total of three sick ups and fourteen food spills, all of which were Hank's problem. Everywhere he ventured he got dirty looks, even from the "performers" at the freak-show which, due to political correctness, had recently been renamed the "oddities tent." Hank supposed he looked rougher than normal, but it still annoyed him when people gave him dirty looks, especially kids. Hank hated kids.

Over the course of the afternoon, he had also spotted three girls who resembled Holli--although god knew his long-lost ex-girlfriend wouldn't look half as good nowadays--and he couldn't help but glance, maybe even leer at, them. He didn't know why he periodically thought back to Holli. He hadn't loved her as much as he'd lusted after her and she had been a real pain in the ass. She'd yelled at him when he didn't pick up his clothes or do the dishes--women's work, in Hank's opinion. Before the drugs, his ma had always done that stuff. Holli had called him a lazy no-good bum when he asked her to buy him some clothes--even though she had the waitressing job and she knew plenty well that he couldn't get as much as a bag-boy gig. She'd go out with her friends and accuse him of being jealous when he demanded to know her whereabouts. Worse still, she didn't like him going out with his buddies and as much as glancing in another woman's direction--but he was a guy, that was his nature. She'd try to talk to him when he was watching TV or interrupt his favorite song on the radio; petty and annoying crap like that could drive a guy crazy after a while. Occasionally, he'd blown up at her, screaming loud enough to shake the pavement they stood on. She'd said she was scared of him, but he'd never hit her once, even when he really wanted to and she'd damned well deserved it.

He'd been happy when he'd made the decision to hop a freight-train out of town and leave her without as much as a goodbye--subsequently ensuring no weepy dramatic scenes--and he never sought her out again, but he'd never forgotten her either. The chick had really gotten under his skin and every lookalike he saw, even decades later, hit that fact home hard.

* * *

By the end of the day, Hank was desperate for a drink and ambled hurriedly into The Captain's Daughter Bar like it was the only refuge in a storm. The big blonde broad behind the counter, who bore more than a passing resemblance to Miss Piggy, recognized him on sight and instantly reached for the whiskey.

Hank had been making the bar his last call of the day for the entire three weeks he'd been in town. It stayed open until 3am and it was close to the no-tell motel he'd holed himself up in, unwilling to shack up with the rest of the carnies in the communal trailers. Hank didn't much care for the other carnies; most seemed shady and on more than one occasion he'd had his liquor stolen. Hank found that, on average, you met a nicer class of person offsite in bars and motels or, hell, even down skid row.

Hank nursed his liquor at the counter and pretended not to notice the blonde bar chick checking out the huge scar that ran down his right arm. He'd gotten it in a bar fight several years before, but he'd been so drunk at the time that he couldn't even remember exactly what the fight had been about. He eventually took his drink to a table in the back corner of the room. The couple sitting beside him smelled vaguely of chocolate chip cookies, Hank supposed they worked at the bakery across the street.

He loved the smell of chocolate chip cookies. They reminded him of his mother. They had baked together when he was little, before she discovered LSD. Those had been the good old days. He had never known his father-- by all accounts, he'd been a booze hound--but his mother had done her best. Sixteen years old or not, she'd been a good ma...until she met a long-haired loser named Doug who introduced her to the commune where she'd started experimenting with every hallucinogenic in existence. Doug left her shortly after crossing her path, but his legacy lived on via her addiction. By the time Hank was ten she couldn't take care of herself, let alone make him cookies. He was surprised social services hadn't taken him. He had, as they say, fallen through the cracks.

He ran away at fifteen. He never saw his ma again but he had called in to check on her periodically. She stopped answering when he was seventeen. At eighteen, he'd gone home to see her only to learn that she had gotten into increasingly hard drugs, specifically crack cocaine. She'd OD'd and died in the back aisle of a rundown movie theater. It was a sorry end for a girl who had grown up singing gospel. Then again, Hank always assumed that it was the church that had destroyed her; his super-religious grandparents had surely driven his mother to rebellion. There was a reason she had never let him meet them.

His mother's death had crushed Hank with depression and he went back on the road; traveling and working to keep himself busy and dull his senses to anything but the basic instinct to survive. He'd met Holli a few months later. She came from an even more screwed up background than he did and they had bonded over their shared dysfunctions. During those late-teen years, Hank got to enjoy what most people considered "normal" coming-of-age experiences--going miniature golfing, necking in the back of movie theaters, dancing and, of course, going on carnival rides. But then he'd started drinking and Holli started bitching. When she claimed that she was pregnant he cut and run; crushing her dreams of the glorious white-wedding and nice picket-fence house.

Hank's dreams hadn't come true either. He'd always wished that he could sing because being a lounge singer seemed a hell of a lot more comfortable than being a carnie, but he didn't have the range. Nowadays, his dreams were far more modest. He hoped to move to Oregon where the weather was cool. He hated the California heat and the blistering sunburns it granted him no matter how much lotion he slathered on whenever he could afford it and remembered to use it. Of course, he'd have to work a long time more before he could settle down anywhere. The Oregon plan, just like the lounge singer aspirations, was merely a pipe dream.

He drank until he couldn't see straight and refused to get up until he was being hurried out at closing time. The night was dark but warm. Hank staggered outside, vaguely aware that the motel--and its comfy bed--was only three blocks away but he was tired and groggy so three blocks might well have been thirty miles.

There was a park across the street from the bar. Well, perhaps nothing as grandiose as a park but it was a patch of green trees and shrubbery separating the town from the highway and it looked like a nice quiet place; an ideal location to camp out in warm weather.

Hank stumbled across the street and fought his way through the thick foliage. He found an ideal spot to lie down against a thick sturdy tree trunk and allowed himself to sink onto the mud and grass, using one of the tree's mossy roots as a pillow. Within a minute, he was asleep and dreaming of Holli.

She was standing in the carnival concession stand, serving up popcorn. She turned to look at him and, surprisingly, she wasn't pregnant this time. She was still slim and pretty; smiling and laughing in the way that had initially attracted him to her. She was his *Jolly Holli*--god, how she'd hated it whenever he called her that...but she always smiled whenever he did so. She was wearing a 1950s-style apron like the one his mother had owned. Dream Holli picked up a scoop of popcorn and strutted over to him, putting a little sway in her step and rocking her hips in the way that used to drive him wild.

"Here, sugar, have a treat," she said in a sultry tone that he'd only heard during their intimate moments. And 'sugar' had been her nickname for him, how could he have forgotten that?

She approached him, eyes sparkling. But now she wasn't holding popcorn, she was holding grapes which she hand-fed him eagerly, giggling in a charming girlish way as he obediently swallowed them down.

Suddenly, in the distance, Hank heard a commotion. Banging and crashing--and, oddly, the unmistakable sound of digging--and what seemed like bright lights going off in the corner of his eyes.

There's been an accident, he thought and tried to turn towards the concession window expecting to see a ride collapsing in flames. But Dream Holli would not be ignored. She threw aside the grapes and rushed at him, taking his head in her hands and kissing him deeply and passionately.

Her lips on his didn't feel like a dream and neither did the heat of her body as she pushed against him. It had been a long time since Hank had felt anything even remotely intimate and the shock of it jolted him awake. He was expecting to find himself alone or--somehow--reunited with Holli. What he didn't expect was precisely what he saw. *Something*--some monstrous *thing*--was lying on top of him and had attached itself to his lips.

Hank tried to scream as he jerked his body violently upwards. With all his might, he used both his moderately muscular arms to propel the creature away. The force of the shove sent its warm body sailing backwards, letting out a gluteal gurgle of rage that was somewhere between a cry and a roar.

Hank abruptly got to his feet, shaking and coughing. His throat was raw and sore but his head was clear; whatever oblivion the alcohol had afforded him was completely spent. Before he could step forward, the creature lunged at him again.

Hank wasn't young but he was strong and accustomed to working on crews that erected rollercoasters and stands that sometimes weighed a total of three-hundred pounds. Using all of his might and considerable girth, he pushed the creature downwards as it attempted to crawl up his chest. It struggled fiercely and emitted outraged shrieks as he punched and stomped it repeatedly. When it was completely still, he turned and ran for his life.

His panic was intense and primitive. He ran towards the edge of the woods and nearly cried out with joy and relief when he saw the streetlights. He tripped and collapsed onto the ground and kissed the concrete before rising again and making a beeline towards the motel. He wasn't twenty feet down the street before he started to second-guess the incident.

He had been drunk and he was notorious for having deeply troubling and incredibly realistic dreams. Monsters didn't exist, so surely what had just occurred was nothing more than a particularly intense nightmare.

You've got to stop drinking. It's killing you.

Then, another thought came to him. It was crazy and rash but also impulsive and impossible to ignore.

Go back to the woods. You'll see there's nothing there and it's all in your head and then you'll make a pack to quit the booze.

Before he could talk himself out of it, Hank turned around and walked back towards the woods, guided by the streetlights and the faint glow of the full moon. He expected to find nothing but his own footprints but--to his utter surprise--the creature was still lying where he had left it, unmoving.

Hank approached it tentatively, strongly assuming that it was dead. In the light of the moon he could see that it was gray and covered with flabby skin with only the faintest of hairs covering its body. He instantly envisioned photos he had seen of naked mole rats although he couldn't remember precisely where he might've seen such pictures.

The creature was vaguely humanoid with an oval shaped head, two arms, two legs, and feet and hands that ended in four digits with sharp talons. It was naked but seemingly sexless. Its nose was a tiny lump with two nostrils and its mouth was akin to an octopuses' suction. Its closed eyes were nothing but two tiny slits. It looked dead but it was breathing, Hank could see its chest rising and falling rhythmically. Apparently, he'd only knocked it unconscious. Most importantly, it was not a figment of his imagination. The thing--whatever it was--was very, very real as was the fresh hole under the shrubs that it had unearthed itself from.

It'd make a fortune on the circuit, Hank thought suddenly, envisioning crowds lining up outside the freak-show--or "oddities tent" as the PC police had seemed fit to deem it--to get a glimpse of the strange thing with the weird anatomy.

As he stood under the trees in the dead of night, Hank Bott realized that he'd struck gold. He decided right there and then that the creature was coming with him.

He had a small bit of duck-tape in his back pocket; he had learned from many years on the job to always kept it handy. He carefully bent down and tied the thing's arms and legs together, praying that it wouldn't suddenly wake up and start fighting. He briefly considered carrying it out of the woods, but if anyone happened to be driving by and saw him, they might think he was abducting a kid. Then, they might try to stop him or call the police. Worse, they could try to take his prize for themselves.

Hank decided he needed a sack and quickly shuffled out of the woods. A bus stop was just down the block and a garbage can was situated beside it. Hank spilled out the thankfully sparse contents onto the street, grabbed the hefty plastic black bag, and sprinted back to the woods. He was afraid that the creature would be gone--or awake and furiously chewing through the tape-- but it remained lying bound and silent. Hank scooped it up and shoved it into the sack. He tied the top but poked a tiny hole in the side. He didn't want to suffocate it; whatever the thing was, it was more useful to him alive than dead.

He lumbered back to the motel with the garbage bag slung across his shoulder, hyper-attentive for any feelings of movement from within the plastic. The creature didn't stir but Hank's back groaned.

Once back in his shabby room, Hank opened the bag and stared at the unaware creature. It was smaller than he'd initially thought; perhaps it was a baby and he was now, by default, its surrogate parent.

Maybe it was trying to get milk from me or something, he thought, remembering how he had awoken to it suckling him.

The biggest question was, what exactly was it? An alien? A prehistoric creature? A mutant? A badly deformed bear? The last option seemed the least likely, Hank knew what bears looked like and this sure as hell wasn't a bear. Perhaps it was some kind of mole, it had dug itself out of the ground and it looked mostly hairless. Moreover, maybe it was a mole with a birth defect that made it big. Gigantism--that was a real condition. Hank had known a guy on the freak-show circuit who had it and he had been damn near eight feet tall.

"Moles are mammals just like humans, aren't they?" Hank said aloud, trying to be logical. "I bet they can get the same thing."

Moles could also be fierce so Hank realized that he would have to be extremely careful. For all he knew, the damn thing had rabies.

Before the drugs took over her life and addled all the sense in her head, Hank's mother had instilled the importance of hygiene in her only child. Undoubtedly, she'd be horrified by how rough he lived most of his adult life, but enough of her good early influence had stuck with him so that he always carried certain items with him like tooth paste, a toothbrush, a comb, nail clippers and a nail file. Now that he had the *thing* in his possession, Hank had never felt more grateful for his mother's advice.

He retrieved the nail clippers and nail file and gently removed the creature from the bag. While it was still out cold, he clipped its nails nearly to the quick-- which took excessive effort since the thing had nails as strong and thick as a hawk's talons--and then checked its mouth, intending to file its sharp little teeth down to non-threatening stubs. Curiously, it had no teeth nor tongue. The pursed sucker and slack line seemed to be its gab's only two modes.

Maybe it's so young that its teeth haven't grown in yet, Hank thought, holding onto his "baby" theory. Yet out in the woods the thing hadn't felt like a baby and it had fought with the strength of an adult.

Like a mother protecting its cub--or a cougar, Hank thought and shivered.

He didn't much care for wildlife. When he was a boy, he'd once walked too far into the woods at dusk trying to escape Jeb, one of his by-then-perpetually-high mother's especially violent boyfriends, only to find himself face-to-face with a mountain lion. It had been maybe two feet away from him and it had growled and bared its teeth threateningly. Hank never forgot the feeling of sinking dread, truly believing that he was about to be torn to shreds. Instead, the big cat had turned and ran back up into the mountains from where it had come. Hank, for his part, heeded its warning and steered clear of those woods since then, preferring to hang out at the arcade whenever Jeb--among others---stopped by. Now here he was, several decades later, crossing paths with another creature of the forest. But this wasn't a passing occurrence--this was fate. Hank felt it in his bones.

"What's your name?" he asked suddenly. It was a silly question; even if the thing had been awake it wouldn't understand English. Hank brayed nervous laughter; wild animals didn't have names and now that it was essentially his pet, it was up to him to christen it.

Holli was the name that he automatically associated with females, but how the hell did he know it was a girl? He didn't, but he figured calling it a "she" would play up the cuteness angle--appeal was a central component to every good act.

"Whaddya want your name to be?" Hank asked the creature. "What'd you look like?"

It seemed only fitting that the name somehow rhymed with Holli.

"Lolli? Ollie? Molli? Polli? Nah, none of them are right for you, doll.... Wait, that's it! Dolli! I'll call you Dolli! We're gonna make a fortune!"

Somehow, having a name for his captive made Hank feel better about his plans for the future which were--admittedly--newly formed and shaky. Yet the most pressing problem at hand was what to do with Dolli for the rest of the night. Exhaustion was quickly overtaking Hank and he wasn't about to cuddle up next to the unconscious pile of skin.

As small and cheap and dingy as it was, the room did have a bathroom. Hank decided the best course of action was to put Dolli back in the bag, put the bag in the bathtub, shut off the light, and close the door. For good measure, Hank also slid the bed-stand table in front of the bathroom's entrance and--noticing it was a little rickety--duct-taped the perimeter of the door.

"If it can get outta there I'll rename it Houdini," Hank told the empty room before tumbling into bed.

He awoke slightly after 10am to the sound of growls and bangs. Dolli was awake. Hank was relieved that it hadn't slipped into a coma and died, but he was also wary of the commotion it was kicking up. He was hopeful that whatever neighbors he had in adjacent rooms weren't the curious type--or the type to go complaining to the cops--but if animal control came, he would probably just get a fine, at worst. What made him a little nervous was the idea of losing control over his potential meal-ticket. What made him *really* nervous was the daunting task of facing it again when it was conscious and, apparently, extremely pissed off.

Hank armed himself with the skinny bedside lamp and used a pillow as a shield; it was a poor means of protection but better than nothing. Maybe he would get lucky and Dolli would turn out to have an insatiable appetite for feathers.

Hank was wrong about the feathers, but he was right about Dolli's mood; the thing was pissed off to no end. The second he opened the door it lunged at him, although its initial furious strength seemed diminished and its gait was loopy and off-kilter.

It's probably got brain damage.

For the first time he realized that, although there were no traces of blood, a portion of the creature's skull was dented inwards. Still, it attacked and growled in its odd way, breathing laboriously. Intimidated, Hank pulled the shower curtain down and wrapped it tightly around the protesting creature. It was a flimsy plasticly fabric but, with nails clipped, Dolli couldn't manage to break free. Hank pulled the ensnared creature to him and held it tightly, rocking it soothingly until it was calm. He'd known an organ-grinder once who calmed his ill-tempered monkey in the same way and it worked, within five minutes Dolli was still and quiet and breathing normally.

Hank realized that he couldn't go back to work until it was trained. As he sat upon the grubby tiles and rocked his inhuman ward, he decided to call Morton and say that he was sick and then spend some time training Dolli in the little bathroom.

I'll say I got the shits, no one'll question that.

The carnival was in town another four days, that would be more than enough time to get the thing under control and then catch a ride to the next town with Blake in his beat-up old pickup truck. Of course, how he was going to get Dolli into the truck without Blake noticing was another problem he had no way to solve as of yet.

* * *

Hank had traveled with the carnival for years and he had shacked up at the motel more than once. The owner was a dowdy dude named Mitch who covered his office with girlie magazine centerfolds and he was used to Hank. He knew he had steady work and could pay his way so he probably wouldn't mind letting him stay on the sly for a couple of days, as long as he paid up before rolling out of town.

I can borough some bucks off Blake, Hank decided. *He owes me for bailing him out back in Dade City.*

Of course, the whole reason Blake had ended up in a Floridian jail cell was for being involved in a bar fight that Hank had started, but he opted not to dwell on that.

The one concrete part of the plan that Hank could bank on was sleeping pills. He had gotten a bottle a few years back when he'd gone through a period of insomnia but it had cleared itself up before he even finished half the bottle. He didn't like to touch drugs on account of what had happened to his mother. Booze, sure, but never drugs. Part of the reason he avoided the carnie trailers was because he knew most of them were jacked up on one concoction or another--or at least they used to be, the carnivals had started testing more in recent years--and he'd seen enough chemical ruination to last him a lifetime. Since the ability to sleep had come back to him naturally, he had only used three sleeping pills but if they were strong enough to knock out a big man like him, then half of one would surely be enough to knock out Dolli.

Over the next few days, Hank stayed holed up in the room; just himself, Dolli and the last thirty bucks he had to his name. He spent the days gaining Dolli's trust through food and gentle pets--much like he'd once wooed Holli with sweet words and fast food hamburgers--and only snuck out to get grub at Taco Bell when he was sure that Dolli was asleep...whilst securely locked up in the bathroom.

By the third day, despite the beating he'd administered upon their initial meeting, Hank and the odd little creature he called Dolli had developed quite a rapport. It loved tacos and seemed to have as much of an affinity for the tortilla bread and cheese as it did for beef and chicken.

Hank did not fare so well on the greasy diet; as the days went on his stomach grew increasingly wretched and twisted. Oddly, when he showed signs of pain, the creature seemed to be compassionate, even tender. One evening, it approached Hank, reached up its dully-clawed hand, and rubbed his belly. It was moving, something his mother might've done when he was little and LSD was yet to be introduced into her life, and it nearly made him tear up.

After a mere few days, he was sure that he had tamed the thing enough to trust it...to a certain degree, anyway.

* * *

Hank had a sizable cardboard box that he took around with him from town to town, mostly to carry his tools and bulky coat and anything else that wouldn't quite fit in his aging suitcase. He emptied those contents into plastic bags and laid a blanket in the box, encouraging Dolli to get used to lying down in it which didn't take much effort, the creature seemed to like curling up in the box and sleeping soundly in the confined space. Holli had owned a cat that had done the same.

On the day of the carnival's moving, Hank fed Dolli a big breakfast of tacos and fries laced with a ground-up sleeping pill. As expected, it took effect nearly instantly and dropped Dolli into a deep slumber. Hank dragged the box into the bathroom, secured the door, and headed off to the site where he disassembled rides and packed up stuffed toys and made enough money to cover the motel debt in full. Yet the whole time he worked, he thought of nothing but Dolli.

What if she overdosed?
I hope she's not having a reaction.
She could get gas pains!
I wish she was with me.

Over the course of their time together, he'd gradually come to think of Dolli as a "she" and not an "it."

He got Blake to give him a ride back to the motel and he used his crappy stomach as an excuse to burst into the bathroom, desperate to see Dolli. He fully expected to find her lying there dead...but instead she was still sleeping peacefully and breathing deeply with seemingly no complications at all. Hank was elated. He was keenly aware that he was starting to develop strong protective feelings for Dolli, nearly paternal. He closed the box lid and packed it carefully into Blake's truck along with his other meager odds and ends.

They high-tailed it out of Modesto, California, by midday. Blake drove down the freeway blasting country music, chain-smoking, and cursing out Tammy Lynn Brown, a ticket taker, for not giving him the time of day even though she was damn near thirty years younger than him.

Normally Hank sat gunshot, drank a beer, and nodded his head to the music while occasionally grunting in agreement of whatever Blake was ranting about. He'd never noticed how badly he drove; the disregard for the speed limit, the sharp turns, the veering in and out of lanes...in the past it hadn't even occurred to him that Blake was a dangerous driver but now, with precious cargo like Dolli on board, his perception had changed.

By the time they reached Sonora nearly an hour later, Blake was ranting at and about Hank who had commented on his lackluster driving skills one time too many.

"Next time, find another ride!" Blake spat as they pulled into the big field where the carnival would soon stand in illuminated glory.

Hank wasted no time in grabbing the box from the backseat and running to the side of the pickup, out of view of everyone, to peek inside. He'd been sure that Blake's screaming was going to awaken Dolli--hell, the whole trip he'd been expecting her to pop out of the box and scare Blake so bad that he'd crash the car and kill them all--but she was still slumbering deeply; still not stirring but breathing blessedly steadily.

I've got to get to the motel, he thought, remembering the little hole in the wall he had stayed at last year, not two blocks from the fairgrounds.

Hank gathered up his other scarce belongings and sprinted to the motel before anyone could stop him. Once Dolli was secured in the bathroom of the locked room, Hank returned to the carnival and spent hours setting up. As he was helping to hammer the walls of the House of Mirrors together, he spotted Mystic Mike arrive in his fancy trailer, dressed to the nines, and sipping on an iced tea. Guys that grand never had to do the hard labor. Hank hoped that this would be his last go-round as a lowly roadie.

* * *

It took Dolli more than sixteen hours to wake up. Hank's relief outweighed his exhaustion and he used the day's pay to buy a king's feast at the local greasy spoon. He and Dolli ate together on the bathroom floor, sharing grunts of approval. Hank called in sick the next day and slept in with Dolli curled into his side, lying her head on his pained stomach as if she sympathized with his discomfort.

The next day, he brought her to Morton.

Even while wide awake, Dolli traveled well in the cardboard box. Hank waltzed into the double-wide trailer that Morton called his office and set the box down on the desk, disrupting his bosses' afternoon coffee break.

"I want to be part of the show," Hank declared, trying hard not to guff at the look of utter surprise on Morton's face.

"Are you on the sauce?" Morton screamed. "What the hell do you imagine--"

Before he could finish, Hank opened the box and took Dolli out. She promptly snarled at Morton who recoiled so quickly that he nearly fell off his chair.

"What the hell is that?!"

"Dolli, my business partner. Although, I guess you'd call her more of an *attraction*."

Morton stared at him, wide-eyed and disbelieving.

"What the fuck is this, Bott? A puppet?"

"Does it look like a puppet to you?"

Morton stared at Dolli, a shark-line grin spreading across his face. Hank knew what Morton was thinking; he had rigged enough carnival games for him to know exactly how he schemed.

He's fixing to get rid of me in some "accident" and then keeping her for himself.

"This little beauty came to me out in the woods, I trained her and I know how to handle her. I guess you could say I'm her surrogate parent. I'd make sure to keep the rubes safe because she's not always friendly to strangers."

Morton narrowed his eyes, challenging Hank. "Really? She looks sweet to me."

He extended his hand and leaned forward. As if on cue, Dolli growled and swatted at him. Hank could've kissed her but instead he pulled her back.

"Told ya," he said, giving dejected Morton his best shit-eating grin.

At that moment, a ripple of pain shot across his abdomen; the indigestion flared up at the strangest of times. Dolli sensed it and nestled into him, laying her head against his torso and emitting purr-like sounds.

The seeming display of affection convinced Morton of their bond. A crook he was, but he was also a businessman and he saw the potential in Dolli. That day, he signed Hank on and agreed to give him and his foundling a place in the Oddities Tent.

The news traveled fast around the small world of the carnival's inner circle. At first, no one could believe it; workers didn't become performers overnight...but that's precisely what Hank had done.

Morton arranged a space for them in the freak-show section between the "mermaid baby"--which was really just a dried out fishtail sewn onto an old taxidermy monkey head--and the skull of a unicorn which, Hank knew, had been created by a particularly gifted sculptor who could carve anything out of animal bones. Morton met him when they were in Dallas a few years back, and from then on, the "unicorn skull" had been a valued part of the show. Next to those two unremarkable items, Dolli was even more enthralling.

Banners bearing their names were placed throughout the fair: *Hank and Dolli, the Darling of Darkness.* According to Morton, Dolli looked just threatening enough to pass for a baby demon.

"The spiel is that you nearly died in a bar fight and ended up in hell for five minutes before the paramedics brought you back and this thing followed you to earth," Morton had explained whilst chewing on the end of an unlit cigar. "That kind of tale will attract every horror buff in the state."

Yet it was the carnies, not horror fans, who first flocked to see her--all except Mystic Mike, Hank supposed he rarely concerned himself with the oddities. Blake was in utter disbelief that he had unknowingly transported "the freak"--as he termed dear Dolli--all the way to Sonora and tried to swindle a percentage out of Hank who promptly told him to go fuck himself.

* * *

Over the course of the carnival's run, Dolli showed well and drew bigger crowds by the day. At first, people came to simply stare at her as she sat on a pedestal and watched them. Shock, awe, revulsion...Hank watched the faces of the pimply teenagers and the fat women in sundresses and reveled in the delight of getting rich off of their dollars, their morbid fascination, their greedy curiosity.

On the day before the fair moved out of Sonora, Mystic Mike paid Hank a visit. Hank wasn't surprised, he'd been drawing bigger crowds for days.

"I suppose I owe you congratulations on your success," Mike said, approaching Hank. "You and that mechanical doll have got a good act going."

"Dolli's no doll," Hank retorted. "Take a closer look."

Mike took a step closer, locked eyes with Dolli, and then jumped back as if he'd received an electrical shock.

His head jolted slightly and his eyelids flickered before snapping open and darting their gaze between Hank's rumbling belly and Dolli. He was quivering slightly, looking as if he'd just seen a bad premonition. It was the least composed Hank had ever seen him look.

"Get rid of that thing, it's not normal," Mike commanded with a distinct tremor in his voice.

"No shit, Sherlock, this *is* the *freak show*."

"I mean it!" Mike shouted. "It's not of this world...it's something else...something bad."

"Oh, gimme a break, she's weird looking but docile as a lamb!"

"You have no idea."

"And you do? So, go ahead, tell me! Spill the beans!"

"I... I just sense something," Mike whispered. "It's strong, bad...Get rid of it. Put it back where you found it."

He was backing up as he spoke and, when he got about ten feet away, he turned and ran. Hank thought the whole thing seemed staged and scripted, like a scene from a bad horror movie. Mike might've been a smooth operator, but there was no way in hell Hank believed that he had any actual powers.

Mike never came back to see Dolli. In fact, shortly thereafter, he signed up with another carnival and headed out to the east coast where he subsequently made a fortune. His absence made Dolli the star attraction in the non-ride category of Morton's traveling carnival.
She was enjoying the attention and got easier and easier to train. She would dance if Hank put on music--she loved Elvis and Jefferson Airplane which were, incidentally, Holli's favorites too--and she eventually permitted Hank to dress her up in bonnets and tutus and cute little gowns. Sometimes her fans even sent him clothes for her to wear; Dolli was developing quite a cult-following.

Their earnings allowed them to move into a single trailer, then a double-wide, with full amenities and fancy furnishings. Best of all, they didn't have to share with anyone but each other.

* * *

Hank should've been on cloud nine, but Dolli was becoming quite a handling. She demanded constant attention and refused to leave his side, clinging to him like a shadow. She had developed a fascination with Mardi Gras beads after being presented with one by a fan, and demanded that Hank supply her with an increasing number of necklaces and other assorted shiny things.

Her appetite was insatiable and she preferred greasy fast-food meals and chocolate milkshakes at midnight. If Hank was slow to supply her with anything she wished, she growled at him so ferociously that he feared her.

As the time went on, Hank's stomach rumbled and extended. His feet swelled, his back ached, and he gained two-dozen pounds in the span of three months. At times, he felt frustrated, used, and unappreciated, because Dolli had a mile-wide selfish streak.

She'd rip up newspapers--a favorite pastime--and leave him to pick up the pieces. She'd throw her milkshakes at the wall just to see them spatter--it was akin to a sport for her--and then watch in satisfaction as he scrubbed up the mess. She was addicted to info-commercials and threw things at Hank's head when they ended in the wee hours, blaming him for the ceasing of her amusement. Similarly, she lashed out accusingly at him whenever a song ended. When it happened during showtime, Hank put up with it because the rubes loved it. In private, it wasn't nearly as tolerable.

She'd ignore him, or hide on him, but if stepped out of the trailer without her for a moment she'd launch into shrieking frenzies. Needy...Ungiving ...She was, in all honesty, quite difficult.

But she could also be sweet, especially when his stomach acted up. When the pain became unbearable and he had to lie down, Dolli would lay her head on his tummy, listening to the gurgles and growls within, and caress him so affectionately that all would be forgiven. He couldn't stay mad at her.

Late spring turned to summer which quickly slipped into autumn. Hank ecstatically welcomed the cooler weather and the onset of the Halloween season. In two months--what amounted to eight short weeks--he'd be working on Winter Wonderland displays in the mall; he was already angling to deck Dolli out in red and green and pass her off as an alien elf. Those sets were full of glittery decorations, Christmas trees, Santas, reindeers, elves, candy canes and more sweetness and light than you could choke on. He much preferred the weeks leading up to Halloween where he got to set up horror houses full of blood and gore and live actors who scared the hell out of teenagers.

For the past five years, he had been trying to land a gig as a performer just for the satisfaction of hearing the little creeps scream. He had never been successful but now, thanks to his Dolli, he had secured a whole segment to himself--hell, she was practically the main attraction! Sometimes life did turn out well.

The plot that they had concocted for the Halloween Scream Fest was that Hank was a mad scientist who had created Dolli by combining a giant mutated mole with a deformed bear. It was a goofy premise, but Morton's company had designed their whole getup on it, turning the previous years' "Murder Manor" into "The Lair Laboratory" run by the dreaded "Dr. Loveless" for whom Hank would assume the role. He had never acted before, but he had perfected his maniacal laughter.

He had desperately wanted to work the acting portion of the horror market for years and he had been excitedly anticipating the gig since Morton offered it to him in late July, but on opening night, Hank was in agony. He had gained nearly forty pounds around his mid-section since finding Dolli and his body was fiercely protesting. Had it been any other night, or any other occasion, he would have opted out, but neither Hell nor high water--or a belly ache--was going to prevent him from making his "Dr. Loveless" debut.

Dolli was naked for this show; something she seemed not to mind. She was very fussy about what she wore, and fickle about when she wore it. Hank considered her complacency to be a blessing. She also seemed keenly aware that he was uncomfortable and kept close to him, staring fixedly at his stomach.

* * *

Opening night was packed. Word about Dolli's inclusion in the attraction had gotten out and a line had started to form at three in the afternoon even though the doors didn't open until seven in the evening. Hank was sore, but managed to play his role. Most of the rubes assumed his gasps and wheezes were part of the performance and they screamed and awed over Dolli as if they'd never seen anything grander...or more horrifying.

For the first two hours, things went accordingly. He crackled laughter and Dolli growled and a seemingly endless parade of rubes came and went...and then something snapped inside of Hank's gut.

He felt it tear, filling him with red-hot agony. He fell to his knees and screamed and the gaggle of rubes he'd been ranting at laughed, convinced his wails were part of the script that coincided with the continuous audio soundtrack blaring screams and chainsaws.

But Hank was not acting, he was suffering--dying. Something--*somethings*--were clawing at his insides; ripping through organs and tissues; sending searing white-hot pain throughout his midsection.

"Get help," he pleaded to one of the bystanders, a pudgy girl in a pink top that looked two sizes too small. Yet he couldn't articulate the words, his mouth had filled with blood and as soon as he parted his lips it spilled out onto the floor.

"Ew, that's gross!" the girl declared, not comprehending.

Hank laid flat on the floor, grabbed his belly, and screamed as he was pierced by dozens of tiny razorblades from within. Suddenly, Dolli was standing over him, chattering wildly. She was more alive and excited than he had ever seen her. She patted his stomach. At first, Hank thought she was trying to comfort him, but then he realized that she wasn't patting, she was digging. If he hadn't kept her nails clipped, she'd be tearing into him with a fury.

Suddenly, a realization dawned on Hank: Dolli had impregnated him. The night he dreamt of swallowing the grapes he'd actually been swallowing her eggs, harboring them, carrying them. He had been her surrogate and now her young were hatching.

They were born with their claws intact and sharp. As the first one burst from Hank's stomach he clearly saw the little talons shining in the strobe-lights. The crowd was screaming and laughing and cheering, incredulously still believing that this was all part of the show.

At least I won't die alone, he thought randomly noticing that more and more people were packing into the space.

Hank birthed one monster after another with Dolli dancing around him, gurgling in victory as he lay bleeding and dying. The last thing Hank Bott ever saw were the hatchlings--followed closely by Dolli--running into the crowd. Screams filled the air as they slashed skin and drank up the spilling blood with their strange sucker-mouths. Then the screams started in earnest; panic, chaos, stampede.

Hank closed his eyes and welcomed the darkness. His purpose had been served.

Hexed
Based on the True Story of Rhoda Derry

    I told Rosemary not to get too big for her britches. I warned her about getting ideas above her station. But my begging and pleading amounted to a whole lot of nothing. She was my best friend, the closest thing I ever had to a sister, but she was headstrong. I've since found that willfulness is a trait that's especially strong in beautiful women, and Rosemary was nothing if not beautiful. She thought she was going to marry a prince and change the world while living in a gilded palace. She was pretty enough to court such fancy notions too. Rosemary had long dark hair, pale skin, bright blue eyes, and red lips. I was a pudgy plain lost cause beside her, decidedly destined for spinsterhood and secretly envious of my best friend's good fortune.

    The funny thing is, even though I was jealous of Rosemary's beauty, I wasn't jealous of her life...especially her family.

    Rosemary's grandmama was Old Mimi who everybody far and wide knew was a witch. Oddly enough, the Duggan's were unlucky. For folks who had a witch in the family, they didn't know many protection spells...or maybe it was just that mean Old Mimi hexed her own kin. She was certainly capable of it, that was never in dispute. Rosemary's paw, Joseph, was Old Mimi's son but he didn't seem to care too much for his mama. When he married Rosemary's ma, Rebecca, he moved far away from Old Mimi. Rebecca—or Misses Duggan, as I'd called her—hated and feared her mother-in-law. She filled Rosemary's head with stories of hexes and spells and boiling brews in caldrons. But it went further than that, sometimes Rebecca Duggan seemed to be possessed. On a few occasions right in front of me, she'd taken a crazy turn and insisted that she'd seen a witch on a broom circling the sky or little demons climbing up the walls. I'd witnessed her throw pots and pans at things no one else could see, screaming up a storm the whole time. It scared the heck out of me, but Rosemary took in all in stride. She was used to it. In fact, she told me that sometimes when the mood struck her, Mama Duggan would get ahold of Mr. Duggan's rifle and start shooting at the invisible things she thought she'd seen.

I wouldn't want to be part of a family like that, good looks or not.

The other thing that kept me from being spiteful towards Rosemary was how interesting she was, and wickedly funny. She was also nice which, in my experience, is something of a rarity for beautiful girls. She never judged me on my looks and seemed pleased to have my company. Our friendship started based on location--I lived one farm over from her--and age; she was the youngest of her family and I was an only child on account of my daddy having died when I was a baby. We were the only two girls near the same age around that particular Illinois farmland. But what had started due to circumstances blossomed into a true bond.

We spent hours together and she'd make me laugh with her silly voices and unflattering portrayals of our peers, neighbors, even parents. She could also tell a mean scary story, mostly about witches and spells because that's what she was most afraid of. See, Rosemary really believed in all that stuff. She was scared to death of the grandmama she had never met but had certainly heard plenty about. Rosemary truly believed in her mother's visions of ghosts and goblins. Back then I thought it was just part of her personality, not a warning sign of something bigger and deeper and darker. I reckoned we'd always be friends...until 1850 when we were sixteen and everything went wrong.

Looking back, it's easy to say that it was all because of Caleb Parker, but that's not entirely true, or fair. Caleb was smitten with Rosemary and I never saw him treat her with anything but kindness. I never forgot the way he looked at her because no boy had ever looked at me like that and it made my teenage mind plenty jealous...I feel bad about it now, considering how things turned out. But Caleb was a nice boy, courteous; it was his mother, Naomi, who kicked up all the trouble.

Rumor had it that Naomi was just as much of a witch as Old Mimi. In fact, legend said that Naomi Parker's grandmama and mama were both witches too and that they'd had their fair share of scrapes with Old Mimi. Maybe that's why Naomi hated Rosemary so much, or maybe it was because she didn't want her son to be taken away from her, or maybe it was because the Duggan clan were poorer than the Parkers...not by much, but by some.

Rosemary ran up to me all excited one day a few months before her eighteenth birthday.

"Caleb proposed to me!" she'd squealed, all beaming smiles and giggles. I celebrated with her. Sure, I should've been jealous—I didn't have a bo—but I couldn't help but feel happy for them. I thought Caleb and Rosemary made a good couple. But Naomi didn't agree.

For whatever reasons she had, Mrs. Naomi Parker had no intention of accepting Rosemary Duggan as her daughter-in-law. And so, as soon as she heard of the engagement, she stormed over to Rosemary's house and said the words that would ruin my friend's life.

I was there, celebrating the good news with my friend and drawing up plans for the wedding dress she'd wear. A few of her sisters were with us, 'cause they were going to tailor the dress. One minute everything was nice and cheerful, and a moment later Naomi was banging on the front door, screaming and shouting and making an awful fuss.

I don't know why she did it, but Rosemary opened the door. I guess she wanted to make peace with the woman who she imagined would soon be her mother-in-law. Naomi didn't even give the younger woman a chance to open her mouth. Instead she barged into the house, eyes wild, pointer-finger extended at Rosemary. Her voice was shrill yet hoarse and spittle was flying from her lips, as if she was foaming at the mouth. She had a wild, disheveled look about her which belied her somewhat privileged social standing.

"*You, wretch, will never marry my son,*" she shrieked. "*I forbid it! I'll see him dead first! I curse ye! You'll have no man, no wanes! Instead of lying with my*

Caleb, you'll lie with rats and bugs! I'll see your pretty eyes plucked from your head; your tongue severed from your seductive mouth! Before I'm done with you, you'll speak no more and your lovely figure will be shriveled and hideous! I curse thee, hex thee, call thy faithful Old Scratch upon thee to torment thee until the day of miserable death! You'll woe the day you crossed my path until they lay you in your cold lonely grave, decades from now. You'll suffer, oh how you'll suffer, you harlot!"

Rosemary's paw heard the ruckus and came in from the field. He saw the woman standing in his house ranting madly, grabbed his rifle, and threatened to shoot her dead if she didn't get off his property right quick. Naomi was so worked up that even the sight of the gun didn't faze her none. Instead she gave a rueful little smile, sneered, and spit at Rosemary's feet before turning and making a hasty retreat back towards her home.

The whole encounter had lasted less than five minutes but it had frightened Rosemary badly. She was shaking hard for hours after Naomi left. Witches were a life-long fear of hers and being hexed in her own home was enough to push her over the edge...we just didn't realize how far over the edge she was going to go.

Her mama and sisters said she started having bad dreams that night. Every time I saw her from then on, she had a distracted and faraway look in her eyes. She wasn't joyful or spunky anymore; she was a shell of herself. Making matters worse, Caleb disappeared. He made no effort to see or talk to the girl he supposedly wanted to marry. Apparently, Naomi Parker held a lot of sway over her son.

One day nearing three months after Naomi's malicious speech, Rosemary took a bad turn. We were walking home from the town market. Rosemary had been acting strange all day, twitchy and nervous. She kept looking over her shoulder and mumbling to herself. As we walked past the woods she suddenly stopped, looked directly into the trees, and started screaming. She turned and ran, leaving me trailing behind her.

"Old Scratch!" she wailed. "He's after me! Get him off me!"

As she ran, she batted at her temples, screaming hysterically...and, for just a moment, I could've sworn I saw something dark—shadowy—twirling around her head and shoulders...

But there was nothing there, of course. I chased her all the way back to her house where she burst through the door, jumped onto her bed, and started spinning on her head in the most unnatural position, raving about Old Scratch the whole time. Her family was alarmed and demanded to know what had upset her, but I honestly didn't know. She hadn't been acting right since the day of Naomi's visit.

From there, things got worse. Rosemary saw ghouls and goblins, demons and monsters, everyplace she went. She hollered and wept and carried on until there was no trace of the sweet funny girl I'd known. I tried to make regular visits to keep her company, and I baked her a pie every October for her birthday, but I eventually stopped coming around to see her. She had taken to lashing out at everyone, believing that anyone in her vicinity was a devil in disguise. The way she ranted was bone-chilling, relaying the things evil Old Scratch said to her. Ever since, I've been half convinced that crazy is contagious because, sometimes, when I was standing a little too close to her, I thought I heard something whispering, real low, from behind her...as if one of her mama's feared goblins was nesting in her hair.

I started to keep my distance, but it was still tough to see Rosemary in such pain and her whole family in turmoil on account of it. Her mama took to shooting at stuff on the regular until most of the neighbors considered her to be just as much a pariah as her youngest daughter. I once heard Rosemary's paw threaten to go have words with Naomi, but I doubt he ever did. The last thing the Duggan's needed was a second curse to cut down their patriarch.

For several years, Rosemary's family did their best to care for her, but her condition only worsened. She got more unruly, more deluded, and more violent. As her siblings married and moved away—not wanting their own spouses and children exposed to her behavior—her aging parents had her committed to the Lima Mental Hospital. She stayed there a mere few weeks before the staff declared her incurable and sent her home, claiming that she was too disruptive to the other patients to stay.

In 1860, her mama died and her paw had no strength or money left to look after his deranged daughter. He admitted her to the Jacksonville Township Almshouse. By then, Rosemary had grown thin and gaunt. She'd scratched at her face and pulled out her hair; her beauty became untraceable. At the almshouse, she acted out even more vehemently; insisting that Old Scratch was always with her, keeping her in a perpetual state of withering torment.

The staff at the almshouse responded to her tirades by locking her, naked, in a small wooden box lined with straw. There, she could not grab nor kick nor bite at other patients or staff, but she also couldn't walk or move many of her muscles. Over time, her unused legs drew upwards, her spine became curved, and her misshapen body could do naught but drag itself slowly across the floor during the rare instances of release. While at the almshouse, Rosemary scratched out her eyes and blinded herself. She bit out her tongue and could produce only animalistic gurgles...of course, we knew nothing of this until much later.

I'd attempted to visit her at the almshouse in 1870, but was barred admission. They did not accept visitors and given the shrieks and wails I heard emanating from the bleak building's windows and long corridors, I felt somewhat relieved not to have to enter such a domain. I now feel guilty that I hadn't done more for my friend, despite being unsure of how much difference I possibly could have made. I got a job as a seamstress and, against all odds given my plain looks, I found a good man who loved me true. We married when I was in my mid-thirties. Old for a bride, maybe, but we had four children who all grew up strong and well and we were happy until the day he died, peacefully in his sleep, two years ago at a ripe old age.

As I was living a normal domestic life—as were the other surviving Duggan siblings and even Caleb, who'd gone on to marry a fancy farmer's pretty blonde daughter—Rosemary languished in the almshouse. She lay helplessly in darkness, with nothing but the breeding rats and roaches who shared her haybed for company. Her broken body was sore with bruises from head to toe, she wallowed in her own waste for weeks on end, and punched the teeth from her mouth. All the while, her diseased mind was ceaselessly antagonized by "Old Scratch." She existed that way for more than forty years, and probably would have died that way with no one knowing naught about it, if it wasn't for Dr. Ziegler.

It was the early 1900s and Rosemary was in her late sixties—a considerable age—before young Dr. Ziegler discovered her at the almshouse. Horrified by her circumstances, he rescued her from the vile place and put her under his personal care at the better staffed, better funded, and better managed Barton Asylum. There he enabled her to live clean and free; lying in a bed like any other human being and garbed in soft cotton fabrics. She could never walk or talk properly again, but she smiled whenever Dr. Ziegler spoke to her. She liked him, so she could still feel some joy. Dr. Ziegler fought for the rights of the mentally distressed and used Rosemary's terrible ordeal as an example of the horrors within the almshouses. He invited state legislators to view her case and to secure greater services for the mentally disabled. He also took a photo of what was left of her and published an article about her in several newspapers so the greater public could be made aware of her awful fate. That's how I found her again, all those years later.

I wept when I saw her photo. I couldn't believe what had become of my dear old friend. I convinced my husband to travel with me to visit with Dr. Ziegler and see Rosemary for the first time in decades. He agreed, God bless his soul, and so I got to find out the entire horrible truth about her depressing, confined, life.

The visit to the Barton Asylum was bittersweet. I saw Rosemary again but she was no one I recognized. To alert her of my presence, I softly spoke her name but she didn't remember the sound of my voice. She recoiled in fear when I gingerly touched her face, lashing out as she'd done when the madness took hold—albeit less violently. Age had mellowed her. She calmed only when she heard the soothing coos of Dr. Ziegler who reassured her that I was safe, and I gave her a firm hug before I left. As I embraced her, I felt something slither up her back, towards what was left of her hair...and it was hissing. Before departing, I lowered myself to her level and put both my hands on her face and--to my amazement--she lifted her own gnarled knuckles to my cheeks. Just for a moment, as we knelt in our strange embrace, I saw a flash of the old Rosemary—my Rosemary—in her face and I knew that *she understood that I understood.*

That was in the spring of 1906. I never saw Rosemary again, she died of natural causes a few months later. She outlived her family; all her siblings had died young. Perhaps Old Scratch had gotten to them too. Dr. Ziegler saw to it that she had a fine resting place and a dignified headstone. My husband and I traveled to it once and laid flowers in her memory...I didn't mention that, from behind the gravestone, I was sure I heard an eerily familiar malevolent hissing. I thank God Rosemary met the good Dr. Ziegler and had some peace at the end of her tormented life. Did it make up for her decades of suffering? I think not. Yet her brutal treatment enabled Dr. Ziegler to help close that dreaded almshouse and advocate for better care of the insane and infirm. And so, Rosemary did get her wish. She made a difference, became known, is remembered...just not in the way she ever could have imagined, or ever would have wanted.

It's now 1926 and I'm an old, old woman who'll be meeting my maker soon. Maybe I'll see Rosemary on the other side, well and witty as we were when we young. Yet one thing chills me to the core whenever I think of it, even all these years later...everything Naomi said the night she hexed Rosemary came true in ten-folds. The experts say madness is an illness of the brain...but I'd be more wary of bewitchments.

I'm sure Rosemary would agree.

Decoy

"God damn it!"

Earl's voice was overpowered by the resounding *boom* that echoed through the trees. In the span of one hour he had wasted four bullets shooting at squirrels that were too fast for him. Earl hated to waste bullets since they cost money—something he held in exceptionally high regard.

"I thought I had that one," he snarled. "I've got to get something before this day's over."

Rob looked around anxiously. Technically, they were still on camp grounds; the section of the park where visitors were permitted to set up RVs, picnic, and barbeque. Hunting was strictly prohibited in this area but Earl didn't seem to care. The legal hunting grounds were over three miles away—much deeper into the woods—and Earl wasn't fond of walking. Besides, it had rained earlier that morning and he was not keen on getting his brand-new Eddie Bauer boots soaking wet.

Rob wasn't exactly comfortable hunting so close to the campsites but it was late November, not mid-summer, and the number of campers had dwindled considerably. Still, all it would take would be one stray bullet and one very unlucky bystander to land both him and Earl in serious trouble...the kind of trouble that could earn them both prison sentences.

"Come on, let's go check the salt lick," Earl muttered and resumed his clumsy stride, stomping through the thick underbrush as if he was Godzilla strolling through a city.

"Man, I don't know—" Rob started to protest but Earl cut him off abruptly.

"If we get something, I'll give you most of it," he sneered, turning his head to glance back at his friend. "Lord knows you need it more than I do."

Earl had done well for himself. He had come up in the world as the owner of a successful loan business and he raked in over $200,000 a year...a fact he never let Rob —or anyone else—forget. Earl took every chance he got to flaunt his wealth or comment on Rob's less privileged circumstances. Occasionally it grated on Rob, but not nearly as much as most people would expect. He and Earl had come from similarly middle-class backgrounds and they had known each other since they were kids. In fact, they had met at a summer camp located not too far away from the woods that they now hunted in. As they grew up, Earl had sought wealth and power and college degrees. Rob was content merely to graduate high school and embraced a simple blue-collar existence as an exterminator. The profession might never make him rich but it damn well paid the bills. Still, securing a hunk of deer meat would be like getting a weeks' worth of free dinner and Rob wasn't fool enough to refuse that.

He followed behind Earl, listening to him cursing nature and wildlife. His mood only got worse when they snuck up to the salt lick—devices Earl frequently used as decoys to entice deer into the crosshairs of his gun—and saw not as much as a fawn.

"God damn it!" Earl repeated, this time slamming his fist into the soggy earth. Earl was not a man regaled for his even temperament. "What the hell is going on out here today?" he ranted. "That's my best salt lick and those stupid things are supposed to love salt!"

Rob shrugged. "Maybe they're on to us."

Earl shot him a disgusted look. "Aw, shut up. They're dumb animals. They don't know nothing about anything."

Rob shrugged again but said nothing. He wasn't fond of animals but he had studied behaviors in pests like rats and mice and, although he annihilated them without pause, he had to admit that they probably were a lot cleverer than most people believed.

Earl guzzled water from his canteen and then rested his beady eyes on Rob. "You better not be turning crazy like that Packer woman."

Rob snorted laughter.

"It's not funny!" Earl retorted, sounding truly annoyed. "The only reason that woman's still alive is because murder is illegal. I swear if you start going down her road, I'll shoot you dead! It'll be a mercy killing."

"Fair enough," Rob replied. "Remember, the Packer woman hates me even more than she hates you. I'm an exterminator; she's picketed outside my house for Christ's sake."

Meryl Packer was an ardent animal rights activist who made it her mission to pester anyone who so much as ate hamburgers. Over the years Rob, the town's sole exterminator, had become her main target but it was Earl who was her true nemesis. Even though Meryl frequently annoyed Rob, he was usually able to shrug her behavior off or, if it got really bad, threaten to call the police. Earl, however, never backed down from a fight. Two years ago, Meryl had made the mistake of scolding Earl for killing God's creatures when she found him fishing in the local lake.

Ever since then, Earl had taken every opportunity to insult her and rail against her. He had even admitted to Rob that every time he killed something, he imagined that it was Meryl. Rob knew the feeling. He often fantasied that the rats he poisoned were actually his ex-wife, Darlene, and her whole crazy family.

Rob rubbed the back of his neck which was stiff after a whole day trekking through the woods. Heck, his back and legs and arms were stiff too. By now, the sun was starting to set and he was aching to get home.

"We better pick that salt lick up and head on back," Rob said.

"No!" Earl hissed. "It's not even half dark yet! Deer come out in the evening and I'm waiting right here until I get one!"

Rob surrendered and settled into the underbrush, trying to make himself as comfortable as possible. Looking at Earl, no one would ever suspect how stubborn he could be or how much of a bloodlust he had. Earl *enjoyed* killing. He didn't do it as much for sport or food as he did just for the sheer power of deciding if something would live or die. Rob reckoned that Earl had some kind of fixation with power. That was probably why he had strived so hard to become a business owner: to have control over his workers. Yet power obviously didn't make Earl happy; he was, in actuality, the angriest man Rob had ever met. Of course, he would probably be perpetually angry too if he was cooped up in a sterile office all day long.

Most of the people on my job are rich kids from silver spoon type families, Earl had confided on one hunting trip. *They all view me as being inherently beneath them even though I'm their boss. They never even offer to buy me coffee! How's that for a lack of respect?*

Rob strongly assumed that most of the people at Earl's job were afraid of him. In fact, most folks were. Rob was the sole exception and the only person Earl ever willingly hung around with. That was an irony in and of itself since, back in their younger years, Rob had been the troublemaker. He had started drinking in his late teens and had ended up in barroom brawls and in and out of jail throughout his 20s. Earl had never visited him in jail nor paid his bail but, whenever Rob got out, Earl hadn't shunned him. Earl viewed Rob as beneath him and that was precisely why he liked him—he enjoyed having the upper hand, the clean record. Earl was a bully but a silent and insidious one; mean as poison.

Earl liked causing mayhem and, to a lesser degree, so did Rob. In essence, they were friends for weird reasons: they both hated most of the townspeople, they both liked hunting, and they both had no other friends or family who would speak to them. In short, they fed off each other's dysfunction. Rob knew that Earl liked using his gruff appearance to scare his white-collar employees which, Rob supposed, was kind of complimentary given his pride in his rough-shaven appearance. For his part, Rob knew that Earl was the go-to person to think up nasty —and impossible-to-prove-in-court—ways to torment Darlene. Earl loved tormenting Darlene just as much as Rob did, mostly because, deep-down, Earl was mad at women in general. Ladies would go out with Earl but only to use him to get free dinners, something akin to taking his money.

Over time, he had become disdainful of women and a self-professed lifelong bachelor. Rob honestly wouldn't be all that surprised if his friend eventually turned into a serial killer. Now nearing 40, Rob was doing fairly well. He had been off the booze and out of fights for the better part of a decade—which was especially lucky for Meryl Packer who he probably would have shot down dead in his younger, hazier, days.

As Rob lay in the woody underbrush an hour ticked by...then another...no deer came but the sky got darker and darker.

"Come on, let's go," Rob pleaded. "We have to get rid of that salt lick. I don't want another fine!"

"No!" Earl retorted.

Rob felt his temper rising. He and Earl had been fined on their last hunting misadventure after a park ranger discovered them using duck decoys and calls to entice mallards in a strictly 'no-hunting' zone. The judge had fined the two men equally but Earl had insisted that Rob pay both bills despite having much less money. *They're your decoys, not mine!* Earl had shouted accusingly. The worst part of it all was that they hadn't as much as grazed a single fowl.

"If we get fined, you're paying both this time," Rob declared.

Earl waved his hand dismissively. "Shut up! You'll scare the deer!"

But there were no deer. Ten minutes passed... fifteen...twenty...nothing.

"God damn it!" Earl shrieked for the third time that day as he jumped up and kicked a tree stump. "Of all the rotten luck! What a goddamn waste of a day!"

Rob watched Earl's tantrum and wondered exactly how he hadn't yet garnered any kind of record for assault. As he got older his temper was worsening. Knowing enough not to say anything contradictory, Rob stood and picked up the untouched salt lick.

"Come on, let's get going," he said as gently as possible.

Earl was armed and very frustrated. When he got frustrated, he got angry and when he got angry, he was unpredictable. Rob most definitely did not want to come across as combatant or belligerent in any way. He hoped the situation would defuse itself and, thankfully, it did. Earl gave the tree trunk another hearty kick and then shuffled, defeated, toward Rob with his eyes downcast.

"Waste of a day," he mumbled again.

* * *

At first, they were sure of where they were going. They had parked Earl's fancy maroon Lexus SUV in the campsite parking lot which should have been only about four miles away from where they had placed the saltlick... but after forty-five minutes of walking deeper and deeper into the forest they had to admit that they had made a wrong turn somewhere.

"This doesn't make any sense," Rob declared as he stared at the old compass his father—a seasoned hunter—had given him. "We're going north; we're supposed to go north, so why aren't we finding the car?"

Earl was taking his frustrations out on his cell phone.

"Piece of crap," he snarled. "I paid good money for this and now when I need it the GPS craps out!"

"The trees are thick here so they probably block out the signal," Rob replied.

"Trees shouldn't bother something worth $700 bucks," Earl retorted. "When we get back to the lot my car better be there! A lot of the godforsaken hillbillies around here would just love to drive off in it!"

Rob didn't comment. Earl constantly worried about his expensive car getting stolen; it was almost like an obsession or a paranoid fixation. His extravagant SUV was his pride and joy in a part of America where most people drove around in ten-year-old pickup trucks. Earl especially liked showing it off in the poorer sides of town but whenever people looked at it with envy, he whipped himself into a frenzy imagining thieves everywhere.

"We must be going the wrong way," Earl stated. "If my top-of-the-line phone can't get a reading then your old compass is about as useless as tits on a bull. Come on, let's try this way."

Earl brusquely turned to the right and headed down a narrow path. Rob reluctantly followed, unsure of what else to do. They got about a quarter of a mile down the route when the ground suddenly gave way. As branches cracked and mud slid all around them, the hunters lost their footing and plummeted, screaming, down a rocky embankment. They hit the bottom hard, both of them scratched and bruised and bleeding.

"You okay?" Rob asked as soon as he got his bearings.

Earl nodded. "I think so."

"Nothing's broke," Rob declared as he stretched and studied his arms and legs. Relief washed over him when he felt no sharp pains—but then he heard the "crunch" of something in his pocket. His father's compass was crushed.

Earl took one look at the crushed compass and immediately pulled out his iPhone.

"God damn it," he screamed in horror when he saw its cracked screen.

"Relax, you've got the insurance," Rob snapped. Earl had told him all about the fancy policy when he had boasted about getting the new phone.

"Screw the phone! This isn't about the phone," Earl shouted. His tone was one of fury mixed with panic. "We're gonna die out here! Hell, it's amazing we survived that fall! What are w—"

Suddenly, Rob heard something in the distance.
"Shh! Shut up!"
Earl's brow furrowed. "Don't you dare tell me—"
"Shh! Don't you hear that?"
"What?"
"Voices."

Earl shut his mouth and listened. Further down the road it certainly sounded like a whole bunch of people were talking although their words were indecipherable. Rob couldn't even tell if the language was English but it at least sounded human which was better than hearing wolves or bears.

"It's coming from that direction," Earl said, cocking his finger southward.

Rob nodded suspiciously. "Sure is, but it doesn't make sense. The campground is the other way. That path leads deeper into the woods."

"Aw, we don't know that! We got so mixed up walking around these parts that we don't know which way is right or left," Earl reasoned. "I don't know about you, but I trust my ears."

With that said, Earl started off down the pathway. Rob followed. He had heard the voices too and even if the other folks turned out to be lost as well at least they could share supplies.

* * *

The hunters walked longer than they expected to as evening turned into twilight, hindering visibility. The trees seemed to get thicker on both sides of the increasingly narrow path. Strangely, the further they walked, and the seemingly closer they got, the more the voices died down.

"Something's not right with this," Rob said uneasily.

"What do you suggest we do?" snapped Earl. "Turn back? Lie out in the mud overnight?"

"I just don't like—"

Rob's words trailed off as the pathway suddenly ended and revealed a circular grove in the trees. It was a camp.

The campsite wasn't large but it was laid out well. There was a tent on the right and an aging blue pickup truck sat on the left, its rusty sides glimmered in the light of a campfire which blazed amber embers in the center of the grounds. Curiously, a misspelled sign hung from one of the trees leading into the area. It read: *Welkome to Kamp*.

Earl chortled when he saw the message which was sloppily written in red paint.

"Someone's not the brightest crayon in the box."

"Or it was written by a kid," Rob suggested before adding: "Kids are stupid."

"Agreed."

"Where is everyone?" Rob asked. "It's gotten awfully quiet."

"HELLO?" Earl called out loudly.

No response.

"Is anybody here?"

Silence.

"We're lost! We could use some help!"

Nothing.

"They must be out hunting," Earl declared.

"At this time of night?" Rob protested. "You can't see anything! It's practically fully dark now! If it wasn't for that fire, I would hardly be able to see my hand in front of my face."

"Maybe they have those infra-red glasses," Earl suggested.

"If they have that kind of money why is their truck in such rough shape?" challenged Rob.

"Don't know, don't care," Earl replied. "It's getting cold. I'm gonna see if they have some blankets in the tent. You check the truck and see if there's a phone or a walkie-talkie or something in it to call the park rangers."

Rob gulped. His stomach was tied in knots of dread. It was an instinctual fear that he couldn't quite pinpoint the basis of but there was a basic *wrongness* about the current situation.

"I don't like this."

"Neither do I. One day we'll look back on this and spit. Come on, let's at least get some supplies. I could use some grub."

Earl and Rob stepped into the campsite. The hairs on the back of Rob's neck immediately stood up; he was sure that he saw movement between the trees out of the corners of his eyes. He quickly turned his head but saw nothing but stillness and shadows.

I'm going crazy, he thought as he approached the old truck. First, he checked the back bed. Nothing was there but fallen leaves. Then he went around to the driver's side door and peeked in the window. His nervousness rapidly intensified when he saw the dusty conditions of the interior.

No one's been in this thing for years, he thought. On impulse, he grasped the door handle and pulled. To his great surprise, the door yanked open.

At that very moment Earl screamed ear-piercingly. Rob whizzed around just on time to see the tent being pulled upwards, his friend imprisoned in its center. Rob instantly realized that the tent was actually a net in disguise, suspended by ropes set high in the trees.

"It's a trap!" Rob screamed, terrified.

He wanted to run but his legs felt like jelly. Then he lost his balance and fell backwards into the truck. As soon as the weight of his body hit the front seat the door slammed shut and locked, caging him.

"Hey! Hey, let me out!" Rob screamed as he banged against the window with all his might. His efforts were fruitless, it didn't budge. Obviously, the door and glass were much stronger than they looked. Rob was suddenly keenly and uncomfortably aware that he probably looked just like the raccoons and possums that he frequently trapped, clawing at the walls and hollering without a hope in hell of escape. Despite the griminess of the window, he could see Earl struggling in the tent-net, screaming loud enough to wake the dead. They had been lured here, enticed by food and shelter, the way mouse traps enticed mice with cheese.

This is a decoy; the whole thing was set up to capture us.

But, why? Moreover, who?

Rob's horrified mind immediately conjured up images of serial killers and homicidally territorial backwoods hillbillies. Then he noticed figures emerging from the forest. There was a whole tribe of them—about a dozen in total—tall and hairy creatures that walked like men but resembled apes, females and children among them. Most carried spears or guns, objects probably taken from past human victims. All of the creatures were looking excitedly from the car to the tent, visibly pleased to have caught two prime pieces of prey. They chatted to each other in an odd dialect, their speech patterns and voices sounded vaguely human but their tones and actual words were much more guttural—much more *prehistoric—*sounds. Rob had never seen anything like them before but he knew exactly what they were: Sasquatches. Big Foots.

Earl had always claimed that animals were stupid and, for the most part, Rob agreed with him...but there was an undeniable intelligence about the sasquatches which emerged from the woods as well as an awful *humanness.* These creatures clearly weren't human but they looked vaguely human, they sounded vaguely human, and they could obviously plan out traps and use tools—including weapons—the same way that humans did. Perhaps they couldn't understand human language or read human words but they could mimic just enough—like writing "welcome" and "camp" only mistaking the sound of the letter "c" for "k"—to trick people...the same way that hunters could trick deer and ducks. Rob had once heard that human beings and chimpanzees shared about 98% of the same genetics. Perhaps these sasquatches were even closer genetic matches. Perhaps they were even smarter than chimps, more aggressive, more secretive, and—unlike the mostly vegetarian apes—carnivorous. Just like humans.

You're dreaming! This can't be happening! Calm down, Rob scolded himself as he watched the sasquatch tribe gather under the tent-net in which Earl was suspended. *If these things really existed there would be more pictures! Evidence! Proof! They're nothing but legends.*

But sometimes legends were enough. A few of these creatures had been caught on camera over the years. The fact that people had refused to believe in them was unfortunate since the proof had been there for years. Heck, "Big Foot" had become a pop-culture icon!

Whatever they are, they're thriving, Rob thought as he observed the group. They all looked healthy and at least one of the females was noticeably pregnant.

Several of the small ones (*the children*) were hopping around excitedly as they pointed up at the tent. Its fabric was wiggling wildly in the air, illustrating Earl's desperate struggles. Suddenly, one of the creatures—a big youngish looking male (*the alpha*)—sliced through the rope that held the tent in place. It promptly crashed to the ground with a resounding BANG! Rob winced as he heard Earl's wail of pain emanate from somewhere inside the cloth. He must have fallen at least sixteen feet.

The sasquatches lunged at the tent straightaway and tore at the material, eager to reveal Earl. Confined inside the truck, Rob clearly saw the entire horrible scene illuminated in the light of the fire. Earl had broken his leg in the fall. He was bleeding and whimpering and, when he saw the creatures, he bawled and tried to run. His face was a mask of misery and fear and his pained gait was pitiful to watch. Yet the sasquatches showed no mercy. Most of them pointed and laughed at Earl's pathetic getaway attempt. The sight made Rob swell with fear. Whatever these things were, they were cruel. They could have helped Earl, his leg was surely salvageable, but they obviously had no intention of doing any such thing.

To Rob's revulsion, the big male that had cut down the tent handed two of the little one's spears and pointed toward Earl, encouraging them. The young ones rushed at him, howling and hissing and snarling. Earl shrieked again—his eyes huge and agonizingly petrified—as the small sasquatches descended upon his downed body and stabbed him repeatedly. Blood spewed. Earl flailed his arms and kicked his legs, still struggling for survival even in his final throes of death.

What the hell kind of thinking species would let kids see something like that, let alone do it? Rob thought. Then he remembered that his father had taken him out hunting before he was old enough to walk to the store alone. He had made his first kill—a squirrel—when he was seven and his father had taught him how to skin the body and cook the meat right then and there. It had been a brutal and bloody experience but it had also been exciting and thrilling. How many times had he and Earl laughed at the fear in some deer's eyes, or the seemingly funny unbalance of an injured gait, just before they administered the final blow? How many times had they bonded or had a laugh or enjoyed themselves amid another creature's pain and fear and suffering? The answer was simple: a lot. They had behaved just like these creatures plenty of times.

Two of the adult female sasquatches started undressing Earl's body. They carefully folded the clothing —saving the fabric to use as tents or blankets, no doubt— and then started to carve up his flesh. Rob watched, sickened, as they jammed bits of Earl's thigh onto sticks and roasted them over the fire. Apparently, sasquatches liked the taste of cooked meat—barbequed, roasted, grilled —just like their human prey.

While the females prepared Earl's remains, the two young sasquatches and a handful of adult males started making their way to the truck where Rob was being held prisoner. Sobbing in fear, Rob hopelessly tried to hold the door shut to keep them out, already knowing it was a losing battle even before they flung him out onto the dirt and stabbed the life out of him.

The last sounds Rob heard was their guttural language and hiss-like laughter but his final thought was more peaceful, almost serene: If there was such a thing as reincarnation, he was going to spend his next life devoted to the anti-hunting cause, just like Meryl Packer.

Ensorcell

It had started with a word. *Ensorcell.* Pollyanna had first overheard it when she was a child, playing with her Barbies in the spacious parlor as her mother prattled away on the phone to one pageant organizer or another.

"She'll absolutely ensorcell everybody, she's a natural!" Adeline gushed every chance she got, always eager to promote her daughter.

Pollyanna asked her mother what the strange word meant one day shortly thereafter while they were waiting at yet another terminal to board yet another plane to go to yet another beauty pageant.

"It means to enchant or fascinate or absolutely bewitch," Adeline had said, beaming. "It's what beautiful girls like you do to anyone who looks at you."

Pollyanna had felt special. Not everyone had the power to ensorcell. Of course, ensorcelling could go many different ways.

* * *

Adeline Marbury had first come upon the word "ensorcell" in an old book of fairy tales. She had frequently escaped into books as a girl to escape the insufferable mundaneness of her daily life.

Pollyanna was named after an unabashedly cheerful character from an old book. She was named so because Adeline lived by the mantra that it was important for girls to *smile;* looking pleasant was part of being beautiful...and smiles impressed the judges, which *was* the primary objective, after all. Whether it was her smile, or her pearly white teeth, or her bleached blonde hair, or her perfectly manicured fingernails, immaculate makeup, and shimmery skimpy costumes, Pollyanna had won the judges over time and time again. She had trophies and ribbons to prove it.

Pollyanna had been enrolled in beauty pageants since she was three years old. Her mother had started prepping her for a life of pageantry practically since she learned she was pregnant with a girl.

"You're blessed to have these opportunities darling," Adeline Mayberry had told her only child time and time again.

Adeline had seen beauty as the begin-all and end-all to having a successful life. She had been an undeniable beauty in her day, a true Georgia peach: blonde haired, blue eyed, slender, pale—central casting for supermodels. Yet she had also been from a solidly working class and strict religious family. Her momma wouldn't let her wear makeup even when she was sixteen. Instead, Adeline had spent most of her youth stocking shelves and working the cash register at the family's general store.

Adeline's escape came when she was sixteen and met Doug Jahn—nine years her senior, a law school graduate, and hailing from a respectable family of old money. Moreover, Doug was the only heir to his recently deceased father's fortune. He and Adeline crossed paths at the county fair and, the way Adeline told it, Doug had been smitten—even downright *ensorcelled*—with her from the moment he laid eyes on her. The way the local gossips told it, Doug was desperately seeking a pretty, prim, and proper wife to distract folks from his questionably quirky behavior, especially his weirdly close attachment to a local waiter named Bob, who was also mysteriously still single well into adulthood.

Adeline practically dragged Doug down the aisle, eager to escape from the drudgery of the store. After they married, she zealously spent money on clothes and makeup and dolling up the sizable colonial mansion that Doug had purchased for them. Two years into the marriage they had Pollyanna, their sole child. Adeline reveled in making her parents beg to see their only grandchild. Needless to say, relations were strained.

If Adeline enjoyed decorating her house, she absolutely delighted in adorning her daughter in every frilly, fancy get-up she could find. Beauty pageants were the cornerstones of Pollyanna's childhood. Her mother told her over and over again that learning how to apply makeup, strut walk, and feel comfortable in sequins was her best chance of finding success.

"You're so pretty Polly," went Adeline's mantra, "you're gonna be a rich man's wife and live like a queen all your life, just wait and see."

Pollyanna loved both her mother's praise and the way she glimmered when she was standing under the stage lights in full costume. Initially, she hadn't enjoyed the spray tanning, or sitting for hours getting her makeup done, or attaching wigs and extensions to her bleached hair, or the weird sensation of acrylic nails, or the way the fake eyelash glue stuck her lashes together...but whenever Pollyanna had dared to have a meltdown, her mother matched her tantrum tit for tat.

"I'm trying to secure your future, so stop being such an ungrateful brat!" Adeline would shriek, alongside similar statements, until they were both in tears. Over time, Pollyanna stopped fighting. She didn't like to upset her mother and, when she was a good girl, she got a Barbie doll. Adeline said that tall, thin, blonde Barbie was a good role model.

Pollyanna's grandparents were horrified by their grandchild's relentless pageantry involvement. Decidedly *not* ensorcelled with glitz and glamour, they vehemently protested what they considered the sexualization of their sole grandchild from toddlerhood onward. Yet every time they complained—or dared to utter a single critical comment—Adeline distanced herself further until there was no relationship left and, subsequently, no further protests. For his part, Doug said nothing about anything. Since his marriage he had stayed away from Bob but got closer to the bottle. He lived in the same house, but Pollyanna rarely saw him. When he died of liver failure when she was six, neither she nor Adeline shed many tears.

After Doug's death, Pollyanna's involvement in pageants increased dramatically. She could afford to enter bigger and grander contests everywhere from Texas to California to Las Vegas. Pollyanna loved traveling but she loved performing more. Singing and dancing had become her forte and joy; she knew no greater thrill than performing on stage and hearing the audience applaud.

I've ensorcelled them, she would think to herself, smiling ear to ear whilst taking a bow. In her spare time, Pollyanna constantly practiced her routines and that dedication had been her downfall.

When she was fourteen, Pollyanna lost her balance while twirling on the patio. She fell awkwardly and banged her head hard on the brick-coated ground. She split open her forehead, broke her nose, and knocked out two front teeth. The doctors at the emergency room said she was lucky to have avoided a concussion, but her mother couldn't be comforted.

"You've ruined your life!" Adeline sobbed when she saw the stitches embedded within her beautiful daughter's forehead. "Who's going to want you now?"

Those words stung Pollyanna more deeply than any said before, but she hadn't responded. There was nothing to say.

A dentist implanted two false teeth that looked and felt real and her nose healed cleanly leaving no trace of the accident...but the scar on her forehead remained. Despite her initial outburst, Adeline didn't turn her back on her only child; much to the contrary, she did everything in her power to find a cure. She took her to specialists and applied every type of healing cream on the market...but nothing completely erased the deep scar that the injury had placed upon Pollyanna's otherwise flawless skin. Pollyanna participated in three pageants after the accident but didn't win a single one. Even the professional makeup artists couldn't cover the mark and the other contestants—and their mothers—pointed and snickered audibly. Adeline finally decided to stop entering the pageants, but she refused to stop searching for a remedy.

"You'll be right as rain soon, sugar, don't you worry," she'd tell her daughter. Pollyanna was skeptical to say the least.

Yet the remedy was found at a big makeup convention in New York City. Adeline and Pollyanna didn't go every year, but whenever they did make the journey to The Big Apple, they enjoyed themselves immensely. Traditionally, they spent a day or two at the show and the rest of the week seeing the sights of the city, especially

Fifth Avenue. Yet the first trip they took to the makeup show after the accident was not nearly as leisurely. It was a stone-cold mission to regain glory.

They didn't find glory, but they found Ilona Muntean. She was manning a stand at the back row of the exposition which should have been inconspicuous but which somehow commanded attention. From the moment Adeline and Pollyanna spotted the stand they were drawn to it like moths to a flame. The woman presiding over the ensemble of bottles and jars introduced herself as Ilona and she was gorgeous; she possessed an enviable beauty that any aspiring model would kill for. She also promised that her potions could transform plain women into beauties and make gorgeous women irresistible.

From the moment Pollyanna met Ilona, she knew that she had found the person who would most alter the course of her life. It wasn't a feeling she could explain, but there had been a definite connection to Ilona—an *allure*—that even the most professional of photos could not capture.

Ilona spoke with a singsong accent that was as alluring as the scents of her perfumes. Pollyanna couldn't remember exactly what had been said initially—it was as if she'd been half lulled (ensorcelled) to sleep—but she did remember Ilona approaching her with sympathy-filled eyes and gently brushing back her long bangs, exposing the scar.

"A scar is imperfection, yes, but I fix," she'd cooed in clear yet broken English. "Sit down, I make disappear."

Pollyanna had done as instructed and allowed herself to be lathered with creams and gels as Ilona's bewitching voice told her and her mother about all of the benefits of her creams and serums. With a sly smile, she called them potions. Pollyanna didn't know exactly how much time had passed, but when she rose from the chair and looked in a mirror, her scar was noticeably lighter. The next morning, it was gone.

Adeline and Pollyanna had shunned the rest of the city and spent every day at the makeup convention, huddled around Ilona's booth, talking to her and buying up her stock of beauty treatments. Ilona told them she was from Moldova but lived in New York. After the convention closed, she had even invited them to her apartment for tea.

The apartment was more akin to a penthouse. It was big and fancy and full of ancient-looking art; clearly Ilona's beauty business had served her well. Once, whilst searching for the bathroom, Pollyanna came across a darkened room that smelled of incense. There were old scrolls and paintings hanging on the walls depicting demonic entities. There were also many photographs of misshapen, disfigured children...most of whom appeared to be female. Pollyanna had let out a yelp of surprise and stumbled backwards. Then Ilona was next to her, speaking words of comfort.

"This my dark collection," she explained. "Demons... the ugliness I fight with my mixtures. Photos show children I support by charity...Them I cannot cure."

Whilst the scattered photos and disturbing artwork seemed weird, scary, and unsettling, Ilona's explanation was convincing. And so, Pollyanna had simply shut the door and thought no more about it.

By the fifth day since making her acquaintance, Adeline and Pollyanna felt as if Ilona was an old friend. It was difficult to go back to Georgia. They had to purchase extra luggage to carry back all the bottles and elixirs they had secured. They also kept in near-constant contact with Ilona via email.

Months passed. Pollyanna entered and won three pageants, her flawless features ensorcelling the judges as expected. Ilona provided Adeline with creams to fight the insidious crow's feet that were infringing around her eyes and Adeline clearly liked the results she saw when she looked in the mirror. Yet Pollyanna noticed her mother looking frailer and more drawn by the day; at times it looked like she had aged twenty years without realizing it. Of course, Adeline refused to see a doctor. After all, she didn't feel sick. In fact, she didn't seem to notice anything but positive improvements.

"We've got to focus on becoming Miss America," Adeline told her daughter. "And modeling. You're almost an adult. Now all these doors are opening for you. In two or three years, we'll be in Hollywood! Can you imagine your name in lights, sugar?"

Pollyanna could and it sounded good. After all, plenty of models—especially supermodels—went on to act.

Yet, no such things happened. Instead, Pollyanna's world was turned upside down one morning five weeks after her eighteenth birthday, and six months after returning from New York, when she found her mother lying in bed, cold and dead. The doctors said it was a massive aneurysm.

Adeline was promptly buried next to her husband and Pollyanna was left alone and devastated in the big house with ample money...and having no idea what to do with herself. In desperation, she called Ilona for advice. Expecting merely comfort, she was surprised by Ilona's generous offer.

"Come, you be my assistant," Ilona had said soothingly. "I have room in house, you stay here. You be model, yes?"

It sounded too good to be true...but Pollyanna recalled Ilona saying something about having a hard time finding suitable help. Pollyanna *did* like the excitement of the city and she *was* intrigued by all the modeling opportunities it offered, and so she promptly gathered her things and got on a plane. She didn't bother selling the house; she assumed that she would likely come back to Georgia from time to time.

Life in New York was ensorcelling; a whirlwind of conventions and parties and modeling shoots. Pollyanna met celebrities and got interviewed by modeling magazines; she even walked the runways during fashion week. Yet after a few months, all the excitement started to affect her. She felt tired and noticed that her skin didn't look as rosy and healthy as it once had. She awoke one morning and discovered several gray hairs protruding from her scalp. Ilona, who never seemed to age past thirty-five or so, laughed at the younger woman's panic and handed her a supplement to drink. For the first time, it didn't seem to work. Pollyanna continued to feel listless, *old*.

A few weeks later, Pollyanna's graying hair started to fall out in clumps, her back ached, and her feet felt oddly numb. She wanted to see a doctor but Ilona said all she really needed was fresh air.

"We go my country," she said. "It nice there, we settle you."

Ilona brought Pollyanna a plane ticket and the two of them traveled to Eastern Europe. Pollyanna didn't enjoy the flight. She felt feverish and sore in ways that not even the comforts of first-class could abate. Ilona assured her—as well as any flight attendants who dared to inquire—that she would be fine and Ilona was so convincing, so soothing and soft-spoken, that everyone believed her without further question.

Pollyanna barely remembered landing. She didn't recall exiting the plane, collecting the luggage, or anything about the airport. She couldn't recall hailing a taxi or journeying into the city, but she *did* remember Ilona practically carrying her—with seemingly superhuman strength—into a grand building that was more castle than mansion. Apparently, Ilona had more money than she ever let on.

Ilona brought Pollyanna into an ornate bedroom and laid her down to rest amid a sea of plush pillows on a lush mattress and silk sheets. Pollyanna didn't know how long she slept or how many days went by. She was in and out of consciousness, vaguely aware of Ilona coming in and out of the room. She was made to swallow unusual tasting drinks and rubbed with intoxicatingly scented ointments. Oddly, she vaguely recollected signing paperwork...but she had no idea how to differentiate between dreams and reality. The word "sleep" was gently cooed seemingly continuously, compelling her to periodically drift back into darkness.

At some point, Pollyanna regained consciousness. She felt very weak and very sore...and very *strange*. She tried to move her legs and agony instantly shot through her back. She crumpled, feeling discombobulated, *wrong*. Her head felt as heavy as lead and her body jerked abnormally as she used all her wane strength to move toward the edge of the bed. She felt stray strands of hair lace her fingertips as her hands gripped the bedsheets. To her horror, she realized that her teeth were lose and her tongue was badly swollen...something was seriously amiss.

Pollyanna groaned. It was painful to move but she had to get to a mirror, she had to see the state that she was in. Then she would call for an ambulance. She obviously needed a doctor desperately.

She fell from the tall bed awkwardly, landing hard on the floor with a sickening thud. She cried out; her ribs throbbed and she couldn't get her footing. Her eyes couldn't quite adjust in the darkness of the room, but she realized that her legs were tiny and thin—almost mangled—as if they had shriveled up into her. Gathering her slight strength, Pollyanna pulled herself along the floor. Her arms practically screamed as she stretched them outward; their muscles were clearly reducing and weakening just as her legs had.

In the distance, Pollyanna saw a dim glint of light. She understood that she would not be able to stand up and look in a standard wall mirror, but there appeared to be an old and shiny suit of armor in the corner. It was surely reflective enough to let her assess her condition...alas a distance of twenty feet might as well have been twenty miles. Huffing and groaning with effort, Pollyanna slithered across the floor and struggled to the foot of the well-polished knight's armor. Nothing could have prepared her for the vision staring back at her.

She was skinny, her eyes were sunken into her gaunt face like those of a skeleton. She was mostly bald and her lips were cracked and caked with blood. Yet it was the state of her body that elicited a scream of horror—her legs were indeed withered, and her arms were starting to retract unnaturally, and her spine was curved crookedly, rendering her into a misshapen lump of humpbacked flesh.

Suddenly the bedroom door burst open. Pollyanna threw her head to the floor, crying out as the sudden burst of light assaulted her irises. Then Ilona was standing over her, looking younger and fresher than

Pollyanna had ever seen. She didn't look thirty-five, she looked twenty-two at most.

"Hospital..." Pollyanna tried to say only to discover that she could not speak. Whatever had happened to her had made her incapable of articulating words or emoting anything more than guttural gurgles.

*Shhh...*Ilona crooned and, for just a moment, she *changed*. For the first time, Pollyanna saw Ilona for what she really was—an ancient crepe-skinned skeletal witch with eyes as black as coal; more demon than human. Pollyanna recoiled in terror and blinked hard. In an instant, Ilona was back to her beautiful self, staring down at Pollyanna ruefully, undoubtedly understanding exactly what she had just seen. One thing was immediately clear: Ilona had ensorcelled her...completely, truly, and utterly ensorcelled her. Adeline had been right; Ilona was certainly something else...something else entirely.

"You go now," she lulled mockingly. "You served me well, beauty."

And so, Pollyanna found herself carted off to an institution where she was locked away with other pitifully deformed beings. She recognized several of them from the photographs she had seen in Ilona's Manhattan apartment; images of their pathetic existences displayed like trophies. She supposed her own photograph was now a cherished part of that macabre collection.

Pollyanna tried to explain what had happened to her, but like all the others, she could not speak coherently. Cruelly, photos of Ilona were displayed upon the walls of every room. After all, she was the primary patron of the asylum...the same establishment which she populated with a never-ending daisy-chain of global victims whose homes she acquired and fortunes she stole along with their youth and health and beauty. Without outright murdering her victims, Ilona nonetheless took their lives.

With no family left to claim her or declare her missing, Pollyanna remained in the asylum. Her vision and mobility decreased, but compared to some of the other older patients, she was in good condition.

Among the victims, Pollyanna was indeed a beauty.

Beastie

Matt Brewer was a bad kid, a *"there's something wrong with him"* kind of kid. People were afraid of him and that was just how he liked it. As a child, his behavior had been off-putting but not by intention; Matt simply acted out the urges to kick and scream and bite and punch that he was not able to control nor contain.

When he was five, he got banned from the playground for pushing other children down and causing a dozen scrapped knees in two weeks. When he was seven, he had nearly drowned his young neighbor in the pool after an argument over a float. That had been his first and last invitation to a birthday party. He had done these things knowing that they would upset—*unsettle*—the adults, but he had done them purely on impulse, *instinct*. Yet as he got older, he started to cultivate his image as a weirdo, a creep. He liked keeping people at bay. Making others uncomfortable was the ultimate power rush.

Matt supposed that there probably was something wrong with him. Other kids—even the tough-talking jocks—didn't experience delight from shooting squirrels with B.B. guns and lacing bread with poison just to watch pigeons suffer through death throes...those were hobbies that Matt savored alone.

He didn't care for others. He had no friends and that was how he liked it. People irritated him. Once, when he was ten, his mother had finally given in to peer pressure and attempted to force a friendship upon him with Fred, the awkward and gangly grandson of her portly co-worker, Barbara. Both boys were close to the same age and both were misfits so the adults naturally assumed that they were kindred spirits who would obviously become fast friends.

They assumed wrong.

Matt and Fred had been left alone one sunny summer afternoon. The "play date" started out in the overgrown backyard of Fred's ramshackle house but quickly led to both boys sneaking off into the woods after Matt suggested that it would be fun to go digging for worms to put into the refrigerator. He giggled just imagining the horrified screams of Fred's granny when she opened the fridge and discovered the withering muddy mess of worms stocked upon the shelves.

Fred had simply gone along with the plan. He was almost catatonically agreeable but Matt still regarded him as an annoying third wheel. He couldn't walk briskly through the foliage and said he disliked nature; he also mentioned being unable to swim. And so, when they got to a rocky stream, Matt hadn't been able to resist pushing Fred into the water. He had landed with a hard splash and Matt giggled wildly as he watched the other boy flail about shrieking. When Fred finally managed to stand up, he was sobbing and stuttering and seemingly trying to cuss Matt out.

"You're a j-j-jerk!" Fred managed to utter before he looked down and saw nearly a dozen leeches stuck to his legs. The sight sent him into a gale of hysterics. He stomped through the woods so frantically that he fell and shattered his ankle with an audible snap. He lay there, hoarse from screaming and crying, with his ankle bent unnaturally to one side and the leeches sucking away at his pale legs. Pathetically, he begged Matt to help him.

"I bet you're sorry you called me a jerk now," Matt stated calmly as he walked away.

Ignoring Fred's pleas for help, Matt spent the next two hours collecting the fattest juiciest earthworms he could find. He then returned to Fred's house and put them in the fridge. He laughed uproariously when Barbara woke from her nap and opened the fridge and screamed like all the demons in Hell were after her. Matt had snickered until his sides hurt and then ran two blocks home before he was spotted.

It was at least three hours before anyone inquired about Fred's whereabouts. Barbara called Matt's mother at 8pm and Matt confessed that they had gotten into an argument and he had left him in the woods earlier in the afternoon. He failed to mention anything about the leeches or the broken ankle. The adults discovered those realities when they found Fred babbling and bloody at the edge of the woods. He had to be taken to the hospital. The police chief had come around to Matt's house but Matt denied any involvement in the injury.

"He was okay when I left him," Matt insisted very matter-of-factly and the police left. No one could *prove* otherwise and, besides, he was only ten...old enough to know that the authorities couldn't send a minor up the river.

Fred and Matt never had another play date and Barbara stopped working at the Shop 'N Go right after that so Matt's mother ceased mentioning her and her feeble grandson in conversation. In truth, Mildred Brewer never said much, period. She was a quiet woman who spent most of her life stocking shelves or tending to the garden. She didn't communicate well with her only child, but she always defended him. She also defended her husband. Local gossip said he had run off with a carnie; Mildred said he had been the victim of a kidnapping. Either way, he was out of the picture.

As he got older, Matt was left alone more as his single mother worked longer hours. Matt supposed that was because she preferred the store to being home alone with him. By fourteen, he had been banned from the local pool, forbidden from entering the ice cream parlor, was on the mall security's watch list, and removed from school. Mildred said he was being persecuted which was arguably true; after all, he never did anything overtly violent. The lifeguards couldn't *prove* he'd unhooked Carrie Linley's top in the crowded wading pool. The ice cream man couldn't *confirm* he'd thrown the dead rats under the tables. The mall guards didn't actually *witness* him ogling women in the underwear department. The fidgety school principle couldn't even cite a *specific* reason to bar him except to say that he didn't "seem to get along with the other students" and freely offered him an online class option. Matt readily accepted it. He liked the solitude of the internet.

The internet had, in fact, opened many doors for Matt. He discovered BDSM and rape fantasy websites. They changed his life. The idea of having such power—such control—over a helpless female was more enticing and exciting than anything he had ever imagined.

Sometimes on his rare excursions into town, he'd spot some limber little peer and stare fixedly at her. Carrie Linley was his primary target of untoward affection and it was she who had fanned the flames of his addictive desire.

"Ugh, you're such a beast," she'd sneered at him whilst pushing past him at the Memorial Day Parade.

Yes, a *beast*. Matt liked the sound of that. He even started creating misshapen figures—*beasties*—out of clay. One day, he decided, he would become a serial killer and leave a grotesque figurine with the body of each victim. That goal gave him something to look forward to.

Matt also looked forward to seeing Carrie. He knew just how to make her notice him. She liked animals and volunteered at a local wildlife rescue center. If he caught a bird and then broke its wing, he could call the rescue when she was on duty and say that he found it and was trying to help it. When she came to get it, he would lure her into his house. He would give her cake and a drink laced with his mother's sleeping pills. Carrie would doze off and he would be able to cop a feel. He wouldn't fuck her—he knew all about DNA evidence—but she wouldn't be able to *prove* anything if he merely fondled her. Besides, he was only fourteen. It's not like they could try him as an adult.

And so, one warm June day Matt descended into the woods with his slingshot and a few rocks. He would catch a bird and injure it, but not kill it. For this hunt, he needed live bait. Matt expected to secure a feathered victim within ten minutes...but the forest was oddly silent. He walked in deeper and deeper, mindful of how easy it would be to lose his sense of direction.

Suddenly, he heard an inhuman roar followed by the rhythmic sound of thuds and breaking branches. For the first time in his life, Matt felt fear as something heavy slammed into the back of his head. He fell to the ground and blacked out. The next thing he knew, sharp claws were pawing at him, tearing his clothes to shreds and slicing into his skin. Matt screamed in pain and looked up to see a huge, hairy, red-eyed, and horribly menacing creature staring down at him. Matt whimpered and tried to back away, but his aching head and throbbing body refused to budge. Then the creature roughly grabbed him by the neck and swung him upwards; seemingly snickering at his dismay.

Matt stared into the creature's bright, unblinking, eyes and registered both intelligence and an absolute lack of emotion. He hoped it would simply bite his head off and end his agony--and humiliation--quickly, but instead it threw him over its shoulder and carried him back to its cave.

The creature didn't devour Matt. Instead, it tied him up with leafy vines and left him lying naked on a filthy bed of leaves. It enjoyed caressing him, exploring *every inch* of him, and worse...*much* worse. Matt had always assumed that sexual gratification was enjoyable, but there was nothing gratifying about their unnatural couplings...at least, not in his opinion; its appetite was quite insatiable. The more unsatisfied he was, the more he cried and screamed and begged and pleaded, the more zealous its passions became. Occasionally, it would beat him with a sharpened stick until he cried out and, over time, he learned to feign enjoyment, as if he shared its euphoria. He expected it to become pregnant and eventually present him with a half-breed little beastie, a monstrosity that walked the line between human and missing link, but no such thing occurred. There was lots of baby making—or what constituted for mating in the realm of its depraved lair—but never a baby born.

After what seemed like forever, Matt's cries—pleads for assistance which he managed to mask as howls of pleasure—attracted the attention of another beast. It entered his captor's cave to gawk and grunt at him and when its back was turned, Matt's tormentor bit into its neck ripping out the jugular and splashing Matt with its hot gooey blood.

Matt's kidnapper devoured its cannibalized victim and made a nest out of its bones in the dark recesses of the cave. As expected, Matt soon found himself splayed across that very boney bed being vigorously defiled; blacking out from exhaustion and disgust was his sole escape from the misery of his slavish existence. The creature sporadically threw Matt raw scraps of meat which he desperately devoured. As a reward for each meal granted, he obediently (begrudgingly) offered his body to the creature who readily accepted time and time again. And so, it went on, time and time again. Their non-consensual union remained steadfast. Matt soon realized that his bedfellow was encouraging of his cries; it liked luring other creatures of its kind into the cave. It liked dispatching them. It liked savoring their flesh.

Inhuman victim after inhuman victim met its end after being lured by Matt's presence. Days turned into months and months turned into years. Matt's fate was sealed; he was the beastie's bait.

Reaper

Arnie saw the shadowy figure first and, shortly thereafter, Matilda said she'd seen it too. Both the janitor and lunch lady described it as a guy in a hooded robe holding a big knife. *"Looked like one of 'em Satanists!"* Arnie quivered—and that was enough for the principle to hit the alarm button and get the lockdown underway.

I wasn't the first to see it, but I knew exactly what that figure was and what it was doing at Lakegrove Academy. It was Death and it was looking for me.

This was an age-old fight; at least age-old in my terminology because it had been going on since I was born...actually, to be precise, it had been going on since I was in my momma's womb.

The first time Death came for me was when momma was five months pregnant. She slipped on ice, fell forward, and damn near squashed the life out of me. She was kept on bed rest for the next four months and had me healthier than anyone expected, despite the fact that I was three weeks premature and had a weakened immune system. The funny thing was that momma, by all accounts a practical woman, swore up and down that something pushed her hard and knocked her to the ground on that icy day.

"I saw Death looming over me—over you—and I decided I wasn't gonna let him take you," she always told me very matter-of-factly. Momma was never one to pay much heed to the paranormal, she was a good Baptist woman—a pastor's wife—even though she had been raised by a self-professed Voodoo priestess.

The second time Death came for me I was two years old. I was on the swings in the rusty old playground behind the bad-side-of-the-tracks apartment complex that we called home. Gunshots rang out and I felt a sharp stinging pain across my forehead. I fell off the swing, fully aware of the blood pouring over me. Momma was screaming. And, in that moment, I saw something hooded and dark hovering over me.

I wasn't shot, just grazed, and I got out of the hospital with nothing but a bandage. Momma and daddy said it was God and all his saints that had saved me, but the accidents kept coming. My guardian angel worked quadrupole duty every single day to keep me off of Death's doorway.

I fell down the stairs when I was three and I nearly drowned at four. At four-and-a-half I barely escaped being struck down by a drunk driver who careened up on the sidewalk at two in the afternoon. I got mauled by a pit bull at five and, two weeks later, I almost got stabbed by a crackhead who was hallucinating real bad. And then there were the asthma attacks—those were damn near daily.

Momma and daddy and my grandparents and aunts, uncles, cousins and neighbors prayed and prayed but, by the time of the knife attack, my momma knew something was seriously wrong. Without telling my daddy or his kin, she took me to see my other grandmother—her momma, granny Gail.

Now, here's the thing about my momma: she was good and kind but she was also proud. She liked to focus on the positive things in life and ignore the negative, which is why she avoided discussing granny Gail as much as possible. I don't know exactly what transpired between them, but my momma left home at sixteen and never looked back.

Momma said granny Gail was a hoodoo woman 'cause she used her powers for bad more than good. But she also knew the ins and outs of Voodoo, a healing religion, and when I kept experiencing all these misfortunes momma took me to see her.

Granny Gail wasn't none too keen on my daddy, a passionate preacher from a long line of clergy, but she still had enough mercy left in her soul to take pity on me. She cast some sort of protection spell and, whether it was that Voodoo or the blessing of the Christian lord, I managed to not only survive, but thrive. I never got sucked into the badness that went on in my neighborhood. I attended church every Sunday and sang gospel hymns and shouted praises proudly in my best hats and matching outfits.

By the time I was seventeen I had survived a car crash, a house fire, and a tornado. But I was happy, content, and safe for the most part...aside from the odd freak injury and bouts of terrifying dreams. My life was stable with momma and daddy and the church as my pillars. I fell in love with dancing and won a tap dance championship the same year I graduated high school. I earned good grades but I knew I couldn't afford college without going into serious debt...the kind I reckoned I would never be able to climb out of. Instead, I decided to go into a trade. I'd always wanted to be a cop but momma's nerves wouldn't stand for it so I instead I got a job as a security guard at an elementary school. I don't have children but I like being around them. Once I even saved a kid who was choking. It feels good to make a living protecting folks.

'Course, for all my righteous ways, I also got some vices. Specifically, I like to gamble. I'm not sure where it comes from, but I reckon it's got something to do with how many times I've lucked out and avoided Death and disaster. Plus, I've always been lucky on lotto cards and the occasional poker game. I never won nothing real big, a couple of grand here and there, and I suppose that can be chalked up to the blessings of granny Gail who was rumored to have run underground gambling dens for decades.

Ironically, it was the gambling—my sole vice—that led to this whole mess. I saved my pennies and spent spring break in Las Vegas where I had me a proper winning streak. The first night, I hit $5,000 on the one-eyed jacks. On the second night, I nabbed $6,000 spinning the roulette wheel. I figured the casino was gonna get suspicious so, on the third night, I decided to go ahead and find a new location. I walked down the strip, trusting my instincts to lead me to the right casino, and my impulses led me right to The Blue Banshee.

It was a little hole-in-the-wall joint in the darkest backstreet off the strip; about as far removed from the glitz and glamor of The Luxor and The Bellagio as you could get. I don't even know exactly how I found it but it was like I was led there on instinct, by fate.

It was dark and smoky and I should've had my guard up or—better yet—high-tailed it outta there, but instead I walked right over the poker table and sat down amid a questionable looking crowd of long-haired bikers and bald ex-cons. Far off in the corner was a figure in a black hoodie, I couldn't see his face—hell, for all I know it was a *her*—but it seemed somehow familiar to me. Not comfortable, but *familiar* nonetheless.

Time ticked by as I played and won one hand after another. Finally, it was down to just me and the hooded figure. We battled it out in silence except for the clatter of chips and the shuffling of cards. I finally prevailed through pairs of black eights and aces...the legendary dead man's hand.

The hooded figure jumped up then and glared at me —even though I couldn't see anything but a deep black hole of nothingness in the hollow where there should've been a face—and that's when a streak of pure fear shot through me 'cause, in that moment, I knew why I recognized the hooded dude; it was the same figure I saw out of the corner of my eye every time I had an accident or barely escaped injury. It was Death, and I'd just cheated it outta a whole lotta money.

I jumped up and collected my winnings as quick as I could—fully expecting that hooded *thing* to chase me down, but it just stood there, an empty socket staring fixedly in my direction.

I walked outta that shabby little casino so fast that I was nearly running. By the time I was two blocks away I thought I'd gone crazy and imagined the whole thing, figuring it was just some down-and-out weirdo in a too-big shirt...but then I saw it outta the corner of my eye. It was following me but I didn't see no gait, it was as if it was gliding towards me instead of walking, hovering off the ground like a ghost.

And that's not all...as I walked, people started bumping into me. A rusty old sign from a liquor store fell and nearly hit me on one street and, on the next, several streetlight bulbs suddenly burst and rained glass and embers down on me. And the whole time that thing stayed behind me in hot pursuit; instigating accidents.

My momma taught me every prayer in the book but she didn't know that I had also taught myself a bunch of Voodoo protection spells and I started reciting both them and the Lord's prayers over and over again, willing that thing away. I ain't never been so frightened but, through one prayer or another, I lost it. The crowds dispersed, the streetlights stopped flickering, and I got back to my hotel. I didn't waste no time packing up and renting a car and getting outta dodge as fast as I could.

I drove hundreds of miles that night, fully anticipating to be killed in a wreck, and I was too scared to look in the rearview mirror in case I saw that dark hooded *thing* hitching a ride along with me. I looked straight ahead and kept reciting the combined prayers for hours on end until I got home safe and sound...myself and my winnings secure. I got my house blessed and then adorned each room with gris-gris and made every attempt to lay as low as possible. And it worked, nothing happened.

That was seven months ago. I'd gotten comfortable. And then, today, *this*. I know what this is. I've been found.

I always knew Death would catch up to me; I'd cheated it once too often. Whether or not the grim reaper in the school is the same one that's been after me since childhood I can't say. Heck, for all I know there's a whole species of these damn things running around all over the world, but the one roaming the halls is certainly the same one I met in Vegas. Of that I have no doubt. Beating Death with a dead man's hand in the recesses of Sin City was just the final insult—the last straw. Apparently, even Death's got its limits.

And so do I; I ain't going out without a fight.

Over the years, I'd become fascinated by Death—or grim reapers or dark angels or whatever you want to call them. How they're depicted in art with the long flowing robes is accurate, which makes me think I'm far from the only person they ever took a shine to and pursued without capture for years on end. It's like Death was as fascinated by me as I was by it; although I can't imagine why. I ain't got no artistic skills. I can't showcase it in paintings, or sculpt its image out of clay, or pay homage to it in lyrical ballads…but, I can face it.

The school's empty now except for me, which is befitting given my duties. Alarms are going off and I can hear sirens in the distance. We don't have much time. I stop square in the middle of the hallway and call out to my longtime companion, both nemesis and muse.

"I'm here, hellion! You come face me and I'll face you!"

And just like that, it stands before me. No bright lights or smoke or big black wings flapping. One moment I'm alone and the next, it's here. That's all. No fuss, no bother, and no face; just that empty black hole of nothingness. Its scythe is sharpened to a point though—no wonder the school officials were expecting a blood bath.

Without warning, Death throws its blade to the side and reaches toward me. Okay, it's finally taking me. I should be scared, but I'm not. I've lived a good life aside from the gambling. Surely, I'll get to heaven and see Jesus and momma and daddy. It won't be so bad.

Death's bony hands grasp mine. They are cold. It twirls me to the left and then to the right. I open my eyes expecting to be soaring towards the next life, but all I see is the faded yellow bricks of the school hallway. Death twirls me again, then dips me. The damn thing is dancing with me!

"Is *this* what you wanted, a *dance*?"

I can't help but laugh…it's not wise to laugh in the face of Death, but it—this particular grim reaper, anyway—doesn't seem to mind. It doesn't even seem too interested in getting its money back. Instead, it tangos. Perhaps it's confused, or insane, or maybe the afterlife really is just one big party and they're all like this under the grim veneer.

I've taken dance classes most of my life; first as a hobby and then as an exercise regime. I know damn near every dance under the sun. Perhaps *that* was part of its unwavering fascination with me. Regardless of the reason, I'll give it this dance and offer it more. If it appears in my house again, I'll even put on some records. Why not? Blue

Oyster Cult's *Don't Fear the Reaper* is one tune that immediately comes to mind.

I can beat Death at cards, dance with it, court it—heck, even tempt it—but I ain't gonna escape it forever. It knows that as well as I do. But it seems like I can temporally elude it and hold onto my precious life force for as long as possible. Maybe a few days, maybe a few decades. We'll see.

I can't defeat Death, but I might be able to join it in my own good time when I'm ready. Let it dance to *my* tune and not the other way around. Live a little. Until then, I'll get on its good side.

Tracker

"Do you *have* to go? Are you *sure* it's really necessary this time?"

Alannah had been standing in the doorway, a thin silhouette illuminated by the bright glare of the hallway light behind her. He remembered thinking that she looked like nothing more than the wisp of a shadow resting against the doorframe. Her voice was steady but her eyes had been wide with worry. She had been watching the news or, worse, googling it...finding every minuscule terrible detail to run through her mind, over and over again and again, indefinitely. Initially, she had encouraged him. As the deadline approached, she clearly had second thoughts.

The reports were startling; inhumanly vicious even for a continent infamous for war and poverty and violence. *Witch children*...the words crowed internally, jarring even when not stated aloud.

"I'll be fine," he had said, wrenching himself away from his half-packed suitcase to rub Alannah's shoulder in a half-crocked attempt at comfort. "I've been to Nigeria before. The vast majority of the people are nice, they appreciate the services we provide. They're poor, they need help. Not unlike the Irish only a few decades ago."

Now he wished that he had listened to his wife and cancelled the trip and never ventured away from Eire. It had been bad—worse than anything he could have expected. And while he wasn't one to support superstitions, the old woman *had* spooked him.

* * *

John Brennan was widely considered to be a decent man, a hardworking man, a caring man. He trained as a doctor at Cork University, then returned to his home county of Donegal. He preferred to keep to the West or South of the isle, its hills were in his blood. Granted, he had come to enjoy the occasional week-long holiday while in college, where he and a group of friends would book cheap flights to Paris or the Canary Islands. By the time he entered his Masters program, he had developed an acute taste for travel so joining Doctors Without Borders seemed natural. He liked to help people, he wanted to see the world, and for a good long while it was a fine arrangement. For over two decades, he traveled to South America, Southeast Asia, Africa, and Eastern Europe. He helped people and it was fulfilling, addictive even.

Back in Ireland, he set up a small dermatology practice where he cured people of rashes that were often itchy and annoying or occasionally painful, but nothing compared to what he saw in the slums of the Philippines or the favelas of Brazil. For many years, he had spent months at a time traveling with Doctors Without Borders, volunteering for assignments with little mind to the logistics. After all, he had no pets, no children, no wife.

Then, when he was forty-eight, John met Alannah. He first spotted her in Galway, during the annual Puck Festival. She had been standing with one of his patients, of whom she was a cousin. They got acquainted and, although he didn't believe in love at first sight, there had been a spark, a keen interest that didn't let up.

Alannah was forty and looked younger but had resigned herself to a life as a spinster. She had taken care of both her parents in their final years and had sole custody of her then fourteen-year-old nephew. Her sister and brother-in-law had been killed in a drunk driving accident years before. John vaguely remembered the story being all over the news when he was in his third year at university.

They dated casually for two years before marrying and, during that time, John spent more and more time at home in Ireland. He eventually warmed up enough to nephew Tommy to legally adopt him, even though the boy was already seventeen at the time. And then, a year after their wedding, Alannah announced that she was pregnant. She had been forty-three during her first and only pregnancy and there had been no expectations of conception nor any fertility treatments. "A miracle baby" everyone said, even as the experts warned of the increased risk of Down Syndrome and physical ailments.

But Eoin had been born healthy and happy two months prior to his mother's forty-fourth birthday. For the first year of his son's life, John had stayed in the country. Then, two months ago, he received a call from Doctors Without Borders, asking him to render his services to Nigeria. Those in the organization knew of the troubles, even though the media hadn't announced them to the global masses yet. John initially balked and claimed he couldn't leave Alannah when Eoin was still so little, but the pay they were offering was twice the normal rate and business at home had been down since the economy slowed...and then, before a week had passed, the news reports came blazing across the screen. One was more horrifying than the next.

"If they think you can help, even a little, then you should go. If it wasn't for the little one, I'd go with you," Alannah said one evening as she watched the reports with an utterly stricken expression. She was, at her core, a humanitarian and the news was too shocking, too brutal, for her to ignore.

Children were being accused of witchcraft, cast out of their homes, left to die of starvation in the streets at best and, at worst, subjected to violent chaotic "exorcisms" performed by self-proclaimed pastors and, when those failed, tortured or killed by their own families. Nollywood, the Nigerian version of Hollywood, continuously released a number of witch-themed horror movies starring young children; profitable fictions with real-world implications that accelerated the situation to new heights with every new premiere, spreading mass hysteria and unprecedented levels of violence. It was horrifying, nearly unrealistically gruesome, but it was also an undeniable fact and taking place in Akwa Ibom state...which just so happened to be a stone's throw away from John's assignment.

* * *

The plane landed on time and his taxi arrived uneventfully. From the backseat, John sat slouched and stared at the lush green foliage of the jungle trees whizzing by as an updated rendition of that creepy old *Iko Iko* song blared from the cab's speakers. The nature was breathtakingly beautiful but the overall landscape left a lot to be desired. Every few feet stood a rusty sign advertising a church that promised fortune and good health through prayer and fees. The communities along the Niger Delta were particularly poverty stricken and adhered to sermons that blended Pentecostal Christianity with indigenous beliefs. Between "thou shall not suffer a witch to live," the ancient societies' omnipresent terror of enchantments, and the astronomically high rates of sickness and hunger, it was hardly surprising that accusations of witchcraft ran rampant. What was surprising was that it was the smallest and most vulnerable who were most often blamed.

In the past two years alone, thousands of children were accused of practicing malicious witchcraft and were starved, beaten, chained up, or even set on fire. According to the locals, some parents had even attempted to behead their "possessed" children with saws or bury them alive. Youngsters who managed to survive the initial accusations were cast away from their homes and left to wander among the *skolombo*—street children—who gathered on the sides of roads and sheltered together in abandoned buildings; shunned by all but each other...and the rescue groups.

The reality of the situation, the raw relentless horror of it, made John feel queasy and dissociated; trapped in a nightmarish world of poverty and fear, delusion and suffering, that he did not recognize as real life. It was all so far away from Ireland, so alien, that it was difficult to comprehend that the two countries could possibly exist on the same planet. Yet he continued coming to Nigeria for the simple fact that most of the people he encountered were friendly and welcoming and delighted to have a doctor tend to their ailments. The majority made the trips worthwhile, but encounters with the minority were sobering and frightening.

His assignment was scheduled for nine days—seven of them actively treating patients—and the first three had been hectic yet standard. A seemingly endless line of people seeking creams and vaccines and pills to cure illnesses that had been eradicated in almost every other part of the world flocked to the medical tent.

Yet John had taken the job to help those most in need, the castaways and pariahs. No child labeled a witch would come anywhere near the tent, knowing that the throngs of crowds would lose all presence of pleasantness at the sight of them. And so, after closing the tent practice up one evening, John ventured out onto the streets, searching for the *skolombo*.

Sam went with him. The Niger Delta was dangerous for Westerners at the best of times and after nightfall it was borderline suicidal to go walking alone. Yet Sam understood the draw. A tall, compassionate, aid worker of Ibibio origin, Sam and John had met and become friends during John's first trip to Nigeria nearly two decades earlier. As a local, Sam understood the nature of the city and knew all the dwelling spots of the banished children.

On the first night, they found seventeen of them, ranging in age from four to sixteen, routing through the trash in a back alley near a road where food vendors sold their wares in daylight. Tattered, bedraggled, and some nearly feral, they were nonetheless happy to get bottled water, food, and much needed ointments and medicines; John strongly suspected that most of their ill health was due as much to parasites as neglect.

For the next two nights, John and Sam ventured out after dark tending to the witch children. John would never forget their shallow faces and sad eyes and scars. The little boy in the torn blue shirt with scald marks all over his leg. The girl with a machete gash across her cheek. The toddler whose bare feet were so blistered that he could barely walk. John came to think of them as the innocent damned.

On the third night of his nighttime exploits—his sixth overall evening in Nigeria—he was confronted. A group of young men surrounded him and Sam and the castaway children and started shouting accusations at them about "helping witches." It had been unnerving since, instead of dispersing, the young men had grown from three to five and then to seven. The children sensibly scattered into the night and Sam had started shouting at the young men in their (his) native Ibibio, warning them not to become violent or they would anger aid workers...people who had the kind of political clout that could end in arrests. That was enough to diffuse the situation, but they shot menacing glares back over their shoulders. The look of utter conviction in their eyes frightened John...they truly believed every word they said.

The encounter haunted him, disturbed him in the deepest recesses of his mind. It played over and over like a broken record, making it difficult for him to focus on his patients. On his last evening in Nigeria, a Sunday, he asked Sam to take him to one of the infamous nighttime masses at one of the more fervent churches. Sam initially hesitated, citing that John's white skin and blue eyes would make him stand out like a sore thumb, but John insisted and persisted and that was how he found himself outside of the Redemption Through Faith Church an hour after sunset.

It was a large white building that had been assembled to look like a palace but built with easy-to-come-by materials. It was brightly lit though, with countless gold-trimmed crucifixes and statues of Jesus and Mary and the apostles positioned everywhere. At the front center of the church was a stage where a pastor preached to the congregation about the dangers of witchcraft—at turns inciting them to dance or sing or clap or pray aloud, arms and legs jittering and twitching as the spirts of dark left them and the spirit of light entered. It was chaotic yet controlled; the room buzzed with the nervous dangerous energy of extremism.

John was raised Roman Catholic so he recognized most of the icons, the prayers, the songs...yet this was altogether different from the serene and often droll masses of Ireland. It looked jovial, but there was a violent harshness to the words, an accusatory theme that ran through the vein of the crowd. A paranoia. And, over again and again were the words magic, witches, hexes.

John stayed to the back, watching as the enormous crowd swayed and chanted and cheered. At one point, a group of adults ran holy water over a crying confused toddler. The water, they hoped, would free the child of the wicked they claimed had bewitched him. It was all so familiar yet alien—Christianity through the scope of much older, more ancient, and apparently more potent beliefs. None of the priests John knew led masses like this.

Yet the presiding priest was no man, the clergy was a woman, Pastor Esther Adeyemi. She spoke with fury and excessive animation, driving her congregation into frenzy with every annunciation. It was as if she had bewitched each and every one of them, hypnotizing them to slavish servitude until they hung on her every word, as if spellbound by enchantment.

For the duration of the ceremony, Pastor Esther Adeyemi paid John absolutely no mind, seemingly unaware of his presence. Yet, towards the end, she glared at him from the stage. Her eyes met his directly and sent a chill straight down his spine. Aside from her gaze, she said nothing to him and made no motion towards him from her perch upon the podium.

"Let's go," Sam said with urgency and pulled at John's arm; clearly noticing the pastor's eyes upon them. John wanted to move but felt as if he couldn't, like he was frozen in place. The sermon ended abruptly with the congregation still dancing and chanting and hailing the Lord feverishly. Under the lights, it looked more like a scene from a nightclub than a mass. Pastor Esther Adeyemi seemingly glided off the stage and hurried down the aisle, parting withering worshippers like Moses had parted the Red Sea. Within seconds, she stood before John. She was tall for a woman, over six feet, yet she towered above him as if sixty stories higher than he. A teenage boy trailed behind her like a small security guard.

"You don't believe my words, eh?" she snapped at John, forsaking any greeting or pretense of politeness. Before he could utter a sound of response, she extended her pointer finger and poked him, her hard eyes beaming with loathing. "Don't even try to deny it, I can hear your thoughts! The Lord has given me powers that you *Oyinbo* don't understand!"

Oyinbo, John knew, was a term used to describe westerners, whites, outsiders. Clearly, Pastor

Esther Adeyemi didn't like such people in the vicinity of her church.

"You question my God-given abilities, eh?" she continued, despite his utter lack of comment. "I see witches and wizards! I protect people from them. But you...*you aid them!*"

She spat the final three words so viciously that others noticed. John felt suffocated as he realized that he was surrounded by Pastor Esther Adeyemi's parishioners, all of whom were staring at him suspiciously. Pastor Esther Adeyemi was also staring at him even more intently, seemingly reading his mind. Her eyes burned with rage.

"You offer them food, clothes, medical assistance," she hissed. "I see all! You go under the cover of darkness to assist the cursed who plague us! Those who killed their own mothers, those who spread famine and disease, those who feed on human flesh! You like them? Are you one of them, Oyinbo? Do you come to Africa to destroy us like your ancestors tied to? Is that why you come to my church? To challenge me? To size me up and report back to the possessed? Are they your masters now? Eh?"

She continued her triad but suddenly, despite the absurdity and menace of the situation, John felt his temper rise. His mind flashed back to all the children he had seen on the streets—starving, scared, traumatized beyond all hope, most of their lives ruined before their ages reached the double-digits. And, before he knew it, he was shouting at Pastor Esther Adeyemi.

"Are you fucking mad?!" John roared in her face but his voice was dulled by the music and praises of the large congregation around them, most of whom were blessedly unaware of the exchange. "They're just children! Innocent vulnerable children! They don't cause illnesses, or hunger, or death but you reap all of that upon them!"

The pastor's eyes were wide, brewing lividness, and something more...something sinister coiled beneath the surface of her dark smooth skin. Clearly, she was not used to being challenged or spoken to in such a way...but John proceeded. Staring her down, he pointed at the teenage boy behind her.

"Look at that boy there! How is he so different from the children you condemned? How do you know *he* doesn't fly around at night on a broom and cast spells and eat flesh? How do we know *you* don't?"

"That's my son!" Pastor Esther Adeyemi shrieked, completely losing her composer for the first time. "Don't you dare accuse my son of any such things you ignorant akata!"

This time John knew he had gone too far, pushed her over the edge, but he couldn't seem to stop. Seeing her get so angry, so unnerved, was recklessly satisfying.

"Everything you say, it's all nonsense! Anyone can accuse anyone else and, at a word, their life can be over! Does that seem Christian to you? Does that seem like what Jesus would do?"

He expected her to start screaming, perhaps even physically launch at him, but instead she leaned back and smiled ruefully, sizing him up. Over her shoulder, her son offered the same smirking grin.

"Oh, you mind your words," she nearly whispered through clenched teeth. "You know nothing of me, of my people, of Africa. You want to condemn me? Condemn my son? Protect the witches that hex our followers?"

She was speaking through grit teeth but still grinning; the effect was nothing short of demonic. She took a step forward and Sam practically jumped back. John, however, stood his ground even as she reached out and clamped her hand onto his bare forearm. In a hurried whisper, she started reciting something in a language he didn't recognize—it wasn't Yoruba, but it could have been Igbo, or Urhobo, or Hausa, or Ibibio or more than 500 other possibilities. Whatever it was, Sam recognized it; he gasped audibly as she uttered it for all of three seconds. As soon as her strange chant was complete, Pastor Esther Adeyemi released John's arm.

"Leave this place," she commanded and, for just a moment, John swore her eyes flashed red.

Then Sam was dragging him out of the church, practically running. He was shaking all over and wouldn't speak until they had made it back to their campsite which was conveniently protected by armed guards.

"What was that all about?" John asked and managed to utter a little laugh even though his stomach was in knots. For the first time, he realized that he too was trembling.

"She hexed you," Sam gulped. "That was no prayer, that was older, darker. I didn't understand half of it, but it was bad. She is no woman of God, no matter what her followers think."

"I'm glad I'm leaving tomorrow," John replied. "I do believe I've overstayed my welcome."

"You need help!" Sam urged. "We need to get you to a healer. It will cost money but we have to disperse whatever she did or—"

John snickered. "No way! Come on, Sam, she's just a con artist. She probably made up half those words."

Sam stared at him, obviously terrified. John was astounded, he had always fancied Sam as a pragmatist, a realist. Much like himself.

* * *

That night, John had nightmares. He couldn't remember any of them upon waking, but they were all rooted in the jungles and involved children and potions and blood and witches...of course, witches. Clearly, the encounter with the less-than-delightful pastor had affected him more than he initially thought.

* * *

Monday

A little after sunrise, John gathered his packed bag and headed for the airport. Sam bid him a polite farewell but wouldn't hug him as usual; it was as if he was afraid to touch him.

"Be careful, you're marked," he warned.

On the way to the taxi, and on the drive to the airport, John noticed more roadside stands selling gris-gris and voodoo wares than he had ever seen before. He also felt eyes upon him, as if everyone in the markets he passed through could see the mark on him. Even the cab driver seemed nervous and uneasy in his presence. He didn't even attempt to make small talk and kept glancing into the rearview mirror, as if he expected John to attack him at any moment.

I'm being hypersensitive, John thought. *I'm tired. I'll sleep on the plane.*

Yet sleep did not come easily. John got to the airport and paid the driver who took the money and promptly peeled off as if he was participating in a rally. John checked into Aer Lingus and waited patiently at the terminal but he couldn't relax. He tried to read the paper and browse the shops, but he couldn't shake the sensation of unease.

As soon as he claimed his seat on the flight, he noticed the stewardesses looking at him oddly, as if they too sensed a general sort of *wrongness*. He put it to the back of his mind and tried to sleep, but he couldn't get comfortable. He spent the entire ten-hour flight tossing and turning whilst vainly attempting to nap. At one point, he opened his eyes and jumped visibly, surprising the middle-aged woman sitting beside him. For a split second, he saw something dark and shadowy slip underneath the seats adjacent to him. Then it was gone, and he closed his eyes again, and unwillingly replayed the scene at the mass over and over whilst desperately wishing it would recede from his memory permanently.

* * *

The plane landed at 7:20pm on Monday evening. John felt discombobulated as he walked through Dublin Airport and was glad to have no time zone difference to adjust to nor any bags to collect; he always took a sole carry-on whenever he traveled alone.

Alannah was waiting for him with Eoin in her arms; he saw them as soon as he stepped out of the terminal gate. The sight of them made his heart flutter and, for the first time since its occurrence, the incident in the church was firmly pushed out of his mind.

Eoin looked bigger. It sounded strange because John had only seen him nine days before, but the time had made a difference. Looking at his son's smiling face reminded John of the Nigerian children he had seen on the streets. Few of them smiled.

Alannah was reaching out to place Eoin in John's arms when she stumbled. For a horrible moment, Eoin was falling towards the tiled floor before John caught him; his quick reflexes had remained even as he descended into middle age.

"Whoa, gotcha there, lad!" John crooned to Eoin who nestled into his chest, seemingly oblivious to his close-call. John turned his attention to Alannah.

"Are you all right?"

"Fine, fine," she jittered nervously. It was obvious that she was not fine. She was rigid and her eyes were lit with worry.

"Alannah, what's the matter?"

She inhaled and looked away. "Nothing, not really. We just had a bit of a scare on the way here and I suppose I've not fully recovered yet."

"What happened?"

"Eoin nearly got hit by a car."

"Where?!"

"Right outside, in the car park. He got away from me and darted right out into the aisle. A car was coming around the corner, it looked like it was going too fast and I thought he was going to get struck dead-on but the driver stopped just in time. The breaks literally squealed. The woman driving was even more shaken up than I was."

She was sort of laughing, sort of smiling, but only barely managing to mask her fear and shaky voice. John enveloped her with his free arm.

"It's okay, love, nothing happened. The wane's got a good guardian angel."

Alannah allowed herself to lean towards John, encasing Eoin between them. She nodded in agreement, but had tears in her eyes. She was shaking slightly. The near miss must have been very near indeed...John had never before seen his wife so spooked.

"It's not just that," Alannah said, pulling away and taking the baby so John could readjust his bag. "Eoin cried all night, he never does that. It frightened me. I thought he was sick or having an aneurysm or something and then to have this car thing, I grabbed him and that car stopped just on time..." She trailed off, then offered a wan smile. "I'm just glad to have you home. We all missed you."

"It's okay, love," John crooned. "These things happen. Babies cry and Eoin isn't used to the big city. He's excitable at the best of times. We just have to watch him much more closely here."

* * *

The exiting of the airport was uneventful, as was much of the four-hour car ride back to the west. John insisted on driving; he was a notoriously bad passenger. Eoin cried and fussed most of the way, which was very unusual. He normally slept on car trips.

"I hope he's not colicky," Alannah said after numerous unsuccessful attempts to comfort the child. John nodded grimly, Eoin had not had issues with colic before and he hoped he wasn't starting. It was a bad dose.

Eoin's incessant crying was unnerving and harping on John's already frayed and tired mind. A few times he glanced at his son via the rearview mirror and thought he saw movement darting off from the corners of his eyes. The elusive shadows eventually distracted him to the point that he nearly swerved into a ditch. After that, he let Alannah drive and he took over trying to comfort Eoin. Eventually, both father and son drifted off to sleep.

* * *

John woke up just as Alannah turned into the driveway. A wave of relief washed over him when he laid his eyes upon the familiar white house with the well-tended evergreen shrubs surrounding its base. No sooner had she turned off the car's engine than Tommy emerged from the house to greet them.

"Good to see ya, I only burned half the place down," Tommy joked and gave John a pat on the back. They got on fantastically, but hugging was not part of their repertoire.

"Still doing things half-assed then, eh? My whole nine days away didn't change you a bit."

"He's been working all-nighters at the pub, beside himself with grief missing you," Alannah said, exiting the car and carefully scooping up sleeping Eoin.

"How's the little man?" Tommy asked.

"Don't wake him!" Alannah half whispered half hissed. "He's still fussy."

Tommy's concern could be clearly read in his eyes. John was habitually touched by Tommy's displays of genuine affection towards his young cousin.

"It's probably nothing," John told the younger man. "Just a little bug most likely, it happens to everyone."

Tommy nodded but his expression didn't waver. Soon thereafter he headed off to work. It was already after 11pm.

* * *

John unpacked his sparse bag and had a cup of tea with Alannah. Eoin slept peacefully in his crib for all of twenty minutes before awaking, screaming uncontrollably. John and Alannah took turns holding him as they watched the late-night news. John was relieved to see nothing concerning witch hunts come across the screen, he had enough experience with that subject to last him a lifetime. At nearly two in the morning, Eoin fell back to sleep. Shortly thereafter, John and Alannah collapsed into bed, utterly exhausted.

John was asleep before his head hit the pillow and the dreams started immediately.

He was back in Africa, standing in front of a gaggle of petrified, ostracized, bedraggled children. A group of angry adults surrounded them, Pastor Esther Adeyemi chief among them.

"These children aren't witches! There are no witches!" John shouted.

"No witch, no witch, no witch," the surrounders sang mockingly, pointing and laughing and making faces that walked the line between silly and menacing; disturbing behavior nonetheless. Suddenly everyone's—even Pastor Esther Adeyemi's—eyes grew wide and their faces fell in utter terror. They pointed at something behind John and then turned, fleeing into the jungles screaming in fear. Except for Esther, she didn't run. She stood firmly and her fear turned to glee. Joyously meanspirited, she laughed and laughed and laughed. John wanted to turn around to see what they had seen, but he was glued to the road, unable to turn his body or head. He distinctively heard the *whoosh* of the people running and their screams...or, specifically, a man screaming and carrying on...in English...nearby...and he could smell the fires of hell creeping closer and closer—

John snapped awake and was surprised to register the sunlight that was filtering in through the lacey white curtains. He had clearly slept several hours, but he still felt groggy and disoriented. He heard a THUD and saw Alannah getting up off the floor; the weird whooshing noise had startled her so badly that she had fallen out of the bed and was struggling to get up.

"What's happened? What is it?" Panic laced her words.

John swung himself out of bed and nearly lost his balance, his knees were heavy and his legs were weak from tiredness. Yet the sounds coming from the adjacent room, Eoin's room, brought him right back to clarity of the high-alert variety. It was obvious that something bad had happened, or was currently underway. Eoin was screaming, not just crying but truly *screaming*, and so was Tommy.

John sprinted into his son's bedroom to find Tommy holding the tiny red fire extinguisher from the kitchen. White foam covered the right wall, the one nearest to the crib where Eoin sat scream-sobbing.

"The nightlight went on fire!" Tommy shouted. "I came home and smelled the smoke! Didn't you smell it? Why didn't the fire alarm go off?"

John stared at the wall; the thick foamy coating could not completely hide the blackened circle around the plug which was still slightly smoking. The clown nightlight that Alannah brought for Eoin's first Christmas had melted away into an indistinguishable charred heap. Alannah picked Eoin up and held him tightly to her.

"How could this happen?!" she shrieked. "We just changed the batteries!"

"How didn't you smell it?" Tommy shouted, obviously very shaken. "I came home and the house was filled with smoke. I grabbed this—" he shook the fire extinguisher for reference—"and ran upstairs. The flames were halfway up the wall! Eoin was terrified! How didn't you hear or smell it?"

"We were sleeping," Alannah sputtered. "How could the fire alarm not have sounded?! How is that even possible? It's a name brand!"

"Ah, they're all made in China for cheap," John spat. "It's malfunctioned. I'm going to have a word with the company."

He turned to Tommy who was still standing beside the wall, grasping the fire extinguisher. He was visibly trembling.

"Thank God you came home when you did," John said. "The flames were close to his crib. You saved his life." And then, for perhaps only the second time in his life, he embraced his adopted son. "Thank you."

At last, Tommy eased his grip on fire extinguisher and Eoin eventually ceased crying and Alannah finally stopped shaking. A little over an hour after the incident, John decided to go back to bed, but he checked the fire alarm first. Its little light was green and blinking. All seemed to be in perfectly working order...but then why hadn't it sounded? Even more chillingly, exactly what had started the fire?

Faulty wiring, the words echoed through John's mind like nails on a chalkboard. If the fire had been the result of faulty wiring then it could happen again, at any time, in any room.

* * *

Tuesday

John awoke to the sound of Eoin crying and shrieking at the top of his lungs; it seemed improbable that anything so small could produce such big noise. Eoin had seemingly developed an odd aversion to being left alone; too young to speak but apparently seeing something troubling that no one else did. John gave him a dose of gripe water and that seemed to soothe him. That afternoon, Alannah suggested that a walk down by the seaside would do them all good.

They got Eoin dressed and into the pram without issue, and the first forty minutes of their walk was lovely and relaxing and uneventful. Then, just as they walked past the fish and chip shop, they heard a young woman scream:

"Bailey! No!"

In an instant a large, rambunctious, dog was racing towards them. His tongue was hanging out, his tail was wagging, and he seemed entirely excitably harmless, but he was big. And when he ran past Eoin's stroller, he violently knocked it over, sending Eoin spilling out onto the concrete and promptly restarting his wails.

The girl was horrified. "He slipped the leash! This never happened before! I'm so sorry, is he hurt?"

John was down on his knees beside the toppled stroller, checking over every inch of his son that wasn't swaddled in thick warm clothing.

"He's not bleeding and he was strapped in so I doubt anything's broken. I think he's okay, just rattled."

So was Alannah, who was hyperventilating. A crowd had gathered and the young woman looked as if she wanted to say more, but then a man a block down started shouting in her direction. He had managed to catch the hyper dog and was holding it by the collar. Containing the captured canine looked like a considerable effort.

"We're okay, go on, collect your dog," John said and managed to muster a smile.

The girl sprinted off and Alannah grabbed the handles of the stroller, placing it upright.

"Are you *sure* he's fine?" she asked urgently.

"He's right as rain," John replied. "Look, he's not even crying. Let's take him to the park. A turn on the swings and a go down the slide will do him good."

That decision proved to be ill-fated when Eoin fell and hit his head on the side of the sandbox. Had John not managed to grab his arm and slightly suspend him, thus softening the blow, the injury would have been severe. That night, Eoin nearly choked on his dinner. John had to slam on the baby's back to get his air passage clear.

Eoin, it seemed, was quickly becoming one of the most chronically unfortunate children on the Irish shores.

* * *

Wednesday

John had planned to return to his local practice on Wednesday morning, but that plan derailed when Eoin escaped from his crib for the first time ever. He toddled over to the stairs and quickly tumbled down. John heard every sickly "thump." The accident resulted in a panicked ride to the Emergency Room. Alannah, normally not religious, took along her rosary beads and prayed over her sobbing son in the ambulance all the way to the hospital.

Incredibly, Eoin wasn't badly hurt aside from a few bruises. That night, however, he was not so lucky when he stopped breathing in his crib. On an inkling, John went in to check on the baby and saw his son turning blue. He revived him with CPR as Alannah called 999 to have the child rushed to the hospital for the second time in one day. Initially, Eoin was breathing very shallowly but the paramedics fully revived him in the ambulance.

Apparently, he had very nearly become a victim of Sudden Infant Death Syndrome (SIDS).

* * *

Thursday

Alannah and John spent all of the next day in the hospital under a cloud of understandable suspicion. Social workers and the police stopped by, the garda were required to ask questions when such a small child was repeatedly injured. They even wanted to speak to Tommy. They asked questions, but both John and Alannah knew the guards well, John had even gone to primary school with the local chief, and the authorities knew that he and Alannah would set themselves on fire before they harmed Eoin.

The doctors and law enforcers came to the conclusion that Eoin's accidents were nothing more than ill luck and nothing more and released him after twenty-four hours of observation. Despite all of his misfortunes, Eoin had been lucky in one respect: despite his topple down a steep flight of stairs, he had only minor bruises and a small cut above his lip to show for it. No broken bones, no concussion. It was, by all accounts, something of a miracle.

Alannah said it was his guardian angel.

* * *

Friday

Upon Eoin's return home from the hospital, Alannah wouldn't let him out of her sight. John took the day off, deciding to resume his regular work schedule after the weekend. That night, Alannah insisted that Eoin sleep in their room in a playpen with blankets.

"One of us will have to stay awake and watch him," she said. "He's had too many problems lately and if that SIDS thing happened once, it can happen again."

John agreed entirely.

Later, no one would be able to explain exactly what had happened. Both John and Alannah agreed to sleep in shifts and neither had felt particularly weary—nervous and stressed, yes, but not tired per se—but there was something about the bedroom threshold. As soon as he walked in, the room felt different to John. The atmosphere was heavier and the air seemed sweet and soothing. Somehow, he was registering a sweet melodic sound...like a lullaby. Although she didn't say it, John suspected that Alannah heard it too. Over the course of the evening both their eyelids grew heavy and, unwillingly and unwittingly, they both slumbered.

* * *

Saturday

When they woke up, they found Eoin. He had gotten out of the playpen, walked down the hallway foyer, and wandered into the slightly ajar closet. There, he found the clothes from the drycleaner hung neatly upon the racks. Obviously, for whatever reason, they had interested him because he went to them and got tangled up in the plastic. By the time he was found, he had been dead for about four hours.

It was then that John knew that whatever had been happening to his only child was more than coincidence. He knew that he had closed that closet door carefully and firmly. He had heard it click. Eoin certainly hadn't reached up to open it, and none of the adults in the house had reason to, but *something* had opened the door. To be precise, *something* had opened the door and then lured Eoin towards it, and the plastic, the same way *it* had first lulled his parents to sleep.

John screamed when he saw his son lying limp amid the plastic and started doing CPR, refusing to stop even as Alannah frantically screamed and wailed and beat his back, trying to get a hold of her child, as if her touch alone could resurrect him. It was Tommy who called 999. He helped the paramedics drag John away from his son's already cold corpse.

Eoin was pronounced dead at the scene but his body was carted off to the hospital along with John and Alannah and Tommy. They were all in shock but Alannah had seemingly lost her mind. She ranted on and on, claiming that she had seen shadowy figures circling around the baby since last Sunday evening. When Tommy confirmed that he had also seen *something* out of the corner of his eyes during the fire, John broke down and told his family, and the doctors, and the guards, all about what had happened in Africa.

"I've been hexed," he calmly explained and went on to tell anyone who would listen about Nigeria and the accusations of witch-children and the mass and Pastor Esther Adeyemi; above all, he spoke of her. He had become quite convinced that she was a powerful witch who used her abilities to turn people against each other, feeding off of negative energy and cursing anyone foolish enough to challenge her...foolish men like western John.

The authorities were investigating the case again, Alannah was under sedation, and Tommy was beside himself with grief yet it was Eoin, sweet baby Eoin, who was dead. John's world had collapsed. He felt numb from everything but the ceaseless anguish, the knowledge that he would never see Eoin grow into a boy, a teenager, a man. He would never forge a career, get married, have children, amass a lifetimes worth of stories. Those possibilities had all been taken away. Now what was left was a bleak future of shopping for a tiny coffin, shuffling along with the funeral procession, watching the little casket getting lowered into a tiny grave with a cherub headstone, and the reality that the cemetery was where his only child would lay forevermore. The finality was wrenching.

When he closed his eyes, John could almost hear the evil crackling laughter of "Pastor" Esther Adeyemi. He assumed this had been her intention all along; once he so much as pointed at her son, he had doomed his own. He couldn't imagine anything worse.

* * *

Sunday

Tommy remembered the day that his parents died. Had he not been staying at his granny and granddad's house that evening, he also would have perished in the collision. He was only six at the time, but he remembered sobbing at the sound of the words "there's been an accident" and the surge of anger he had felt when he heard that the drunk driver who had caused the whole mess had escaped his equally crumped vehicle completely unharmed. Yet Eoin's death was worse. Tommy had loved his little cousin as if he was his own. He knew Aunt Alannah would never recover from the loss nor have the ability to bear another child. And John, who had always treated him like a son, the sight of John sobbing and screaming and desperately, relentlessly, fruitlessly, performing CPR on his cold, blue, son's body was a scene that couldn't be erased from thought.

Both John and Alannah had been admitted to the hospital and the doctors had wanted to keep an eye on him too—he was in shock, they claimed—but Tommy couldn't stand the smell of the hospital halls or the grief that permeated so many of the wards. So, he had left and gone to Yvonne's house.

Tommy sometimes mentioned Yvonne in passing. John and Alannah assumed that they were friends, which was not incorrect, but they hadn't any idea of the depth of Tommy's feelings for Yvonne. He had never asked her out on a date, never showed her off to his friends, and had never even properly kissed her, but he saw her every day at work and, over the course of several years, he had come to love her. He was afraid to admit it, afraid to lose her like he had his mam and dad and now his cousin, but he did love her, and she knew it, even if she refused to take that first step and goad him into admitting it. Under her interrogation, he would come clean completely and immediately. Yet women like Yvonne didn't make the first move; she was a traditionalist to her core and doing such a thing wouldn't be proper. Still, Yvonne was unabashedly his best friend and whenever he needed her, she was there.

She let him into her home and told him how sorry she was. The whole county already knew what had happened courtesy of the local news. In the west of Ireland, bad news traveled fast.

Sitting on her couch—or, rather, her parents' couch—shrouded in her arms, Tommy had sobbed uncontrollably, letting it all out. He told her of the way Eoin had suddenly started crying all week and hadn't stopped; something that was completely uncharacteristic. He told her about how he could have sworn he saw a dark shadowy figure hunched up in the back seat of the car when John got home, and then how the house suddenly felt stuffy and creepy, giving him the sensation that eyes were upon him in every room no matter where he went or what he did. He told her about Eoin's ceaseless succession of accidents, the strange fire, the dog, the choking scare...And finally he told her about John's confession regarding his weird encounter with the crazy pastor, a woman he was convinced was a witch. The tale had given Tommy the heebie-jeebies. He wasn't normally superstitious, but the story made sense in the context of the timeline between Eoin starting to cry and fuss and the accidents and the death. Underneath it all, Tommy felt helpless and guilty; he hadn't been able to stop anything or save anyone.

Yvonne let him talk, clinging to him and rubbing her hand through his hair. Eventually she led him into her bedroom and lay down with him, holding him tightly to her—fully clothed, of course. Tommy appreciated the comfort, flabbergasted that it had been allowed under her family's roof. In the traditional west, it was taboo to share a bed before being wed, but he supposed her folks were too logical perceive his crumpled depressed self as a threat to their daughter's virtue.

He was surprised that sleep had come, but he did drift off. When he woke up in Yvonne's arms the next morning, he decided that he would marry her one day and announce her as his girlfriend soon. But first he would have to go to the hospital and check on Alannah and John. He supposed all Eoin's funeral arrangements would fall to him; it was a task that made him feel physically ill.

"I can't go yet," he told Yvonne when she awoke and offered to accompany him to the hospital. "I need to clear me head."

And that was how, an hour later, he found himself driving through the county roads. Yvonne was silently sitting shotgun, supportive but unsure what to say.

"Mind if I turn the radio on?" she inquired after some time.

Tommy gestured between a nod and a shrug, indifferent.

The Belle Stars *Iko Iko* blared through the speakers, Yvonne turned it down but it was still just loud enough to hear over the whispers of the wind. Tommy considered asking her to switch it off; for some reason that song—especially that version of it—gave him the creeps, but then relented. Yvonne likely needed the radio on; it was a distraction, a coping mechanism.

Tommy started to steer the car towards the hospital, knowing he would have to face the grim and terrible reality one way or another. He was thinking about Aunt Alannah and the dead look he had seen in her eyes and what he could possibly say to her and, as that cacophony of thoughts raced through his mind, the entity appeared on the road.

At first, he thought it was a man. It had initially looked like one. It stood on two legs and leap into the road like a man would. But it was far too tall and far too thin and far too solidly black to be a man. It wasn't wearing clothes and it had no discernible features side from a long large frame and a grinning jagged maw. Its sticklike arms ended in talons. It pointed them towards the car. They glinted in the sunlight like swords that would easily pierce through the windshield.

The last thing Tommy thought before he veered hard to the left, slammed the car head-first into a stone wall, and subsequently ended his life, was that the thing in the road was a biped but not a human. In his last moments, he finally understood exactly what he had seen lurking in the backseat of Alannah's car on the day John returned.

Yvonne survived the crash. She would later recant the accident in minuet-detail and describe how Tommy had screamed and swerved as if he was trying to avoid hitting something on the road.

But there had been nothing there at all.

* * *

The news of Tommy's death left Alannah on suicide watch. John was devastated but not nearly as surprised as one might expect. After all, he had legally adopted Tommy. It had attacked the *biological* child first, then the adopted one. Whatever it was, it was efficient. It had ended both of their existences within one week of the casting of the curse. John supposed it had already dissipated back to hell now that its mission was accomplished.

Unsurprisingly, John suffered a nervous breakdown. He abandoned his practice and committed himself to live in care, never speaking to anyone unless it was absolutely necessary. He had told them what happened, there was simply nothing more to say. The bank eventually stepped in and sold the house he and Alannah and Eoin and Tommy had once shared. The new tenants never reported feeling weird or unnerved inside of it. John wasn't surprised, the demonic, otherworldly, entity that had unraveled his life was long gone.

Now there was peace everywhere but inside his head. Sometimes, he still heard Pastor Esther Adeyemi's vengeful laughter. No wonder she knew so much about witchcraft and could speak with such conviction. She knew the practices that she spoke of very well, very intimately.

John knew that he should have listened to Alannah; he should have backed out of the trip. Yet the person whose advice he really should have heeded was that of his granny, a woman who thoroughly believed in magic and spells and all sorts of things that John had once scoffed at. She had told him that nothing was scarier or more dangerous than an angry witch and it was best to stay out of their vicinity. If she were still alive, John would have admitted that she was right about the existence of magic, but explained that she was wrong about witches and vicinities. The scariest most dangerous witch was a pissed off control freak...the precise variety that he had managed to cross to his ruination.

And while some hexes worked within parameters and vicinities, others *tracked*.

Sire

I keep hearing them crackling; I can't see them, but I hear them. At first, I thought it was just a distant wolf howling or my imagination playing up, but now I'm certain that they're here—somewhere amid the trees—maybe watching me, maybe not, but aware of me nonetheless. Them hags are aware of everything that goes on in these woods and I love 'em for it in spite of myself. Their presence makes these nightly camping excursions more interesting, I'll give them that, but I wish I could drag my nice soft bed out here with me. Sleeping on the rooty ground with nothing but a few wooly blankets and a little tarp tent gets really old, really fast. One day, the devil will take me for the things I do for the girls. Until then, my aching body will do the complaining every morning.

I've played out most of my life in these woods, alongside the things that dwell within it. I've lived in fascinated fear of them most of my life, which is funny considering that I started out being enchanted by them. Bone truth is, deep down, I miss them in a strange way. I think about them every day and wonder what would've become of me had I stayed on with them. I suppose it's only natural; man's a curious creature.

I knew they was running around in the woods since I was a boy growing up in a rickety wood cabin on the edge of the trees. We had a small farm consisting of one donkey, ten chickens, two goats, and a cow. We also had a big old hound dog who couldn't herd for nothing but was a darn good watch dog. If anybody came anywhere near the house, old Hank would start barking like he was possessed.

Hank saw them before I did, or *sensed* them anyway. As far back as I can remember, Hank would stand guard right on the edge of the woods line. He'd stare real fixedly and snarl and growl...not just at nighttime either, even in broad daylight he couldn't look into the forest without being on high alert. I reckon they was sneaking around even then—probably had been for over a century by that stage—but I only recall seeing glimpses of them here and there. My very first recollection is seeing one staring out at me from behind a tree. She was old and withered and raggedy and sharp-faced; glaring at me with coal-black eyes. I'd screamed and cried for my momma and she reassured me that it'd just been my imagination. We were on our own out there; we had no neighbors and town was about a hours' walk each way. Surely, there couldn't possibly be no woman in the woods. Momma then turned all angry on my pa and blamed him for telling me the story of Hansel and Gretel and the scary old witch. She said he'd put ideas in my head. Truthfully, he just allowed me to put a name to what I'd been seeing long before I ever heard that old fairy tale: witches. Them things in the woods were witches.

Back then, I didn't know exactly where the coven lived but I knew they wasn't far away and they had a real fascination with our farm. We'd often lose chickens during the night. Mostly they just disappeared but a few times, later on especially, some blood and feathers would be left behind as if in ritual.

Pa said it was foxes but he never sounded none too convinced of that. Looking back, I reckon my father was well aware that bad things lurked in those woods. My momma did too; she'd get all jittery if we was outside and she heard as much as a twig snap. I don't know if she ever got a glimpse of one, but she never missed as much as one Sunday church sermon. I suppose all that praying was her way of seeking protection from a threat she couldn't describe or explain. My folks might've had their suspicions, but they ain't never said nothing to me. Of course, they didn't have to say anything to me. I knew more than anyone else because I had seen more than anybody. Those hags had a fancy for me from day one.

They was always lurking around the woods, but when I was five, they got bolder and started staring in at me from the window. If I had the poor luck of waking up in the middle of the night, I'd get a nasty shock when I looked over at the window to see several of those raggedy women staring in at me, grinning. I woke up screaming more nights than I can count. Momma blamed the fairy tales but I knew them women were as real as the moon.

The old hags could move fast too; they were always away from the window when pa and momma burst into my room.

To be honest, not all of them were hags. Some of them were young—and later several were beautiful, which is really how the whole mess started in the first place—and occasionally they seemed kind and friendly; more akin to angels than witches. I was about four the first time I really took notice of the one who called herself Blythe. She looked to be only a few years older than me and she had a soft smile. At night she'd come to the window closest to my bed (she always seemed to know when I couldn't sleep) and we'd make funny faces at each other—she standing outside and me lying in bed—until I got sleepy enough to doze off. Sometimes she'd hum lullabies to me...just loud enough for me to hear but she never woke my folks.

I liked being an only child and when I found out my momma was expecting I was none too pleased. I went up to the window the night I found out and I tearfully told Blythe about how I didn't want no brother or sister. She nodded at me with sympathy in her eyes and took my hand in hers. She listened close, even though she didn't say nothing. Blythe was as quiet as a spider. I was elated a little while later to hear I wasn't gonna have none, although I was sorry to see momma laid up in bed crying. I understand now that she had—and then kept having—miscarriages and she didn't know why...although I did. I'd willed it without even understanding that I'd done so.

I was twelve going on thirteen when the Civil War started. I was too young to get called up and pa was too old so we just continued life as if nothing was wrong; our neck of the woods saw no fighting and the soldiers didn't descend on our little town neither. I suppose you could say we was real lucky, or we had a little extra "protection."

As the war raged on around us, near but distant, boys only a little older than me was losing their lives every day. As for me, I kept my life but gave my soul to something much worse than soldiers.

Blythe was the start of it, of course, as I always knew she'd be. Her visits to me had become more frequent and they wasn't only confined to the nighttime anymore. It had started when she took to peeking at me from the woods, in broad daylight, as I did my daily chores. Now, they'd always been there, creeping and peeking, but Blythe got close. She wanted me to know she was there. Hell, she was my friend.

I was about seven when our kinship initially started up and over the course of the following five years, we took to playing hide and seek and tag whenever I could sneak away. As usual, Blythe never spoke a word, I don't think she could. Her sisters—I suppose that's as good a thing to call them as any—could speak, rave even, in my language and tongues far older, but Blythe was mute. She was also beautiful and seemed to grow up right with me, except lovelier and lovelier the older I got.

When I was twelve, I started to notice her piercing blue eyes, jet black hair, and magenta lips with increasing interest. She was lithe yet curvy in all the right places. When I was thirteen, I went down to the river to get some washing water for my momma who was having one of her bad spells, a day when she did nothing but lie around the house. That happened more and more after she started losing all the babies. Anyway, while I was down at the water, Blythe crept out of the woods. I smiled at her, thinking she was just gonna stand on the shore and stare at me like she so often did—she never helped me with the chores—but instead she descended into the water, way past her knees, up to her thighs. In the process of doing so, she lifted her skirt high enough to give me a full view of her long legs. I stared and she stopped and looked right at me. She smiled coyly and then she giggled—which was the most noise I'd ever heard her make when she wasn't humming some strange tune—splashed some water in my direction, and darted off back into the woods, leaving me standing there by my lonesome and wishing (*yearning*) for more of her legs and laugh and company.

I saw her again two days later and that's when she offered me the apple. A rare sort of red, savory juicy, I can still feel it on my lips. I suppose that was that was the day of my indoctrination since my absolute *obsession* with Blythe started then. I thought about her constantly, even dreamt about her, and as if she knew it, she started getting flirtier with me. She would still meet me in the woods to play like we had when we was kids—or when I *was* a kid and she *looked* like a kid—but she started flashing her legs at me more...well, at first it was her legs but, over time, she let me catch flashes of other, more intimate parts of her, too. Always from a bit of a distance, mind you, she wouldn't ever stand still long enough to let me touch her—not as if I'd the nerve to begin with, mind you—but she'd taken to touching me whenever she could. She'd jump out at me from behind the trees and stroke my hair, or run her palm down my chest—which drove me wild even with my shirt on—and she'd even reach out and squeeze my leg on occasions when we was sitting next to each other. But if I tried to touch her, she'd stand up and run off into the woods, giggling like the tease she was.

She was driving me crazy and it only got worse when she started bringing her friends—or sisters, or whatever the hell they were—with her. One was more succulent than the next. There was the busty blonde named Anne who wasn't shy about complimenting me and looking me over in a way that made my heart hammer in my chest. Joan was a brunette with black eyes that were as pretty as Blythe blues and she was the *really* touchy feely one. But no matter how much they surrounded me and fawned over me and hand-fed me impossibly fresh apples and grapes, they never let me get too comfortable and they never let things go as far as I wanted. And whenever we was out in the woods together, I'd always spy other shapes creeping about; the old ones lurking. I suppose they were spying on us, making sure all went according to plan.

I'd become so enthralled by the woods that I started neglecting my chores. On a few occasions, I'd wandered home late and my pa had given me a heck of a belting while my momma screamed and cried and begged him to stop. She was disturbed by how thin I'd grown; I hadn't been eating on the regular. My only appetite at the time had nothing to do with food.

Hank, the dog, went first. My pa and I found him all ripped up on the edge of our farm. My pa thought it was a fox, but I thought the slashes looked more like claws or talons—like a lady's fingernails—more than teeth. I can't say I was angry; I couldn't *prove* them women of the woods had anything to do with the old dog's death and it was one less mouth to feed.

My father went next; then my mother. Both were taken by fever. They came down sick without me noticing too much at first—I was mighty distracted most days, after all—but when I saw them sicking up and feverish, I instantly ran to the woods. I screamed for Blythe and the others and I begged them for help; I somehow knew they could make potions. Yet I was just calling into the trees. No one came. I thought I'd been forsaken and walked home feeling sick and panicky...only to find a pretty green glass bottle at my doorway. Relief washed over me like rainwater. See, I still loved my folks dearly and I would've done anything to save them. I made sure both my parents drank from the bottle and then I took a swig from it too. I don't know why I did, I wasn't ailing none, but it just seemed like a good idea at the time.

It was sweet yet it had a sharp aftertaste. I ain't never tasted nothing like it before or since but I ain't never forgot it or what it did. As soon as I swallowed it down, I felt completely relaxed and at peace with everything, which is pretty goddamn weird considering both my parents were dying, but I slept like a baby that night. Within a fortnight both my folks had passed on but I didn't cry or make any fuss at all, it's like I was incapable of feeling sadness. I calmly walked outside in the light of day and started digging two graves. I had no desire to alert the town or setup a church mass...my parents had been happy living on that farm for nearly two decades and they'd be happy staying there for eternity.

As I was digging, I heard branches crack behind me. I turned around and saw Blythe standing there, her big eyes looking at me not with sympathy, but with a kind a longing—a *yearning*—that I ain't never seen in her before. Anne and Joan followed close behind her and all three of them helped me finish the burials and mark the graves with rocks. Then Blythe, who was still my favorite of all, took my hand and pulled me into the woods with Joan and Anne following. Them two was giggling but

Blythe was just smiling. Back then I thought her grin was soft and sweet, but looking back now I realize that there was something wolffish right under the surface.

That was the day my life either began or ended, depending on how you look at it. It was certainly when things got weird though.

Blythe led me by hand through the woods to a cabin that was nestled between a grove of trees and a mountain rock. They took me inside and gave me another sip of something—this time out of a blue bottle—that sent my head spinning in the nicest possible way.

They led me to a tub of nice warm water, which was a rarity back when I was sixteen, and all three of the young ones stripped me naked before scrubbing me down with fresh soap and getting all the dirt and grim off my skin and outta my hair. Blythe was just smiling but Anne and Joan were commenting on how nice and muscular I was. After my bath, they dried me off with a towel as soft as velvet and led me to a nice soft bed. Each one of them took turns making me a man. I was happy Blythe went first because she was special, although as I watched her face contort in pleasure I couldn't help but notice that it was changing, altering...At times it looked like she was about a thousand years old, which should've disturbed me, but I was too wrapped in euphoria to startle.

And that's how things went for some unknown length of time. I stayed lying in that bed all day, drinking their potions and eating their food, sleeping soundly entwined in their plush blankets with my head resting on their soft pillows, and making love to the young ones every night. At first it was just Blythe and Anne and Joan but then there were others and I couldn't keep track of anything and I didn't care that I couldn't.

I was aware of the older women being around. They looked like hags but they cooked well and didn't try to mess with me so I didn't mind them. Occasionally, I'd have a nightmare about sharp-toothed, gaping-mawed, demon-women chasing me through the trees and I'd wake up in a cold sweat, startling all the girls (*coven*) lying around me. Then they'd give me a swig of one of their potions and it would all go away and all would be well again.

Occasionally, I'd come out of my pleasure-stupor enough to notice that some of the girls' bellies were extending; swelling like pumpkins in autumn in a way that could only mean pregnancy. They were growing my children inside of them. That realization initially horrified me so much that I physically recoiled and let out a little scream. They laughed and surrounded me and let me feel their bellies—something was moving inside them, but it felt more like a festering nest of ants then a baby—as they poured more of that sweet potion down my throat and sent my hazy head back into oblivion.

As blissfully out-of-it as I was back then, there are some things I recall. I suppose the war was still going on 'because I'd occasionally hear the sound of lost soldiers roaming around the woods. The ladies would throw a blanket over me to keep me (*their treasure*) warm and hidden (*safe*) before leaving the cabin. I'd sometimes just be able to make out vague voices; conversations that went from chatter to panic to screaming. Afterwards, the ladies would use the scraps of their uniforms to sew themselves new dresses—and prettying the garments up with shiny brass buttons and the occasional ring—and one of the old hags would cook up a nice meaty stew and share some with me. Over the years, I can't count how many times I've had a hankering to taste that delicious meal again.

Other times I'd hear babies crying or gurgling. Some sounded right, like what I assumed a human child should sound like, and others *didn't*. The crying always stopped, sometimes by itself and somethings after I heard a good hard sickening THUD, but it always stopped eventually. Then I'd see the ladies busying themselves around the caldron, brewing up a skin cream that made them all look younger (*fresher*), even the old ones.

Sometimes, I'd catch glimpses of the women nursing babies at their bosoms. Anne and Joan used to do it right in front of me but they wouldn't never let me see the children's (*my children's*) faces. I got a feeling they kept the girls only; they was replenishing the coven. I have no idea how long their kind lives—because I'm now certain that there ain't nothing human about them—but some of the older ones had to be close to the end. Perhaps that's why they needed me.

Blythe's belly never grew. Even though she visited me in the bed most often, and most tenderly, she never grew my seed. I have no idea why that still makes me a little sad—given the horror of what was happening to those (*my*) youngins'—but it does. Blythe's special to me, always will be.

A few times a year, which I now reckon to be the two equinoxes and solstices, they'd leave the cabin and descend into the woods. I was so curious one night that I decided to follow them. I had to gather my strength to get out of the bed and my legs and feet felt cramped and sore since I hadn't been walking in a while. I spied them just beyond the tree grove, all of them dancing stark naked around a big bonfire. I wasn't able to take my eyes off them even though I was scared that they was gonna see me and get mad and crack my skull open like they'd done to most of the babes. Yet after about an hour, Blythe did spot me and did nothing but smile. Later, they all led me back to the cabin and Blythe loved me to sleep while Anne and Joan lounged nearby, lulling a sweet song in a language that only their kind could understand.

And so that's how it was for years; maybe as long as a decade or more. I lived every young man's fantasy and probably would've kept on doing it if they hadn't evicted me.

It wasn't as harsh as it sounds. I always figured that when they got tired of me, they'd simply kill me and eat me like they did to the soldiers and the occasional band of runaway slaves who had the misfortune of crossing the cabin's path. Yet Blythe had other ideas. Although she never spoke, she was somehow the most commanding of them. Hell, for all I know she's the oldest and is just real good at masking it. One day, when I was a grown man with a full beard and fuller belly, she dressed me, and helped me off the bed, and led me out of the cabin. We walked hand-in-hand out of the woods in much the same way that we'd walked into it so many years before. She brought me back to my childhood home. My parent's graves were overgrown, the stones covered in moss, and the barn was barely standing, but a rush of memories came at me nonetheless.

I told her I didn't want to stay here. I begged her to go back to the cabin (*coven*) and the warmth of her bed (*body*) but she shook her head firmly. She handed me a pouch full of sand—or what normal folks would mistake for sand—and pointed outwards towards the farm and the trees and what lay beyond them. Without one word uttered, I'd been given my instructions, assigned my fate. I would've compiled regardless, but I'm mighty glad that she saw fit to give me one final intimate kiss before she slipped back into the woods and disappeared among the trees.

It was strange going back to town. A lot had changed and most folks didn't know me and assumed I was a hobo or a drifter; I hadn't shaved in a while. Pa had been a poor man but a savvy one and he had saved some coins in a mason jar that he'd buried under the porch. I dug it up and had just enough in pocket to get a wash and a shave, some food and a paper. The old feller behind the counter at the general store seemed to recognize me, although he didn't say nothing. It took me a moment to recognize him since, when I'd been there last, he was a man of thirty or so and now he looked like a granddaddy. I sure as heck ain't aged that much. Whatever the girls put into those potions clearly worked.

The paper said there'd been a war, not the Civil War but another one, and now a third was brewing. The country was in trouble, everybody was poor. Money men in New York City were jumping out of windows and out west there was some awful freak of nature going on called the Dust Bowl. It sounded more like a hex or a spell than anything natural, but of course I didn't say that to nobody. In fact, I didn't say one word to nobody then and haven't much since. I'm sure my conversation skills are well and truly lacking.

With my foray into town over, I went back to the farm and spread the sand (*ground baby bones*) all over the edges of my property. I knew damn well it was a protection spell; a long-lasting one at that. I saw how the world was changing when I went into my once-sleepy village; people riding around on machines rather than horses and women wearing outfits that showed off more of their physiques than my momma woulda thought proper...and the town was bigger, a LOT bigger, than it had been when I was a boy. It's only a matter of time before more people come and then folks start walking around those woods.

And Blythe knew it.

We can't let nobody find them...or me. I'll start fixing up my homestead, although I reckon I'm about eight decades old I don't feel or look more than thirty-five or so. I can do it. The work will put muscles on me, just the way they like it.

If the coven needs a place to run to (*sanctuary*), I can provide such safety. And it's not just because if I fail, they'll tear me limb-from-limb and use my parts for potions—which they would, but that's beside the point. There's a reason I built that old farmstead back up, there's a cause behind me camping out yonder every night just to hear the cold-comfort of their calls and rustling, there's a method behind my unending diligence to their preservation.

I protect them, because that's what patriarchs do.

~About the Author~

Meagan J. Meehan is a published author of novels, short stories, children's books, poems and cartoons. She is a produced playwright and screenwriter who has had the honor of seeing her work grace both the stage and screen. She is also a stop-motion animator, curator, an award-winning abstract artist and the founder of the "Conscious Perceptionalism" art movement. Meagan presently works as a journalist and as a college professor focusing on art and writing. She holds a Bachelors in English Literature from New York Institute of Technology (NYIT), a Masters in Communication from Marist College, and is currently pursuing a Ph.D. in Curriculum, Instruction and the Science of Learning from the University at Buffalo (SUNY). She is an animal advocate and a fledgling toy and game designer.

www.ingramcontent.com/pod-product-compliance
Lightning Source LLC
LaVergne TN
LVHW012016060526
838201LV00061B/4337